TONI turned out the light. They held each other very close. Megan could feel Toni's heart beating; it seemed as though it would break through her chest.

"I love you, Toni Underwood," Megan whispered.

"You're my life, Megan," Toni responded softly.

Their lovemaking was long, and sweet, and gentle this night. There was a tenderness between them that hadn't been there for a long time, since the beginning, since when they were just getting to know each other.

Toni lay awake all night holding Megan to her. She wished tomorrow, and the dangers it held, would never come. For the first time in her life, she truly wanted time to stand still.

□ □ □

A Toni Underwood Mystery

Deadly Rendezvous

DIANE DAVIDSON

RISING
TIDE
PRESS

HUNTINGTON, NEW YORK

Rising Tide Press
5 Kivy Street
Huntington Station, NY 11746
(516) 427-1289

Printed in the United States on acid-free paper

Publisher's note:
All characters, places and situations in this book are fictitious and any
resemblance to persons (living or dead) is purely coincidental.

Publisher's Acknowledgments:
The publisher is grateful for all the support and expertise offered by the
members of its editorial board: Bobbi Bauer, Adriane Balaban, Beth Heyn,
Harriet Edwards, Marian Satriani, and Pat G. Special thanks to Harriet and
Adriane for their excellent proofing and criticism; to Joyce Honorof, M.D.,
for sharing her medical expertise; to Edna G. for believing in us, and to the
feminist bookstores for being there.

First printing August 1994
10 9 8 7 6 5 4 3 2 1

Edited by Alice Frier and Lee Boojamra
Book cover art: Evelyn Rysdyk

Library of Congress Cataloging-in-Publication Data
Diane Bunker 1933—
                    p.cm

ISBN 1-883061-02-4   93-087607

Dedication

To Sydney and Cookie.
You encouraged me, pushed me, and insisted I had talent,
when the one who should have, didn't. My loving thanks.

Thanks, also, to my editors, Alice Frier and Lee Boojamra.
Without the two of you my dream would remain
unfulfilled.

1

THE dull ache in her head had persisted for weeks. Squeezing her eyelids shut, she made a futile attempt to blot out the image. But the dead, battered face of the latest victim continued to flash before her eyes. The muscles of her finely chiseled jaw twitched as she clenched her teeth tightly together. Another ragged week had begun.

Lighting a cigarette, she turned her chair around, away from her desk, and stared out the dirty window of her office. The afternoon air was brown with smog. *It's been another hot mother today,* she thought.

She put her heels up on the window sill and leaned back in her chair. Taking a long drag on her cigarette, Lieutenant Underwood closed her eyes once again. How long had it been now? Twelve years, fifteen years? She could hardly believe it.

Toni Underwood had joined the Police Department in 1977, right after graduating from college. She had been full of hope and high expectations then. But in those days, women officers were little more than file clerks and secretaries. Working in the field was considered *man's* work.

She had volunteered for every dirty job, and was determined to prove that women had everything it took to succeed in police work. But often it seemed like a hopeless task. A frown wrinkled Toni's forehead as the memories of the frustration and humiliation she had suffered those first few years on the force flooded her mind.

Eventually, she had succeeded in proving she was smarter and tougher than most other officers. And slowly, she moved up in rank, taking one tiny step after the other.

Sometimes she had wondered if it was worth all the effort. In the last couple of years, she had been pushing herself closer to the edge with each case she took. Each assignment seemed more difficult and demanding. She found herself taking unnecessary risks, for reasons she herself didn't understand.

It was true, she *had* come a long way in a short period of time, but now Toni wasn't sure if she hadn't paid too high a price. The sight of death and brutality could no longer be blotted out when she closed her eyes and fell asleep. It seemed that Megan was the only source of sanity and happiness left in her life.

"Fifteen years, yeah, that's right, it has to be fifteen," Toni said, arguing out loud with herself. "Let's see, I made sergeant in five, and lieutenant six years later. Then I transferred to the city of Riverside P.D. four years ago...so it is fifteen. Fuck, who gives a shit anyway?"

"Lieutenant Underwood," Michael Hayward spoke softly, as he opened her office door.

Spinning around in her chair, Toni stared at him coldly. He was new to the department. A rookie, in his mid-twenties, and already balding. His shy, sometimes awkward manner, and puppy-dog eagerness to please irritated most of the seasoned officers. They had tagged him the *Pillsbury Doughboy.*

"Lieutenant Underwood, here are those papers you've been waiting for on the Lewis case."

"How many times have I told you to knock before you come into my office, Hayward?" Annoyed, she grabbed the manila folder out of his hand.

"I'm really sorry, Lieutenant. I just...well, I knew you were in a hurry to get them, so, I guess I forgot. It won't happen again." He lowered his gaze to the floor.

"It's okay, Hayward, just don't do it again. Now get out of here," she ordered.

She watched him through the Plexiglass window of her office as he returned to his desk, which was located in a remote corner of the squad room.

Shaking her head, she couldn't help but feel a pang of sympathy for him. She knew what it felt like to be different, and not accepted as one of the *boys. Why the hell would someone like Hayward want to be a policeman in the first place? Better toughen up, kid, or you're gonna get eaten alive around here*, she thought.

Then, standing up, Toni stretched her long, muscular six-foot body. She flexed her upper arm muscles a few times, while stretching her back in an effort to relax the tension in her shoulders. Then she sat back down behind her desk.

Unconsciously, she ran her fingers through her neatly cropped dark brown hair. Taking a deep breath, she focused her attention on the file Hayward had just handed her. *Okay, the Anita Lewis case.* Opening the folder she began to read.

A picture fell out. Toni caught it before it hit the floor. The name Anita Lewis was neatly printed on a piece of tape beneath the photo. The battered body of a nude Caucasian female lay on a table. *God, what a mess,* she thought. She had already seen the body down in the morgue earlier that day, but the brutality of this type of crime still made her sick. She could feel her eyes tear up as she tucked the picture behind the pages of the report. After pausing for a moment to harden herself, she began reading. A deep furrow formed between her eyebrows as she engrossed herself in the scant report.

Anita Lewis was the third woman murdered, within as many months. Same MO, same cause of death: knife wounds to both eyes, with the weapon penetrating the brain. In addition, she had been severely beaten. There wasn't much to go on. No suspects, no witnesses, and no solid clues in the report. Toni shuddered inwardly.

The same was true of the others. The murders had only four things in common so far. The victims were all women between forty and forty-five years old. The bodies had all been found in isolated spots along Highway 60, on the outskirts of Riverside. The automobiles, all abandoned in Palm Springs, were expensive luxury models. And each one was a rental.

"It looks like there's another sick son-of-a-bitch out there, taking his god damn hang-ups out on women," Toni said out loud.

Angry, she got up and headed for Captain Morris' office. After knocking, Toni opened the door. Captain Morris looked up from his mound of paper work and motioned for her to enter.

"What's up, Toni?" His deep voice boomed out.

"Why the hell do you always give *me* these cases?" She threw the file down in front of him. Once again, she could feel her shoulder muscles growing tense. "Why the hell can't I get a nice gang shooting, or robbery homicide?" she complained.

"Now, Lieutenant Underwood, we both know you're the best we got for these types of cases," he said in a condescending manner. Then he leaned back in his worn brown leather chair which squeaked with each change in body position. "Shit, anyone else would give up before they even got started. You know that. You've got that special something that just won't say 'Uncle.' What more can I say?" Captain Morris smiled at her, his round fatherly face glowing under the fluorescent light.

He was well aware of Toni's reputation for not always following established guidelines and proper procedures. She had a certain propensity for independent action...when the situation called for it. Yet she had never stepped over the line far enough to be suspended.

"You know this kind of thing gives me nightmares, and pisses me off," Toni grumbled, waving her hands in the air in frustration.

"That's why we give them to you, Toni," he calmly answered.

"You know I got vacation time coming. I might just take it, and dump this whole mess in your fat lap."

He'd heard this threat many times before. Captain Morris sat straight up in his chair, a wide grin spreading over his face. "I know you, Toni. As messy as it is, this is just your cup of tea. You would've quit the force years ago if things had gotten too easy for you, and you know it." Then his smile disappeared. "This one is bad, I grant you that, but we need the best we got on it, and that's you. The press is already pounding on my door, and the Chief wants results, not excuses. Now, what have you got?"

"Not much," she answered with a sigh. "Read it for yourself."

Picking up the manila folder, Captain Morris began reading. The light from his green shaded desk lamp reflected off the paper. He slipped his reading glasses over his broad nose and his dark eyes followed each line, slowly and deliberately, as though he were branding every word into his brain. When he had finished, Toni noticed a slight tremble to his hands and beads of sweat stood out on his upper lip.

"You're right, Toni," Morris commented. "But there is one thing that stands out here—none of these women were raped. Whatcha think about that?"

"Yeah, I caught that right away, but that's happened before. Some of these sick bastards can't get it up. I'm sure you know what I mean." She gave him a mocking smile.

Morris became dead serious. "Okay, Toni, this is how it's goin' down. I want you to take a team and retrace the steps of all these women, and I mean, everything. Find out if they had anything in common—from lovers, to cheating husbands, to when they last took a shit. You know the routine."

"Yes, sir," Toni snapped.

Taking out a handkerchief, Morris wiped the sweat from his lip and chin.

"Are you okay, Harvey?" she asked frowning.

"Yeah, sure. Why do you ask?"

"I don't know, I noticed your hands shaking a bit and you're perspiring." She liked Harvey Morris, and was truly concerned.

"Must be a touch of the flu, or maybe it's just that this job is finally getting to me. Too damn many problems to deal with, and I can't seem to solve 'em all."

"Sounds like you need some R & R, Harvey, " Toni quipped, trying to sound casual. She knew he hated too many personal questions, including ones about his health.

Ignoring her last comment, he commenced once more with his discussion of the murders. "I'm assigning you four men. We have to stop this before the press rips us to shreds. Now, I've already talked with the Chief of Police down in Palm Springs. When you're through organizing the team here, you're heading there. Sergeant Murphy, of the Palm Springs Police Department, will be working with you from that end. The Palm Springs P.D. will be informed you're on loan to their department. The Chief has assured me you will have a free hand and they will cooperate with you in every way. Our first priority is to find the connection among these murders, since they all took place between Riverside and the desert towns." Toni opened her mouth to speak. "Don't say a word. That's the way it's gonna to be, and that's it!" Captain Morris handed the file back to her, and resumed reading the papers on his desk.

She turned and left the room without another word. Toni knew Harvey well, and he was worried. Returning to her office, she was suddenly very tired and depressed. She stood in front of the window again and touched her forehead with the palm of her hand; she realized she had broken out in a cold sweat. *God, am I having an anxiety attack? Gotta get out of here.* Grabbing her grey blazer off the back of her chair and adjusting her gun holster, she quickly left the building. All she wanted was to go home and see Megan's smiling face.

As the stop-and-go rush hour traffic slowed to a stop on the freeway, Toni's thoughts drifted back six years. She had learned long ago not to fight the inescapable delays caused by the glut of cars on the California freeways. Sometimes these delays worked to her advantage. They afforded her the opportunity to be alone and reflect on her life— past and present. The depression and panic she had experienced in the office slowly began to fade as visions and thoughts of Megan danced through her mind.

Toni had met Megan at an afternoon barbecue party six years ago. Art Winslow was retiring from the department, and Bill Perry had invited all the officers who had worked with Art over the past twenty-five years to wish him well in his retirement.

The Perrys had a wide variety of friends, both gay and straight, and Toni always felt comfortable in their home knowing she could be herself. If it hadn't been this way, she would not have been there on that summer day.

At that time, she was working vice out of the Corona, California Police Department. Corona is a small town compared to most cities in Southern California. Sitting in a valley some thirty-five miles southeast of Los Angeles, it boasts mild year-round weather. Orange groves cover the hillsides, the smell of orange blossoms filling the air in early spring. Old Victorian style homes still line many of the streets, while hundred-year-old pines and oak trees provide soothing shade on hot summer days.

Toni was happy living here. But because the Corona Police Department was small, she applied for—and got—a position with the Riverside force. Toni was ambitious and determined to move on.

Megan both worked and lived in Riverside, yet their paths had never crossed before Art's retirement party.

Bill Perry and Toni had been sharing a story and sipping on their drinks when Megan walked in the room. Toni turned as she heard the commotion coming from the doorway behind her.

"Hi, Megan," Carla Perry chirped as she rushed to greet her newly arrived guest. "Megan, dear, we were beginning to think you wouldn't make it."

Standing in the doorway of the living room was the most stunningly beautiful woman Toni had ever seen. The light coming in through the large window seemed to gather around Megan's shoulders and surround her auburn hair. Flecks of green, blue, and gold danced and sparkled in her hazel eyes as they moved to take everyone in.

She was wearing a lime green sleeveless silk blouse, white linen slacks and white sandals. Her hair hung loose and long over her tan shoulders. For Toni, everyone and everything seemed to fade away and there was nothing in the room but this glorious creature.

"Hey, Toni, are you okay?" Bill was shaking Toni's arm.

"What? Oh, no I'm all right, just swallowed an ice cube, that's all," she replied, blushing.

Mesmerized, she watched as Megan went from one person to another hugging and greeting the other guests. Was it her imagination or was Megan slowly working her way across the crowded room toward her?

The beating of Toni's heart began to feel as though a jack hammer had been turned loose in her chest.

Carla Perry was saying, "Come here, Megan, I don't think you know Toni Underwood."

Oh God, here she comes. Toni thought. *Jesus Christ, I hope I don't make a complete fool of myself.* She took a deep breath, and presented a cool appearance.

Megan was standing directly in front of her now. Toni had fixed her gaze on the glass she held in her hand. The warm, sensuous scent of Megan filled her senses.

"Toni, I'd like you to meet my close friend, Megan Pollard," Carla said smiling. "Megan, this is Toni Underwood."

Slowly, Toni raised her eyes to meet Megan's. Neither of them moved or spoke for what seemed an eternity.

After a time Carla became uneasy and began shifting from one foot to the other.

"Hello, is anybody home in there?" Carla finally asked, looking at the two of them, and then excusing herself as someone called her name.

A smile slowly spread across Megan's tanned face as she extended her hand to Toni. "It's really a pleasure to meet you, Toni," she spoke in a soft voice.

"Believe me, the pleasure is all mine, Megan," Toni almost shuddered. She wondered if Megan could hear her heart pounding beneath her tank top.

Their hands were warm and firm against one another's. Toni never wanted to let go of the smaller hand which now rested in her own.

"Would you like to go outside? There's plenty of shade and a cooling breeze," Toni ask shyly.

"I think that's exactly what I'd like," Megan answered.

From that moment on there was only the two of them. They talked and laughed through the rest of the summer day.

As they exchanged vital statistics, Toni learned that Megan had been a street cop in Riverside before transferring to the crime lab. She had taken night classes at Cal State Fullerton for six years to obtain her degree as a Criminologist. The challenge of piecing together a case from seemingly unimportant clues was something that stimulated and excited her.

It was immediately clear to Toni that this lovely woman had touched a place deep in her heart. A place long ago forgotten. The warm gentle place which had been waiting just for someone like Megan..

After that first meeting, Toni found one excuse after another to *accidently* run into her at the crime lab. She could not stay away. They began having lunch together frequently. Over the passing weeks, the two women discovered they had much in common.

But despite all that Toni had learned about her, she still wasn't sure if Megan was a lesbian, and for the first time in her life, she was afraid to ask. Above all, she didn't want to lose the friendship of this sensitive, warm woman.

Toni jumped as a horn blasted behind her. The guy in a red Toyota truck was waving his arms and making crude hand gestures at her. The traffic had moved ahead about sixty feet. She pulled the car forward, and then stopped again. She stared out the windshield, lost in her thoughts once more.

One day, near the end of August, while they were having lunch at a nearby park, Megan had asked Toni if she would like to have dinner some night.

"I'd love to," she had answered without a moment's hesitation.

"Well then, how about The Chart House?"

As she almost choked on her ice tea, Toni could feel her insides begin to churn. Taking a deep breath, she answered in her most casual manner. "You name the night."

"This Saturday? Say you pick me up around 7:30 p.m.. Just remember, it's my treat."

Toni would never forget that wonderful night.

Dinner had been a blur to her. All she seemed to be able to do was nod her head up and down as Megan talked. She was intoxicated by the warmth and beauty of this kind-spirited, intelligent woman sitting across from her.

"Is everything all right?" Megan had finally realized Toni wasn't eating.

"What? Oh, yes, I'm fine," Toni responded, blinking her eyes. *My God, Underwood, you're acting like a jerk. Pull yourself together, or this woman is going to think this was a big mistake.* "I'm sorry, guess I ate lunch a little late today and I'm not as hungry as I thought." *No, no, you fool. Now she's going to think you're bored. Keep digging, Underwood. Pretty soon you'll be in so deep you'll never find your way out.*

Megan looked confused and hurt. There was a long uncomfortable silence. Both women sat staring into their plates while their food began to grow cold.

Finally, Toni could stand it no longer. She knew she had come to the point where she had to be honest, or lose Megan, for sure. "I find this very difficult to say...but you overwhelm me in a way no one ever has before. I...I feel like a bumbling kid who's always got an upset stomach. Having lunch at the park is one thing, but having dinner with you seems to be a very different matter. I wasn't prepared for this."

"Prepared for what? I don't understand." A slight smile touched the corners of Megan's mouth. The flickering light from the small candle on the table danced in her penetrating hazel eyes.

"Okay, here goes." Toni swallowed hard. "I realize you think all our meetings have just been accidental, due to my work...but they weren't. I planned them. I wanted, no, I *needed* to get to know everything about you. My feelings for you are more than that of a friend...do you understand what I'm trying to say?" Toni stopped and turned beet red.

"Yes, I do. Now, eat your dinner before it's completely ruined." Behind the matter-of-fact answer, there seemed to lurk a hint of humor.

With mouth hanging open, all Toni could do was sit there looking like a stunned duck. Slowly, Megan raised her eyes and looked directly into hers. A moment that held an eternity passed between them.

"You knew! You knew all along!"

"Yes." The soft whispering answer rang in Toni's ears.

Again the sounds of rush hour pierced her reveries. The slow traffic inched forward, and then quickly ground to a halt. *Someone up ahead probably has a flat tire and the looky-lou's all have to stop and take a peek,* she thought in disgust, and then happily slipped back into her reminiscence.

After dinner they had gone back to Megan's place, which was on the ground floor. Toni stood silently behind her as she unlocked her front door. A shy awkwardness swept over her as she followed Megan inside. It was the same feeling she had had during her first real date with a woman some seventeen years ago.

The only light in the room came from a small lamp sitting on the end table next to the couch. Toni's mouth felt dry, and she could feel the pulse pounding in her temples. She continued to follow Megan into the kitchen.

"Would you like a drink or some coffee?"

Megan stopped and turned suddenly, causing Toni to bump into her. Grabbing her around the waist, Toni kept her from falling.

As luck would have it, Megan's breast touched Toni when she pulled her in. The hair on Toni's neck stood up as the hard nipple of Megan's breast brushed across her bare arm.

"I'm really sorry. Are you okay?" Toni asked.

"It was my fault. I shouldn't have stopped so abruptly." Megan's voice was almost a whisper.

They stood together, bodies touching, Toni's arms still around Megan's waist. Megan tilted her head up toward Toni's face, their mouths now inches apart. The moonlight coming in through the sheer kitchen curtains seemed to shimmer against their bodies, enhancing this suddenly romantic moment.

Hesitantly, Toni brought her mouth closer to Megan's. She brushed the soft lips with her own. Megan's mouth opened slightly as she responded to the gentle, whispering kiss. They continued this soft exploration of each other's mouths. Each tingling touch sent them deeper into their growing passion.

Finally, she pulled back and looked into Megan's eyes. They didn't speak. No words were needed. This was the beginning of something new and wonderful, and they both knew it.

Moving her head foreword, Megan placed her mouth in the hollow of Toni's neck. She could feel Toni's pulse pounding against her lips.

Toni's head was back and she uttered a soft moan as the hot tongue touched her skin. This wondrous tongue and mouth slowly moved up Toni's neck until their lips once again brushed and met.

Pulling Megan tightly to her, she kissed her deeply, then drew Megan's lip into her mouth, softly biting it. Their tongues played and danced together. Their bodies trembled.

Suddenly Toni bent over and scooped Megan up into her strong arms; she was as light as a feather. Megan's beautiful 5'6" frame fit perfectly into her arms. As she headed toward the bedroom, Megan nestled her head on Toni's shoulder.

Gently lowering her down onto the bed, Toni bent to kiss Megan's soft mouth once again.

"Wait," she whispered.

Toni looked surprised as Megan rose quickly and walked across the room. She lit three candles which were on the dresser, and then returned to the bed.

"I want to see you when we make love." Then Megan knelt on the bed.

While Toni stood in front of her, Megan's long fingers began undoing her belt. She watched as the delicate fingers slowly slid the zipper of her pants down. It felt as though tiny electrical shocks were running through her flesh as Megan's hands slid inside and around her bare hips. The slacks fell to the floor.

Fingertips traced Toni's back and buttocks, while Megan's tongue softly ran over her belly. She caressed Megan's hair and shoulders as magical fingers began gently massaging her clit. Toni closed her eyes.

Sliding easily through the wetness, Megan's fingers entered her, moving in and out, thrusting deeper with each movement, her thumb continually massaging the wet hardness. Finally, Toni could stand no more, and pulled away.

"I don't want this to end so quickly," Toni whispered fiercely, as she went to her knees on the floor in front of Megan.

One by one, she undid the buttons on Megan's powder blue blouse. Slowly, she pushed it off her suntanned shoulders, revealing the beautiful firm breasts. Toni cupped Megan's face in her hands and kissed her. Then her hands moved down to gently caress the taut nipples. They grew harder as Toni teased and softly pinched them.

Gently kissing Megan's eyelids, cheeks, and throat, she finally drew the firm breast into her mouth. Her tongue traced the nipple.

"Oh, baby," Megan whispered, in a husky voice.

Toni looked up at her. Her mouth was slightly open.

"Lie back." Toni's tone was soft, as she removed her own shirt.

She pulled Megan's legs over the edge of the bed, bending her knees so her feet touched the floor. She undid the blue cotton slacks and tugged them off, and removed the rest of her own clothing.

Tenderly, Toni slid a pillow under Megan's buttocks. She kissed the inside of the firm thigh, savoring the sweet-scent of the flesh which lingered on her lips. Megan shivered as she widened the opening between her legs.

"I'm going to suck you in, and eat the plum you offer, until the juice of your ripe fruit is all mine." Toni's voice was sweet and deep. The sensuous fragrance of Megan once again filled her senses as she kissed the wet hardness. Megan groaned.

Opening her mouth, she drew Megan in. Her tongue rubbed back and forth against the throbbing head as her saliva mingled with Megan's own wetness. Toni nuzzled the head with her mouth, sucking harder and more intently with each breath. Megan's hips increased their rhythm as her passion peaked. And then with a groan and a shudder, she lay still. Delighted to have given her such sweet pleasure, Toni continued her soft kissing and gentle teasing of the ripe pulsating fruit.

"Oh, baby, don't stop."

Sweat ran between Megan's breast, her hair wet against her forehead as Toni's mouth pulled her in once more. Toni's tongue rubbed firmly against the extended head.

Megan twisted the sheets in her clenched fists; she held her breath. Then her total being burst into an explosion of unbridled passion as the juice of her second climax gushed forth.

She lay motionless, breathing hard, her throbbing clit still held in Toni's mouth. It was not easy to open her eyes. Her trip had been long and sweet, and she was not sure if she wanted to return so soon.

"Come up here to me," Megan finally whispered.

Toni crawled up on top of her. Their bodies were wet against each other. As their breasts touched, they shared a long deep kiss.

"Lower your sweet pussy down on my face," Megan whispered.

Moving her body up, Toni straddled Megan's face. She carefully lowered herself to the waiting mouth. Megan's tongue hardened and moved in and out, filling her. Then Megan began licking. Toni put her hands on her thighs, moving her hips back and forth slowly; making it last. She lowered herself again until Megan's mouth consumed her.

Head back, she moaned as Megan sucked her in further. Gently biting, she continued drawing Toni in. Fiery fingers traced the small of Toni's back, barely brushing her skin. This sensation caused her hips to twitch, increasing the sexual pleasure now rushing through her body.

Unable to hold back a moment longer, she stiffened as a burst of ecstasy permeated her very being. A blinding flash of lightning cut across her eyes. Toni's whole body shook. Far away someone screamed.

With a deep sigh of pleasure, Toni rolled over onto her back. Megan snuggled her head on Toni's shoulder. Then, turning toward one another, they shared a soft sweet kiss. Toni brushed the hair back from Megan's face and smiled. Wrapped in each other's arms, they fell into a deep, peaceful sleep, without saying a word.

The morning sun streamed in the bedroom window and fell on the two sleeping women. Toni was first to open her eyes. Megan's head still rested on her shoulder. Carefully, she turned her head. As she looked at Megan's sleeping face, she smiled.

Megan stirred slightly. Her eyelids slowly opened and she looked into Toni's eyes. A sleepy smile crossed her lips.

"Hi," Toni said quietly.

"Hi," Megan replied.

Toni bent and gently kissed Megan's waiting mouth. They embraced and held each other close for a long time, not speaking. Their naked bodies felt cool in the morning air. Their hearts beat together.

"How did you know I was a lesbian?" Megan whispered.

"I didn't," Toni whispered back. "It didn't matter. If all I could have had with you was a friendship, I would have settled for that. I just knew I had to be near you."

A warm tear fell on Toni's shoulder. She pulled away looking into Megan's eyes.

"Why are you crying?"

"I don't know. No one's ever said anything like that to me before. Can two people really feel so much so soon? It scares me."

Toni gently wiped the tears from Megan's eyes. "I'm scared too, but I knew from the first moment I saw you there was somebody special walking into my life.

Within three months Megan moved into Toni's small but comfortable house in Corona. Her easygoing manner and quick smile helped ease the tensions Toni had surrounding her job. Now there was always Megan to come home to, her refuge from the ugliness of the world.

The blaring horns jogged Toni back to reality. As the red Toyota truck pulled out around her and sped by, the driver offered her another crude hand gesture and mouthed something through his window. She smiled at him, waved, and threw him a kiss. *That should send him into orbit. They hate it when you do that.*

She opened the front door at 5:30, and as usual, Megan had gotten home before her. She found Megan standing in the fragrant kitchen, and immediately threw her arms around her. After giving her a big kiss, she continued to hold Megan tight.

"Hmm! What was that for?" Megan said breathlessly after Toni released her.

"It's a long story, babe, but I really missed you today."

"I think I like this being missed routine a lot." Megan smiled broadly.

After planting another big smooch on Megan, Toni quickly went to change clothes. Then, walking into the living room, she flipped the TV set on. The evening news had just started. A piece about the three murdered women was the first story. They hadn't quite dubbed it a serial killing yet, but they were close. Next was the rape of an eighty-year-old woman, followed by the story of a child molester hanging around the Washington Elementary School; he'd already snatched up two little girls.

"Thank God, the son of a bitch didn't kill them." Toni turned the TV off. "I don't know how long I can take this shit before I start killing some of these bastards," she said angrily. She felt helpless and frustrated, fighting against a world growing madder and meaner every day. *A man's world,* Toni thought.

She had been living on the edge for a long time, and she knew it. She tried to keep things from Megan as much as possible and maintain a normal life, but the constant onslaught of rapes, murder, and death were beginning to overwhelm her.

"Come on, honey, dinner's ready, don't watch anymore. You do this every night. Why do you torture yourself?" Megan set Toni's dinner on the table.

"So, what's happening with your new case?" Megan asked, as they lay in bed later that night.

"You've seen the reports, babe. In fact, your people in the crime lab probably know more about some of this shit than I do. Captain Morris has assigned me to the case, and I'm afraid it's really going to be a rough one. One more killing, and we got a serial on our hands." Toni sighed and stretched back on the cool fresh sheets.

Moving closer, Megan's breasts pushed against her. Toni turned. Her mouth touched Megan's, gently at first. Their lips opened, and the kiss became deep and demanding.

The shrill ringing of the phone startled Toni.

"Shit!" she said, reaching for the receiver.

"Don't answer it, baby," Megan whispered in a husky voice.

"Hello. Yeah, this is Lieutenant Underwood." Toni sounded out of breath. "No, I didn't have to run to the phone," she replied angrily, as she glared at the clock. "Hayward, is that you? Well stop apologizing, and tell me what the hell you want at 1:00 a.m.."

Toni reached for a cigarette and sat up listening, a frown wrinkling her forehead.

"I'll be there in half an hour." She slammed the phone down. "We got another one," she sighed.

After throwing on blue jeans, a tee-shirt, and boots, she slid her wallet into her back pocket, clipped her belt holster on and slipped into a light denim jacket.

Then turning to Megan, she gave her one last yearning look. "I'm really sorry, babe, but I have to go. I love ya." She gave her a peck on the cheek, and rushed out into the night.

2

THE rocks and gravel scattered as Toni pulled her white Honda Prelude onto the soft shoulder of the highway, and parked. The woman's body had been discovered just ten yards off the roadway by a trucker when he stopped to take a pee around 12:00 a.m.. The beam from his headlights had caught the feet, which were sticking out from under a large bush. She'd been dumped in one of the numerous ditches along Highway 60, heading east, which leads to Palm Springs.

Three units were on the scene; the officers had cordoned off the area with yellow tape. Toni jumped out of the car, and pulled her lightweight jacket tighter around her body. The night air was warm, but a sudden coldness had gripped her, and she found herself shivering.

"What a barren, lonely place," she whispered.

She walked up to three officers who were standing motionless, staring down at the nude body. One of the cars was positioned so its headlights illuminated the area.

Taking a deep breath, she stepped between the officers and looked down into a face that was not a face. The woman had been brutally beaten. Her hair was matted in blood, teeth were missing from the battered mouth, and the eyes were gone.

She stepped closer. "Has anyone touched anything?" Her voice cracked as she spoke.

"No, Lieutenant," a young officer answered. Toni barely heard his voice.

"Okay, I want everyone to watch where they step. Don't disturb anything. The coroner and the crime investigation unit are on their way."

Toni walked carefully around the crime scene looking for some clue that might have been overlooked, and then, went back to the car to get her notebook. Leaning against her Honda, she began to write. *Time: 2:00 a.m., Tues. 24th of June 1992. Victim: African American female. Name unknown at this time. Same basic MO as Parker, Caldwell, and Lewis cases. Area of body disposal: Highway 60, Riverside. No automobile on scene.* As a matter of routine, Toni kept her own private notes on each case. She continued writing for another two or three minutes before she heard the coroner's van pull up.

"Hi Toni, what's up?" Paul Sholl, the deputy coroner, greeted her.

"We have another body, Paul. I'm afraid it's just like the last three." Toni's face felt like a piece of stone.

"Damn!" Paul replied. "Looks like we got us a serial here, doesn't it?"

"Yeah," Toni answered, grimly following him back to the body.

Paul Sholl knelt down beside the dead woman. The beam from his flashlight gleamed against the light brown skin. After a couple of minutes he stood up. "Can't tell much about this until we get her back to the morgue, but I'd say it's the same MO." Paul shook his head.

"Anybody find anything?" Toni called out to the officers.

"Negative," two responded.

"I found this."

A young officer stepped up to Toni, and handed her a small plastic bag. She held it up in front of the headlights. Inside was a bright yellow feather.

"Looks like one of those feathers they put on hats, doesn't it, Lieutenant? It was lying on her foot."

Toni looked at the young man. "What's your name?"

"Ted. Ted Dawson, Lieutenant."

"Good work, Dawson."

"Thank you, Lieutenant," he answered.

She gathered the officers around her. "Okay, listen up. I want you four to stay here until your relief arrives. The crime investigation team will go over this area with a fine tooth comb. I want the statement from the truck driver on my desk by 9:00 a.m., plus all the rest of your reports. Does anyone have any questions?" Toni looked at each officer. Her jaw muscle twitched as she clenched and unclenched her teeth. Her blue eyes were unblinking.

They all answered, "No, Lieutenant."

The crime investigation unit arrived at 2:50 a.m.. Toni briefed them. As they quietly began the task at hand, Toni sensed that even these seasoned professionals were touched deeply by these grisly murders.

Toni finally opened her front door just as the hall clock chimed six times. She tried to be quiet, but as usual, the door creaked. Megan came out of the bedroom. She was dressed and ready for work.

"Hi, honey." Megan's face was drawn. She had small lines around her eyes.

"Hi, babe. I thought you'd still be in bed." Toni kissed her.

Megan put her arms around Toni and held her tight. "Are you okay?" she whispered.

"Yeah, honey, I'm okay, just beat, that's all."

Drawing back, she looked deep into Toni's eyes. They were like ice. Her jaw was set tight, the jaw muscle twitching slightly. Megan knew this look. Whenever Toni was angry or tense, she worked her jaw. Yes, Megan knew this face well. Toni was into the hunt now, and nothing would stop her until she trapped the murderer.

3

TONI pushed her way through the throng of reporters gathered outside Captain Morris' office. She backed into the room, shoving two reporters aside so she could close the door.

"What the hell's going on around here? It's like a three-ring circus. Every god damn reporter in California must be out there," she blurted out before turning around.

As she whirled around toward Morris' desk, a look of surprise spread over her face. Next to Captain Morris stood the Riverside Chief of Police, and the District Attorney, plus two people from the Mayor's office.

"Sit down, Lieutenant," the captain said quietly. His face was red. He looked like he'd been up all night. "From the look on your face, I assume you haven't been brought up-to-date yet."

Toni continued to stand. "No, sir, I just got in." She blinked her eyes and stared at the men. She recognized them all. Over the years she had either worked with, or had contact with each of them. She fixed her gaze on Captain Morris.

"All right, Lieutenant Underwood, here it is." He never called her Lieutenant Underwood unless he was threatening to fire her, or all hell was about to break loose. She guessed the latter was the case this time.

Captain Morris cleared his throat. "We have a situation here, a situation that has to be handled as quietly and quickly as possible. Mayor Washington's niece, Lana Washington, was our latest victim. She never arrived at his home for a family dinner last night, so she must have been abducted either after work, or when she left her apartment. We didn't get a positive I.D. until 7:00 a.m. this morning."

Before Toni could respond, Chief of Police Abbott interrupted. "Lieutenant Underwood, Captain Morris has informed me you people believe this to be the work of a serial killer. Is that correct?" He walked toward her.

"Yes, sir."

"Captain Morris filled me in on all the details you have so far. Not much, is it?"

"No, sir," she nodded.

Small beads of sweat began breaking out on Toni's forehead. The chief's comments and attitude somehow felt threatening, as though an unwanted challenge was about to be forced upon her.

Chief Abbott was a tall man. His graying hair was cropped close to his head, clothes precisely pressed. Toni always thought he looked like he had a rod stuck up his ass. Chief Abbott believed it was a *man's* world and women like Toni were intruders. She disliked him immensely and she knew whatever he had in mind now would not be good.

He was standing very close as he spoke. She didn't back away. "We have to get this bastard before he kills again. Don't you agree, Lieutenant?"

"Yes, sir," she replied sharply, while maintaining eye contact with him. His breath smelled of stale cigar smoke.

"I recommended that you be placed in charge of this investigation, Lieutenant. I want you to do what's necessary to catch this crazy bastard. You can handle it in whatever manner you deem fit. We will back you with whatever assistance you need. But know this— I want results, and I want them soon! Is that clear, Lieutenant?" He pulled out his pocket watch. "It's 9:00 a.m., and as of now, this baby is yours, Lieutenant Underwood."

"Yes, sir," Toni answered in a self-assured voice.

They all shook Toni's hand as they silently left the room.

She turned toward Captain Morris. "God, Harvey, he sure knows how to pressure a girl!"

"Yeah, he sure does. But the whole department is behind you on this one, Toni. Lana Washington was going to run for the State Senate next year, so you know this is big."

Toni frowned. "Damn. I just read about her in the newspaper this week. Divorced, raised two kids, and still finished law school. A great women's rights attorney. Strong woman, just the kind of person we need up there in Sacramento."

"Remember, if there's anything I can do to help, just yell. You know, I was a pretty good street cop at one time." Captain Morris patted her on the back, and handed her the folder containing what little information they had on the Lana Washington murder. "Who knows, maybe after this case you'll get *my* job, and then you'll *really* be in trouble." He smiled.

"Thanks, Captain." She turned, and walked briskly out into the crowd of reporters gathered in the squad room.

"Good luck," Morris yelled to her.

"We have nothing to say at this time," Toni shouted over the roar of questions, as she shouldered her way through the crowd. "There will be a written statement available to you by five o'clock this afternoon. Now, you'll all have to excuse me, I have work to do." She put her head down and grimly moved forward.

She fought her way through the throng of news reporters to her office and slammed the door behind her, momentarily leaning against it to catch her breath. Letting out a sigh, she walked to her desk and picked up the phone.

"Hayward, get those bastards out of the building NOW! Got it?" she yelled into the receiver as she started jabbing at another extension button on the phone. She removed her jacket with her free hand and tossed it over the back of the chair.

Her jaw worked feverishly as she waited for Detective Walter Green to answer.

"Green, here."

"Walter, I want you to round up Davidson, Hughes, and Hernadez. If they're working on something, tell them to give it to another officer, on my orders. I want you all in my office within thirty minutes. Got it? Oh, and bring in any new information you have on the Highway 60 murders." *I like it, The Highway 60 Murders. That's how we'll refer to these killings from now on.*

"Yes, Lieutenant," Green answered.

Next she buzzed the crime lab. "This is Underwood. You people got anything for me down there?"

"Megan's got something on that feather found at the scene, Lieutenant. Should I send her up?" The voice on the phone responded.

"Yes, immediately," she replied, and hung up.

Toni lit a cigarette and watched from her interoffice window as Detective Green began gathering up the men she had requested. The only one missing seemed to be Hughes. Toni smiled as she caught sight of Megan crossing the squad room toward her.

Megan knocked on the door. "Come on in, babe. What have you got for me?"

"Well, that small yellow feather has told us some things that may surprise you," Megan said. They both sat down.

"Great, go on." Toni leaned forward across her desk, listening.

"First of all, it's not really yellow. I mean, it was dyed. Second, because of its shape and size, we believe it came from a hat. We also found traces of black felt and glue on it. After checking the bits of felt, we discovered a chemical compound which is used in forming and blocking hats." She smiled at Toni, proudly. "How am I doing so far?"

Toni frowned. "Now all I have to do is find a guy who wears black hats with yellow feathers, living in either the Riverside or the Palm Springs area, who gets his kicks out of killing women."

"I'm sorry, Toni, I thought you'd be happy to hear we found something, no matter how small." Megan looked deflated.

"Oh, babe, I didn't mean your information isn't important or good; I was only thinking out loud." Then, apologetically, she added, "I just got out of a high pressure meeting, and my mind's running a mile a minute right now, that's all. I'll tell you all about it tonight."

Toni rose from her chair and patted Megan on the back, giving her neck a tender squeeze. "See you at home. Maybe we can finish what we started last night, okay?" Megan smiled and left. She wanted to know what was going down, but knew better than to ask now.

Walking over to her automatic coffee maker, Toni poured herself a cup of hot black coffee, then returned to the desk. After taking a few careful sips, she picked up her phone once again. She punched in the necessary numbers and waited.

Two rings, and a voice answered, "Riverside County Coroner's Office."

"This is Lieutenant Underwood calling for Deputy Coroner Sholl."

"One moment, please," the businesslike voice replied.

Toni listened as the extension rang. "Sholl, here."

"Hi, Paul, this is Toni Underwood. Got anything for me yet on the Lana Washington murder?" She nervously tapped her pencil on the desk as she waited for his answer.

"Hold on a minute, Toni, I have a partial report right here." After a few moments, Paul Sholl spoke again. "The physical cause of death is the same in this one as in the other three murders, Toni."

"Damn. Then you didn't find anything more than what we already have in these cases, right?" She threw her pencil down in disgust.

There was a long pause before Paul Sholl responded. "Look, Toni, I don't know if this will be of any help. All I can do is tell you that after twenty years of examining dead bodies, I have found that in some cases, certain patterns emerge."

Toni raised her eyebrows, and straightened in her chair. "Go ahead, Paul, I'll take anything I can get."

"Don't quote me on this, but in my opinion, these women were *not* abducted. Whoever your killer is, the victims went with him *willingly*."

"What? God, Paul, what makes you believe that?" Toni picked up her pencil, and grabbed a piece of paper. Her heartbeat quickened.

"Now, remember, this is only my conclusion based on intuition and experience."

"Go on, Paul."

Toni began taking notes as Paul Sholl continued.

"I found no bruising on the wrists or ankles of any of these women. No tape residue or tape burns around the mouth. No skin or hair under the fingernails. And no evidence of any semen. Their cars were clean; no blood, no sign of a struggle, and they weren't drugged."

"So, tell me exactly what all this means, Paul." Her eyes were wide open, filled with excitement. She tried to sound calm.

His answer came quickly. "They weren't tied up or gagged. They didn't fight their attacker. And there was no struggle in the car. In other words, they all either knew or trusted the killer."

"Jesus Christ." Her voice was no more than a whisper.

"Oh, ahh...one other thing, that may be important. I found what appeared to be similar odd-shaped scars on the shoulders of the victims. Could be symbolic of some cult or something, but I'm not sure. But one thing I am sure of, Toni, these are old scars—not new ones. As soon as I'm finished with the autopsies and reports, I'll send everything over to you in a day or two. Then you can check the photos. I hope this helps, Toni, but remember, in a court of law, you'll need a lot more than an educated guess."

Toni blinked her eyes. "I understand...but this *educated guess,* as you call it, is the most helpful information I've gotten so far. I can't thank you enough."

"My pleasure, Toni. Anytime. I'll send my report to your office as soon as I'm finished." He hung up.

Toni sat motionless, staring into space, the dial tone humming in her ear. She didn't know how long she had been sitting there when she heard the knock on the door.

"Come in," she called.

"We're here, as ordered, Lieutenant," Detective Green stated as the four men entered the room. They all stood stiffly, waiting for her to speak.

She rose to her feet. "Good morning, gentlemen." Toni greeted them in an official manner.

"Good morning Lieutenant," they all answered.

"Good, you've all brought note pads. Let's go down to the conference room. I don't want any distractions during this briefing,

my office is too public. Grab yourselves a cup of coffee if you like."
Toni refilled her cup, then headed down the hall at a brisk pace.

After everyone was seated, she stood at the head of the long
conference table, leaning forward on her hands.

"I picked you four men because I've worked with all of you,
and I know you'll give me the best you've got. We, the five of us, are
going to be working on a series of killings which have occurred over
the last three months. Anything we discuss here is not to be repeated
outside of this room." She laid four separate files on the table.

"The latest victim, Lana Washington, was none other than
our Riverside mayor's niece. I don't have to explain the kind of pressure this puts on the department." Toni straightened up and looked at
each of the detectives. "Any information you come up with from now
on will be discussed with me, and me alone. No talking to the press.
No...."

"Excuse me, Lieutenant," Green interrupted.

"Yes, Green," she answered, pointing to him.

"Does that include Captain Morris?"

"Yeah, Green. You got a problem with that?"

"No, ma'am," he quietly answered.

Toni shoved her hands into her pants pockets and began pacing around the room. "Okay, this is how we start. Today, I'll be giving each of you one of these folders. In the folder will be a name, and
all we have, as of now, on the person whose file is contained in that
folder. Your job is to get to know the woman assigned to you as if she
were your other self."

"Is this the only assignment we have?" Hughes asked, fidgeting in his chair.

"You got it, Hughes. I want to know what route these women
took to work. What hairdresser they went to. Where they had their
cars serviced, and when. What cleaner they used. Were they Repub-
lican or Democrat. What organizations or clubs they belonged to. In
other words, I want to know these women inside and out. There has
to be a link, something that these women have in common. The first
three victims all have a scar on their shoulders. Even though Lana
Washington doesn't, I want you to be sure to check on this, and see if

it connects them in any way. You're going to have to interview their families, friends, and associates, and any one else you can think of. Is that clear enough?"

"Yes, Lieutenant," they all replied.

"Early this afternoon the files will be on your desk. Look them over, and if you have any questions call me. My beeper number will be on each file. From now on, we will refer to these cases as the Highway 60 Murders. Are there any questions?" She waited patiently, giving each man a chance to respond. No one spoke. "Now, most of these women are from out of town, which means lots of phone calls to other agencies. You may even have to do some traveling. I will instruct Hayward to set up any arrangements needed. But keep me apprised of your investigations. Now, let's get to work; we got a killer to catch."

She shook each of their hands as they slowly left the conference room. Detective Green remained behind.

"Can I have a word with you, Lieutenant?"

"Certainly, Green. What's up?"

"Just before the meeting, I got information on the rented automobiles the victims were driving." Detective Green paused for a moment to find the fax he had shoved into one of his pockets.

"Go on. Go on," Toni urged, frowning.

Finally, he pulled the faxed information out of his jacket pocket. "Oh yeah, here it is. Seems all but Lana Washington rented their cars in Palm Springs, from V.I.P. Rentals. Ms. Washington had been using her own car."

"That's great, now we have a link as to why the vehicles were found in Palm Springs. Good work, Green." Toni patted him firmly on the back. "Check the airlines, trains, and buses. I want to know how and when these women got into Palm Springs."

"It's not much, Lieutenant."

"You're right, Green, but it's better than nothing."

Detective Green gave Toni a warm smile and walked briskly back to his desk in the squad room.

Her head was pounding by the time she reached her office. Sitting on the corner of her desk, Toni pushed a button on the phone.

"Hayward, I want you to come in here and get the files I have. Then I want the computer crew to pull up all the similarities between these four cases. Be sure every bit of information on each murdered woman is included in her own separate folder. I have a list here of which detective will get which file. I need this data by 1:00 p.m. this afternoon. That gives you two hours.

"Then, I need pictures of all the murdered women *before* they were killed, and three copies of all their bios for myself. I want complete reports from the lab on all the cases in question. Next, I want you to call the Palm Springs Police Department and inform them I will be there day after tomorrow. Are you getting all this, Hayward?"

"Yes, Lieutenant Underwood. Is there anything else?"

"Not right now, Hayward, just get on the stick." Toni hung up the phone. *That's Hayward's forté, detail work!*

She walked to the window, and stared out on the smog-filled city. Just looking into the glare made her eyes water. *I don't know how anyone can live in this day after day,* she thought. *It's becoming just like L.A..*

Like any large city, Riverside had been suffering from growing pains over the past few years. But even with the expansion and new building, much of the city remained old and in disrepair. As she looked out the window she thought about how crime was on the rise, and more and more homeless people were seen on the streets. Toni was thankful she had decided not to move out of Corona when she went to work for the Riverside P.D.. Happily, Corona had held onto its small town atmosphere, and unlike Riverside, the cooling breezes from the west kept the air clean and fresh.

Turning back to her desk, she picked up the phone and called Bill Perry. Gulping down the last of her now cold coffee, Toni waited.

"Bill Perry here," the cheery deep voice said.

"Hi, Bill, it's me, Toni."

"Toni. How the hell are you? I haven't heard your sexy voice in weeks."

"Listen, Bill, I only have a minute, so I'll get right to the point," she said, ignoring his question.

Bill could tell by her tone that this was more than a friendly call.

"What is it, Toni? What do you need?"

"I need a favor. Your house in Palm Springs. Can I stay there for about a week? It's business. I hate motels, so I thought if you didn't have it rented out, maybe I could flop there while I'm on assignment in that area." Toni held her breath, hoping the answer would be yes.

"No problem. It's empty. We don't get many people staying there in the summer. You still have a key, don't you?"

"I sure do, Bill. Thanks a million, I owe you one. I'll see you and Carla when I get back. Megan and I will have you two over for dinner. Talk to ya soon." Toni hung up and let out a loud sigh of relief. *At least I won't have to deal with a god damn noisy motel.*

4

"Good morning, sleeping beauty," Megan said cheerfully, as Toni came shuffling into the kitchen. Her old Mickey Mouse tee shirt hung unevenly over her cotton underwear. Her short wavy hair looked as if it had been caught in a mix-master.

Scratching her head, Toni sat down at the breakfast bar which separated the kitchen from the living room. With her eyes half open, she sipped the hot black coffee Megan handed her. Nothing much registered until she had her first cup. Pouring another cup, she smiled sleepily back at Megan.

Megan hummed as she took the dishes out of the dishwasher.

"How the hell can you be so cheery at 6:00 a.m.? Look at you, you're already dressed," Toni grumbled.

"Because it's hump day. You know...it's Wednesday. And besides, last night is still fresh in my mind. Remember?"

A broad smile suddenly covered Toni's face as her thoughts flashed back.

They had fixed a light dinner of fresh crab salad, hot French bread, wine, and grapes. At 7:30 they carried the meal into the bedroom and had dinner in bed, with candles, soft music, incense...the works. And, as promised, they certainly did finish what they had started the night before.

Fully awake now, Toni threw a pat of butter into the skillet and began scrambling eggs. With her back turned to Megan, she abruptly blurted out, "I'm going to Palm Springs tomorrow, and I don't know how long I'll be gone."

She had discovered long ago, it was best not to tell Megan about anything like this until the last minute. Megan had a habit of gently dictating to Toni what clothes she should or shouldn't take. This way, it saved them both a lot of trouble. Megan wouldn't have enough time to nag too much about her choices. Which helped preserve Toni's sanity.

"Well thanks for telling me, before I just happened to wake up and notice you were gone!" Megan said angrily.

"Now, sweetheart, you know what we go through every time I tell you ahead of time when I have to go out of town. Besides, I didn't want to put a damper on last night. I'll probably be back before you know it." Toni raised her eyebrows and gave Megan her most innocent look.

"Can't you send someone else? I can tell you're really beat." Megan's voice had softened. She stood close to Toni, putting her arm around her waist as she watched the eggs frying.

"It has to be me, babe. The whole god damn city bureaucracy has dumped this in my lap. I have no choice." She took Megan's hand. "Maybe you can come down on the weekend. I'm staying at Carla and Bill Perry's house. Remember what a great time we had there? It's only three days away, how about that?"

"I understand," Megan replied with a sigh. Suddenly the cheerfulness had left her. "I'll help you pack when we get home tonight. And oh, yes, you'd better believe I'll be there on the weekend. I wouldn't think of leaving you alone for too long down there with all those gorgeous women," she said, managing a slight grin.

Toni rolled her eyes back. "Why do I even try?"

She spent the early part of the day making sure Green, Davidson, Hughes, and Hernadez had everything they needed to start their investigations. She told them where she would be if they needed her. She checked through the files Hayward had prepared for her to take to Palm Springs. Everything was in order. After putting them in her briefcase, she headed for Captain Morris' office.

As she approached the door, she spied Hayward near the water cooler. "Hayward," she called out. "Come over here for a minute."

He jumped at the sound of her voice, his face turning red. Quickly, he walked to where she was standing. With a tremor in his voice he said, "Yes, Lieutenant, ma'am."

"Hayward, look at me." Toni put her hand on his shoulder.

Everyone who was close by, stopped what they were doing to listen and watch what was happening.

Toni spoke in a loud voice so none of the curious onlookers would miss anything. "Hayward, I just wanted to acknowledge a job well done. You carried out my instructions to the letter, and I know they would have been confusing to someone who wasn't as efficient."

Hayward looked dumbfounded. His face became even redder, and he blinked his pale blue eyes in disbelief at what he had just heard. Then a wide grin spread over his baby-like face.

"Thank you, Lieutenant Underwood. I did my best."

She patted him on the back and continued on to the Captain's office.

"Hi, Captain," Toni said, as she entered. "I'm leaving for Palm Springs in the morning. Is there anything you need to go over with me before I leave?"

"Not a thing, Toni. Captain Powers of the Palm Springs P.D. has arranged for you and Sergeant Murphy to have full charge of the investigation in Palm Springs. Just keep me up to date."

Toni purposely got home early. Her work shift had varied over the past year and a half, while Megan's remained 7:00 a.m. to 4:00 p.m. throughout the year. She wanted to spend as much time with Megan as possible before she left. With a smile, she saw her bags already packed, waiting in the hallway.

Megan was standing at the kitchen sink peeling potatoes. "What a sweetheart you are," Toni said, kissing Megan on the back of her neck.

She didn't turn around. "I'm no sweetheart. I just can't stand to watch you do it yourself. Nothing you ever take matches. You either take too many of one thing, or not enough. For such an organized person, your packing habits remind me of a small tornado."

Toni laughed. "But that's why you love me so much, right?"

"It's just one of the reasons," Megan answered in a seductive tone. She had already changed into a pair of shorts and a tee shirt.

"Nice pair of legs ya got there, cutie," Toni joked as she left to go change her own clothes.

After dinner, they sat at the kitchen table discussing the murders.

"I don't know what I'm going to discover when I get to Palm Springs," Toni said. "But I pray we get a break in this case soon."

"With that bloodhound nose of yours, this sicko doesn't have a chance." Megan put her arms reassuringly around Toni's neck. "Come on, it's cooled down outside, let's walk down to the park. It'll relax you and help get your mind off of these murders."

The June night was pleasantly warm, and it seemed they could see every star in the sky. By the time they had walked to the park and back, it was close to ten o'clock, and Toni was ready to call it a night.

✦ ✦ ✦ ✦ ✦

The drive to Palm Springs took a little over an hour. The palm tree filled city always made Toni think of an oasis nestled in the middle of the desert. It seemed to spring up out of nowhere. One minute you were driving through a hot, barren land, and the next you were in a lush garden. The freshly watered lawns and flowering shrubs glistened in the morning sun. The long, green fronds of the date palms looked as though they'd been freshly waxed.

Palm Canyon Drive was lined with stately palm trees, inviting motels, and gift shops. The windows of some of the most expensive department stores in the world gleamed, beckoning those with money to come inside.

As she drove along this famous main street, she passed many luxurious hotels with beautifully landscaped grounds. Their huge, green, manicured lawns and flower-filled planters created an illusion of coolness.

With the San Jacinto Mountains serving as a backdrop, the whole place looked like a movie set. Outdoor cafes dotted the sidewalks here and there, and helped to create the casual image Palm Springs wished to project to the tourists. But fine restaurants and expensive accommodations were still the mainstay of this plush resort town.

For the past few years Toni and Megan had been coming here for the Dinah Shore Open Golf Tournament. It was always a wild time, for the whole town would be taken over by lesbians from all over the United States. It was wonderful seeing thousands of women flood the town and make it their own. Many gays lived in Palm Springs year round, so there were quite a few gay and lesbian bars and motels throughout the area.

Turning into the circular driveway, she pulled up in front of the Palm Springs Police Department. As Toni turned the engine off and stepped out of the car, the pleasant illusion of coolness she had experienced driving through town quickly disappeared. A blast of hot air hit her in the face, taking her breath away. The thermometer on the side of the building read 108.

"Shit, it's only 9:00 a.m.. Now I remember why I've never wanted to live here," Toni said aloud as she walked to the front door.

Walking briskly through the lobby, she approached the front desk. "I'm Lieutenant Underwood, here to see Captain Powers," she said matter-of-factly to the desk sergeant.

"One moment, Lieutenant," he replied, picking up the phone. "Captain Powers, a Lieutenant Underwood to see you. Yes, sir, right away. You can go right in, Lieutenant, down the hall to your right."

"Thank you, Sergeant." *Hmm...quite a place*, Toni mused. *So clean and quiet. It looks more like a resort hotel than a police station.* She knocked on the door and walked in.

"Good morning, Lieutenant." Captain Powers stood up and extended his hand to Toni.

Powers was close to six foot four and powerfully built. His hair was dark, with streaks of gray. The light blue Armani suit he wore fit perfectly; not a wrinkle. A set of perfect white teeth glistened against his tan face as he smiled at her. Even Toni had to admit to herself, this guy was quite a hunk.

"I understand we have a big problem on our hands." Powers motioned her to sit down.

"Yes, sir, I'm afraid we do," she answered. "I brought copies of all the information we have on these cases so your office will be fully informed. I'm going to need all the help I can get from your department, Captain Powers."

"Don't worry, Lieutenant, we want this solved as badly as you. Things like this hurt our tourist business, and that's the lifeblood of Palm Springs. Sergeant Murphy will assist you with anything you may need. Hold on a minute." Captain Powers picked up his phone. "Harry, get Murphy in here right away."

Within two minutes the door opened. "Good morning, Captain," Sergeant Murphy said, entering the room.

Toni stood up and turned around. Then her mouth fell open, as she lay her eyes on Sergeant Murphy.

"Lieutenant Underwood, this is Sergeant Sally Murphy." Toni had not expected to see a woman.

Sally Murphy was about twenty-seven, close to five foot five, and a classic blue-eyed blonde. The tan uniform she was wearing was starched and pressed, the pleat in the pants clean and straight. Her long hair was pulled back in a ponytail. Suntanned skin accentuated her clear blue eyes, and like Captain Powers, she had a mouth full of white even teeth.

Jesus Christ, are these people real, or are they all cloned? Toni wondered while shaking Sally's hand. *This one looks like she'd be afraid to pull her gun because it might mess up those long red nails.*

"I've been looking forward to meeting and working with you, Lieutenant Underwood."

Toni cleared her throat. "Ahem...thank you, Sergeant."

"I believe you'll find Sergeant Murphy can be of great assistance in your investigation, Lieutenant." Powers smiled and walked them to the door.

"Thank you, Captain, I'm sure you're right," Toni answered, shaking his hand once more. Then the two women walked out into the hallway.

As Sergeant Murphy led Toni down the hall she said, "We've set up a conference room designed just for this investigation, Lieutenant. It will also double as our office. Maybe if we put our experience together, we can crack this thing before there are any more murders."

There were two desks with several phones, a chalkboard, map, corkboard, and conference table in the room. A computer sat on a table against the wall, along with a fax machine.

"If there's anything else we need, all we have to do is ask. We've already had a few phone calls regarding these murders."

"Oh, and what were they?" Toni asked, raising her eyebrows.

"After the pictures of the murdered women appeared in *The Daily Sun Times*, we received calls from several people who recognized a couple of them, or said they did."

Toni's pulse quickened. "Hey, that's great! Have you talked to any of them?"

"Yes, Lieutenant, but most of them didn't pan out." Sergeant Murphy thumbed through her notebook as she spoke. "The only interesting call came from a Thelma June Richmond. She owns a bar in town, and says she recognizes at least two of the murdered women." Then, she paused and looked up from her notes. "I believe we should question her in more depth as soon as possible. Personally, I've found a good bartender knows what's happening around town even more than the police, in some cases."

"Good thinking, Murphy, and please, call me Toni, I really hate this Lieutenant bullshit, okay?"

"Sure, Lieutenant...I mean Toni." Sally smiled.

Maybe this woman hasn't got her head up her ass after all, Toni thought.

They worked for over two hours setting up the corkboard. On the board they placed pictures of each woman: their descriptions, manner of death, and general background information. Then Toni briefed Sally for several hours to familiarize her with all the details they had so far on all the cases.

By late afternoon they had established a good working relationship. Sally listened intently and seemed to grasp information immediately. They bounced ideas off one another, and in most instances, both reached the same conclusions regarding their best plan of attack. Sally was eager to learn, and Toni liked that.

Rubbing her tired eyes, Toni said, "Okay, Murphy, I've had it for today. I've got to go get settled in and unpack. I'll be staying at the home of a friend of mine. Here's the phone number and address, okay? Give me yours. I'm afraid this will be a twenty-four-hour-a-day job, so we need to be able to reach each other at all times. I'll meet you back here tomorrow at 9:00 a.m. sharp, and wear comfortable clothes, no uniform. First thing tomorrow morning we'll question this Thelma June Richmond. See ya tomorrow." Toni slipped on her light summer blazer, walked out the door, and disappeared down the hall.

Wow, she sure doesn't waste any time. Just hope I can keep up. Yes! I think it's going to be quite interesting working with Toni Underwood. A forceful, take-charge woman, Sally thought. She switched off the lights and headed home.

5

THELMA JUNE shook her head, trying to loosen the cobwebs in her brain. Still groggy from sleep, she sat on the edge of the bed scratching her head and looking around the room.

God damn, it's getting hot in here already, and it's only 7:00 a.m.. Better get the air going right now. And I better move my ass. Got to be at the bar by 8:30 this morning for deliveries. Jumping into a cool shower, she let the water beat on her head.

After getting out of the shower, T.J. looked in the mirror and frowned. *Damn, if I get many more lines in my face everyone will be calling me road map.* At forty-five, the years of hard work and worry showed in her face. Her life had not been easy, what with raising two children alone, putting them through college, and somehow managing to save a little money.

She loved her bar and had always dreamed of having her own business. She had hoped that she and Kathy would enjoy running it together, but that didn't happen.

They had shared a life together for ten years, and then six months after purchasing the bar, Kathy dumped T.J. for a younger woman. T.J.'s heart still ached for the old days, but she managed to put up a good front, most of the time.

She had just opened the front door of the Pussy Willow when Sam backed his truck down the driveway.

"Hey Sam," she yelled. "Boy, you're here bright and early."

"End of da week, always gotta bust my ass. How ya doin' T.J.?" he called back.

Sam quickly loaded his dolly with cases of beer. Thelma June held the door open for him. It was dark and cool inside.

By ten o'clock, all deliveries had been made. T.J. was already tired, but there was still inventory to take and a bank to set up for Sydney, the day bartender. T.J. herself worked the night shift.

The Pussy Willow was a busy place, just outside of Cathedral City. From the street the bar didn't look like much, but T.J. had done extensive interior remodelling. The building sat on a deep lot and ran back from the street. It surprised people to find so much room inside when they entered.

T.J. was bending down behind the long, horseshoe-shaped bar, stocking beer in the cooler, when the unexpected voice boomed out.

"Mrs. Thelma June Richmond?" Toni said, trying to adjust her eyes to the darkness.

The voice startled T.J. Rising too quickly from behind the bar, she hit her head on the counter.

"What the hell? Who the hell's there?" T.J. said, rubbing her head. "Who are you two?"

"I'm sorry, we didn't mean to startle you, Mrs. Richmond. I'm Lieutenant Underwood, and this is Sergeant Murphy. We're here to ask you some questions regarding the four women who were murdered recently. You know, the ones you called the police about." Toni showed her badge as she talked.

"Oh, yeah, sure, what do you want to know?" T.J.'s voice softened.

"Anything you can tell us will be of great help. Let me start by asking how you know these women, and then we'll go from there, okay?"

Toni and Sally sat down on the bar stools.

"I know them from here," T.J. said simply.

"From here?" Sally responded, a surprised look on her face.

"You mean they were patrons of *your* bar?" Toni asked.

"Yeah, anything wrong with that?" T.J. answered, placing her hands on her hips.

"Not at all, Mrs. Richmond," Toni quickly replied. "This *is* a lesbian bar, right?"

"That's right." T.J.'s tone had suddenly become defensive and suspicious. Her mouth tightened and her eyes narrowed.

"Before we go any further, Mrs. Richmond, I'm a sister, so please know I'm not here to hassle you in any way. We're just surprised, that's all. The fact that these victims frequented a lesbian bar is completely new information to us; you can understand why we might be a little shocked," Toni said, smiling at her.

Sally looked surprised. She blinked her eyes and swallowed hard, then continued jotting down notes. A frown slowly spread across her forehead.

"Well, hell's bells! All right!" T.J. burst out, a pleased grin lighting up her face at this news. "Call me T.J., Lieutenant. Now I'm *really* pleased to meet you." She laughed. "Guess we aren't doing so bad after all; one of our sisters being a Police Lieutenant and all. How about a drink, on the house?" She reached for a glass.

"Can't right now, T.J.," Toni said with a smile. "Maybe tonight though, when I'm off duty. Now, back to the murdered women. Did you see every one of them in here, or was it just maybe a couple of them?"

"They've ALL been in here," T.J. answered. "Not all at once, mind you, but over the past year, each one was in here enough times for me to recognize their pictures in the newspaper. Outta town regulars, I always called 'em."

"Did they ever come in with what you might call a date, or with each other?" Toni asked.

"Nope. They didn't come in together. But I saw at least three of 'em either with, or talking to Nicky Clark. I've seen others with Nicky, but their pictures were never in the paper."

"Who's Nicky Clark?" Toni pressed on.

"She's a hard-nosed dyke that lives here. 'Bout thirty years old. Thinks she's hot stuff, you know, one of those butches who believes their shit don't stink. She's bad news, if you ask me. I don't like her. Never have."

"How can we get in touch with this Nicky Clark?" Toni asked.

"Well, I know she owns a guest ranch around here somewhere. I've never been to it, not my cup of tea. Too god damn snooty for me. You know, very expensive."

"Then why would these wealthy women be coming into an ordinary place like the Pussy Willow, when there are so many classy nightclubs around town?" Sally asked bluntly.

T.J.'s eyes flashed daggers at Sally. "Ordinary! Where the hell do you come off sayin' somethin' like that to me? It's pretty clear you don't know diddly shit about lesbians."

"Mrs. Richmond, I'm sorry if I offended you, that certainly was not my intent, I..." Sally hastily apologized.

Toni interrupted before things got out of hand and they lost T.J.'s cooperation completely. "Mrs. Richmond...I mean T.J., Sergeant Murphy simply doesn't understand that when lesbian women are vacationing, they seek out the local lesbian bar so they can mingle and relax among other lesbians." Toni took a deep breath, hoping her words were soothing T.J.'s bruised feelings.

There was a long uncomfortable silence before T.J. spoke. Her eyes were still boring into Sally. Sally kept her eyes down toward her notebook.

"Well, I guess it's okay. These damn straight people just don't get the picture, do they, Lieutenant?" She spoke as if Sally were not in the room.

"I think Sergeant Murphy has the *picture*, now, T.J.. Now, back to what we were talking about. Do you know the name of Ms. Clark's ranch?"

"Let's see, what is that name?" T.J. rolled her eyes toward the ceiling thoughtfully. "Oh yeah, the Lazy Q, that's it. Probably listed in the phone book. From what I've heard, her mother bought it for her a couple of years ago. Her mom's some big shot lawyer in San Francisco, I think."

"Thanks a lot, T.J.. This has been very useful. I think that's all we need for now, so I'll be seeing you later," Toni said. She shook

Thelma June's hand firmly, gave her a friendly smile, then she and Sally left.

The two women were silent on the short drive back to the station. An uncomfortable feeling hung between them.

"Well, Sally, looks like we got some prime info today, what do you think?" Toni asked, as she opened the door to their office.

Looking uncomfortable, Sally blurted out, "Toni, I've got to be honest with you, I don't know much about gay life, or the people in it. I don't know if my input can be of much help."

Toni threw her light blue denim jacket over the back of her chair, then whirled around, facing Sally. "Let's get this straightened out here and now, Sally. I'm a lesbian, have been all my life. I've never hidden that fact from anyone, I'm proud of who I am. And if someone has a problem with that, it's their problem, not mine. I do my job, and I do it well. Far as I'm concerned, that's all that counts. If I can try to understand your world, by God, you *will* try to understand mine. Or you're right, you're useless to me."

Toni walked back to her desk, unclipped her holster from the leather belt on her blue jeans, and dropped it on the desk. Then she sat down and lit a cigarette.

Sally's eyes never left Toni. She stood rigidly near her own desk.

After taking a drag on the cigarette, Toni continued. "Your job here isn't to judge, or decide whether you like my life-style or not. Your job is to help me solve four murders. Their being lesbian or not makes no difference. These women were human beings, and there's a maniac out there who brutally killed them. That's *all* that matters." Toni's manner was firm and straightforward.

Sally couldn't help but be impressed by the simplicity of what she'd heard. She sat at her desk for a long time without saying a word.

Toni got up from her chair and busied herself adding the new information to the board. Finally, Sally got up and walked over to Toni and touched her arm. Toni turned to face her.

Sally began speaking with a slight tremor in her voice. "You're right, you and I have a job to do here. I admit I don't understand a lot of things, but I think we can make a good team. I'll do the best I can to do that job. You may have to be patient with me from time to time, though. Help me see these people from your angle, you know what I mean." Finally, her voice got surer as she smiled at Toni. "So, if we're both through with our own *bullshit*, let's get the bastard who killed these women."

"Hi, babe, miss me?" Toni asked.

It was six o'clock, and Megan had caught the phone on the third ring. She had worked two hours overtime, and had just gotten home from work.

"You know I do. How are things going, honey?" Megan set her shoulder bag down, and took the cordless phone with her into the living room.

"We've had a new development here that's going to blow you away. Would you believe all the victims were involved in the gay life? How's that grab you?"

"You're kidding. How did you find this out so soon?" she asked while sliding her shoes off and then leaning back in the recliner.

Toni sipped her coffee and explained how she and Sally had discovered this important information.

"I was afraid they were going to assign me some *airhead*, but Sal really seems to have her shit together."

"Sal? What's this Sal business? You're not down there two days and already I have to start worrying about another woman?" Megan teased.

"Baby, you know you never have to worry about another woman. She's straight, anyway."

"And that's supposed to make me feel better? The straight ones are the worst!" Megan said, the kidding tone suddenly disappearing from her voice.

"Look, babe, we've only got two days left before the weekend. Then you can come down and check her out for yourself, okay? We can go to the Pussy Willow bar I told you about, and have some fun. I promise I'll take the night off."

There was a long pause before Megan responded. "I can't make it this weekend." Her voice was filled with regret. "We got so backed up in the lab this week, I just can't get away."

"Shit! I'll probably be back before you can get a day off." Toni's voice echoed her disappointment. "It's okay, honey, you know I understand how our line of work can screw up your life. I'll see you when I get home. Don't forget I love you."

"Sweet dreams until we meet again, sweetheart. I love you, too."

When Toni arrived in the office the next morning, Sally was already hard at work.

Looking up, she smiled. "Hi, Toni."

"Good morning." Toni smiled back.

Sally had on skintight jeans and a navy blue tee shirt that left nothing to the imagination. A white linen sports jacket hung on the coat rack near the door. Toni couldn't help but give her the once over.

Okay, you idiot, wipe the drool off your chin and act like the faithful person you are. You'd be in deep shit if Megan were here, Toni thought. Then added out loud, "Watch your step, Toni."

"Excuse me? What did you say?" Sally asked, as she walked over to the corkboard.

"Oh, I just said we look almost like twins today. Except my shirt's a little lighter blue than yours." Toni tried to look busy. She glanced at her watch. *Hmm, only 8:00 a.m.. This gal is really a worker.* Trying to sound businesslike, she asked, "So what have you been doing this morning?"

"Well, for the last half hour I've made sure we have all the information on these women up on the board. Here's what we come up with so far." Sally began reviewing the data they'd collected. "Each one of these women was in an executive position with the companies they worked for. Each was in her early forties. Each one was divorced. At this point, we have to assume all of them had been involved in the lesbian life-styles in one way or the other, and at least three of them knew Nicky Clark. And from what you told me, it may just be they also all knew the killer. How am I doing so far, boss?" Sally looked at Toni, a wide grin on her face.

"Sounds good. I think today we pay a little visit to the Lazy Q Ranch. What do you say?" Toni asked, heading for the door. Sally nodded eagerly, made sure her .45 was in her white leather shoulder bag, and followed Toni out the door.

The Lazy Q Ranch sat at the foot of the San Jacinto mountains, about thirty minutes southwest from downtown Palm Springs. There was nothing around for miles. Like most places built in the desert, it seemed to spring up out of nowhere.

They drove through an ornate white gate, and passed horses grazing peacefully in pastures which spread to either side of the drive. Tall date palms and oleanders lined the long driveway.

The main building turned out to be an impressive two-story ranch house. A wooden sign hung over the door, with the words Thunderbird Lodge burned into it. There were several smaller structures to either side, which were replicas of shops you'd find in an old mining town. A long wooden walkway connected the buildings, and there were twenty or so separate cushy-looking adobe villas scattered among the pine trees.

"Damn, this is quite a setup," Toni whistled.

"Really nice, isn't it?" I believe the pool and tennis courts are in back, out of view of approaching cars."

"Oh, have you been here before?" Toni asked.

"No, but I've seen pictures of it, a long time ago."

"You mean before these nasty queers took it over, right?"

"That's not what I meant at all. Get the chip off your shoulder, okay?" Sally's blue eyes flashed with sudden anger.

"I'm sorry, Sal, I had no right to take that attitude with you." Toni looked at Sally with her beguilingly innocent, please-forgive-me look.

Sally didn't respond.

As they walked silently through the front door, a blast of cool air hit them. It was a relief, as the temperature was 110 outside, and rising. The spacious living room had been converted into a lobby. A stone fireplace ran from floor to ceiling to the left of the entrance. Leather couches and cozy-looking easy chairs were all around the room. Southwestern pottery and lamps decorated the oak tables. The place had a quiet elegance. A tanned woman dressed in western clothes stood behind the registration counter.

"Can I help you ladies?" The clerk asked with a smile.

"Yes, we'd like to talk with Nicky Clark, please," Toni answered.

"Do you have business with, Ms. Clark?" the clerk asked.

"You might say that," Toni responded.

"Well, Ms. Clark doesn't see anyone without an appointment. Our manager, Ms. Anderson, handles all of our guest accommodations and business regarding the hotel."

"I think Ms. Clark will see *us*," Toni answered, showing her badge to the clerk.

"One moment, please." Her hand shook a bit as she buzzed the office. "Ms. Clark, there are two policewomen here to see you."

The clerk was clearly nervous. There was a slight pause while she listened. "She'll be out in just a moment. Please take a seat." She motioned to the plush leather lobby chairs.

"Something isn't kosher here. I can feel it," Toni whispered to Sally.

Sally didn't look at Toni; she was still pissed. Just as Toni turned to speak to her again, Sally hissed, "Here she comes," and quickly got to her feet.

Nicky Clark strode across the lobby towards Toni and Sally. Her faded blue jeans were tight against her muscular thighs and the short sleeves on her checkered shirt were rolled up twice. From a distance, she looked just like a man.

"This one's a hard-assed dyke," Toni said to Sally out of the corner of her mouth. "Better let me handle this."

"Good afternoon, Ms. Clark," Sally said, stepping forward, ignoring Toni's warning completely. "I'm Sergeant Murphy, and this is Lieutenant Underwood of the Riverside Police Department. Would you mind if we asked you a few questions?"

"Concerning what?" Nicky replied, in a deep voice. She undressed Sally with her dark, close-set eyes. Her manner was stiff and aggressive.

"As I'm sure you've read in the papers, and heard, there have been four murders in the Riverside/ Palm Springs areas, and...."

"I don't read the papers."

Sally began again. "I'm sure you've seen something about them on the TV."

"Don't watch much TV either."

Nicky was toying with Sally, and the Sergeant's face was turning red; she was becoming flustered and losing her train of thought. Clearly, Nicky had the upper hand already, and was reveling in it as she stood with her weight on one leg, thumbs hooked inside her pockets, a sneering smile on her thin lips.

Toni stepped close to Nicky. She knew Sally was getting nowhere and losing ground fast. "Look, Ms. Clark, being a resort owner and resident of the area, I would assume you'd want to do all you could to help in this investigation. Something like this could affect your business." Toni's voice was icy, her stare direct and cold. "Am I making myself clear?"

Nicky Clark set her broad, square jaw and stepped back two paces. Toni's straightforward, self-assured manner had worked.

Toni pressed her advantage and continued to prod Nicky. "Now, Ms. Clark, Sergeant Murphy and I have come here with only your best interests in mind. Our informant has told us the murdered women had been guests at your ranch, and that you were seen with three of the women out on the town." Toni put her hands in the pockets of her Levis and forced a concerned look to cover her face.

Then, in a soothing voice, she added, "You're certainly not under any suspicion in connection with these murders, and we certainly don't want to give you that impression. So, as the good citizen we believe you to be, you won't mind answering a couple of questions...right?"

Nicky was clearly in a corner now, and Toni could tell she felt ill at ease and nervous. *No more fun and games, you bitch,* Toni thought, as she smiled, staring into Nicky's eyes.

"Well, I guess I have time to answer a few questions if you think it might help. Follow me." Nicky turned and walked toward her office.

Sally walked beside Toni silently, in awe of how smoothly Toni had maneuvered Clark into allowing them to question her. Toni smiled down at Sally with a smug, I told-you-so expression. Sally couldn't help but smile back. *I Suppose I've got a lot to learn from this woman*, Sally thought.

As they were all sitting down, Toni began, "Now, Ms. Clark, we understand from our source that you either knew, or had contact with, at least three of these murdered women. Is that correct?"

Toni handed Nicky pictures of the four women. She slowly looked at each one. "They do look familiar."

Toni wasn't going to mess around. She knew if she didn't sound firm, yet calm and cool to this hard-faced woman, she'd get nowhere. Nicky would consider anything less than that a sign of weakness.

"I'm sorry, was that a yes or a no?"

Nicky looked up at Toni; her eyes were like ice. "Yeah, I know them."

"And how do you know them?" Toni persisted.

"They all stayed at the ranch during the last year." Nicky's voice was a whisper.

"Pardon me, I couldn't hear you, Ms. Clark." Toni sat forward in her chair. The more she studied this woman's body language and face, the more she disliked her.

Nicky repeated, almost shouting, "They all stayed here during the last year, okay?"

"Were you involved personally with any of them?" Sally asked in a soft manner.

"Yes." Again, Nicky's answer was barely audible.

"Sorry again, Ms. Clark, but we couldn't quite hear your answer." Toni flashed her most solicitous look.

Nicky's face had turned bright red. She knew Toni was being sarcastic.

"Ms. Clark." Sally intervened. "How soon could you get us the records on when these women stayed here, and the length of their stay?"

"Right away," Nicky answered, in a loud voice this time.

"We really would appreciate it if you would come to headquarters tomorrow and give us a detailed statement of your relationship to each woman. You don't mind, do you? I know it's Saturday, but you've been so helpful, and we really need to wrap up these minor loose ends. And of course, if you feel you should have your attorney present, that *is* your right. What time would be good for you?" Sally pulled out her notebook and looked at Nicky. Sally knew they had sucked Nicky into a situation she would now have a hard time backing out of without casting suspicion on herself. She'd caught on quickly to what Toni was doing.

"I'll be there at 9:00 a.m.," Nicky mumbled reluctantly.

"See you then," Sally replied with a pleasant smile.

They walked out of the room, leaving Nicky Clark slumped behind her desk.

"Do you think she knows something that will really help us, Toni?" Sally asked on the drive back to Palm Springs.

"I'm sure of it. Did you notice how she shifted around in her chair? And her voice...she was very tense. Body language says a lot, and this woman's nervous. We're going to make a hell of a team. You catch on fast. Stick with me and you'll learn to handle 'em all." Toni had a big self-satisfied grin on her face.

After they finished scrutinizing all their notes from the visit with Nicky Clark, it was time to call it a day. Sally yawned and stretched.

"Long day, huh?" Toni said, as she followed Sally out, closing the door behind them.

"Very. All I want to do is go home, get out of these clothes, take a hot shower, and relax."

"I have an idea," Toni said as they continued down the hall. "Why don't you run by your house, grab some clothes, come to my place, take a swim, and have some dinner?"

"I don't know, Toni, I'm really beat. Maybe another time, okay?"

"Sure, that's fine, whenever you're ready. The invitation is always open. See ya tomorrow."

Toni realized she was feeling a bit down as she drove out of town toward Bill Perry's house. *Did she say no because she was afraid I might try something, or was she really that tired?* This thought bothered Toni. She didn't want Sally feeling defensive toward her. She liked Sally and hoped they could become friends.

At exactly 9:00 a.m. the desk sergeant buzzed Toni's extension. "Nicky Clark is here to see you, Lieutenant."

"Fine. Send her in, Harry." To Sally, she said, "Get ready, Sal, she's here."

There was a light rap on the door, and then it opened. "Good morning, Ms. Clark," Toni said flatly, deliberately not looking up.

Nicky did not respond.

"Good morning, Ms. Clark," Sally said, shaking Nicky's hand. "Have a seat. Would you care for coffee?" Sally smiled warmly.

"No, thank you, Sergeant."

Sally placed a tape recorder on the table in front of Nicky.

"I hope you don't mind, but we are going to tape our conversation today. Don't want to forget anything, you know." Again, Sally smiled.

Suddenly, Toni rose from her chair and walked to the conference room door. "Sergeant Murphy, I'm going out for a while and check that new lead we got last night." Then turning to Nicky she said, "I'll leave you in the capable hands of the Sergeant here, Ms. Clark. I *know* you'll give her your *full* cooperation. And oh, yes, thanks again for coming in on a Saturday." Before Nicky could respond, Toni turned abruptly and left the room.

Opening the door to the adjacent room, Toni walked in and sat down in front of the two-way mirror.

Nicky leaned over toward Sally, resting her elbows on the conference table. "I don't think Lieutenant Underwood likes me. Is there some reason for that?" she asked in a husky voice.

"Boy, is she playing the part of the innocent to the hilt," Toni mumbled to herself.

"We're trying to solve four very ugly murders here, Ms. Clark, and we're all a little tense. Lieutenant Underwood is very dedicated to this case and sometimes she seems abrupt. I'm sure it would distress her to think you had the wrong idea about her. After all, you're being more than cooperative." Sally smiled encouragingly.

What a line of bull. Sally's getting better at this every minute. Toni grinned as she watched the interplay between the two women.

"Now shall we begin? First of all, please read and sign this Admonishment Statement, and initial where indicated. It's only a formality, and self explanatory." The statement consisted of the basic reading of a person's rights in printed form.

Nicky carefully read the paper, signed it, and handed it back to Sally.

Then, Sally turned on the tape recorder and announced, "Questioning of Nicky Clark. Subject: Highway 60 serial murders, Riverside-Palm Springs. Date of questioning, 1992, Saturday, June 27th. 9:15 a.m.. Ms. Clark, are you aware we are taping this conversation?"

"Yes."

"And this is being done with your full permission?"

"Yes."

"And you've read and signed the Admonishment Statement, informing you of your right to have an attorney present? And you've waived that right, is this correct?"

"Yes." Nicky answered once more. She appeared to be growing nervous, so Sally pressed right on to the questioning before Nicky could change her mind.

"Okay, Ms. Clark, let's start from the beginning."

Nicky sat straight in the chair with her hands on the table and her fingers interlaced through most of the questioning. Sally noticed her knuckles turning white when the question of dating the murdered women was brought up.

After two hours, and two tapes, Sally concluded her questioning of Nicky Clark.

"Thank you, Ms. Clark. You've been most helpful."

Sally rose, shook Nicky's hand, and then walked her to the door. Nicky Clark definitely looked tired, and left without saying another word.

Toni came back into the room. "Well, did we get anything, or not?"

"Don't know yet. Let's get this information transcribed, and get a computer printout so we can go over every detail methodically."

Sally picked up the tapes and headed for the computer room.

That dyke is hiding something, and I'm going to find out what it is. With that thought in mind, Toni picked up the phone. She wanted to fill Captain Morris in on what was going on. Her second call would be to Megan.

6

I'M telling you they don't know a fucking thing!" Nicky's voice was angry. She sat on the edge of her desk, twirling the letter opener in her fingers as she spoke. "All they asked about were the four broads who were murdered. Everything's been put away in a safe place, and no one will touch it until these cops get out of my life. I've spent most of this morning answering their stupid questions, and I'm not going to waste the rest of the day answering yours."

Nicky listened impatiently to the voice on the other end of the phone.

"Get off my ass. If it wasn't for me, you'd have no major connection here, so can it!" She slammed the phone down. The nostrils of her broad flat nose flared as she took a few deep breaths.

Furious, she walked over to the wet bar, pulled a bottle of whiskey from the shelf and grabbed a shot glass. Then, returning to her desk, she flopped down in the leather chair and slugged down two quick shots. After coughing several times, she buzzed the front desk on her intercom.

"Cookie, I'm goin' out, if there are any calls, just take a message."

After downing one more full shot glass, Nicky banged the whiskey bottle down, stomped across the office, and threw open the door. The heels of her alligator boots struck angrily against the terra-cotta tile floor as she strode down the corridor and across the lobby.

Once outside, she crossed the parking area and jumped into her black Jag. The tires squealed against the asphalt as she headed for town.

Cookie stood behind the front desk shaking her head. *"Somebody's* in big shit," she whispered under her breath.

It was 6:00 p.m., and T.J. had just relieved the day bartender, Sydney. While counting out the cash, T.J. thought, *Syd was pretty busy today, maybe I should give her a raise. Ever since I hired her my day receipts have increased. Would hate to lose her, she's become quite an asset.*

Even though it was a Saturday, the crowd usually thinned out until around eight o'clock. There were eight women still in the bar. Four were playing pool in the alcove off the dance floor. Jill Collins was watching the pool game as she sipped her rum and coke, while three other women sat at the bar watching a women's golf tournament on the TV.

Poor Jill. T.J. thought. *Too bad she ever got mixed up with that bitch Nicky.*

Something made T.J. look up from the cash drawer. Someone was standing in the doorway. The bright light coming from outside blinded T.J. so that she couldn't make out who it was.

"Hi, *Thelma June.*" A deep voice thundered out at her. The figure moved further into the room.

"Hear ya got diarrhea of the mouth lately." Nicky Clark stomped up to a bar stool and sat down. The blood drained from T.J.'s face.

"What the hell are ya talkin' about, Nicky?"

"Hear ya been blabbin' your mouth off to the cops about my business." Nicky was glaring at her.

"What business?"

"You know, about the murdered women, and how I knew 'em. Isn't that right? Bitch!" Nicky spat.

"Nicky, I don't want no trouble from you. All I did was answer some questions the cops asked, that's all." T.J.'s hand slowly reached under the bar for her bat.

"From now on, ya old bitch, leave my name outta your conversations altogether, or some unexplained things might just start happenin' 'round here. Understand'?" Nicky was leaning over the bar menacingly, her face inches from T.J.'s. "Now, gimme a draft beer, bitch."

Just as Nicky tipped the mug of cold beer to her lips a familiar voice blasted her eardrums. "Hey, Ms. Clark, you wouldn't be angry at my friend T.J. here, now would you?" Toni slapped Nicky on the back. No one had noticed Toni enter the bar soon after Nicky.

Coughing and choking, Nicky spit the beer out of her mouth.

"God damn, Ms. Clark, you sound like you're gonna die or something. Did you swallow wrong, or what?" Toni hit her hard on the back a few times.

"You just scared the shit out of me, god damn it!" Nicky's face was red, and beer was running down her chin.

"Gee, Ms. Clark, I'm real sorry about that," Toni said smiling.

It took everything T.J. had to hold back the laugh welling up in her throat.

Nicky jumped to her feet, threw two dollars on the bar and split.

"God damn, Lieutenant Underwood, that was great. First time I've ever seen Nicky Clark scared of anyone. Thanks."

"Believe me T.J., it was my pleasure. And please, call me Toni, at least when I'm off duty." She sat down.

"Since you're off duty now, *Toni,* how about a drink, on the house?"

"Don't mind if I do, T.J.. Make it a Miller Light," Toni smiled as she straddled the bar stool.

"Anything new on the murders, or shouldn't I ask?" T.J. said, putting Toni's beer bottle down on a napkin.

"Right now we're just following leads, filling out reports, and collecting information. We really won't know any more until we follow up some more leads. Spent the whole day in the office. That's the part of this job I hate. But without it, I'm afraid we'd never solve a case." Toni took a long pull on her beer.

She casually looked around the bar. Then her eyes rested on the lonely looking young woman sitting near the pool tables. "Who's that girl sitting over there?" Toni gestured toward Jill Collins.

T.J. frowned. "Oh, that poor thing. She's one of Nicky's ex's, or should I say, victims? Her name is Jill Collins. Works at a restaurant in town. She's in here all the time now. Doesn't know what to do with herself, if ya know what I mean. She tried suicide right after Nicky dumped her. We all try to look out for her as much as we can."

T.J. set another cold beer down in front of Toni. Beer in hand, Toni walked over to Jill. "Hi, good game?"

The four women were still shooting pool. Jill didn't answer.

"My name's Toni. Do you come in here often?"

Jill turned and faced Toni. Her sad, blue eyes were framed by a pale thin face; a small scar stood out on her left cheek. The tank top she was wearing hung on her, as clothes do on someone who's lost weight. Her long thin fingers shook as she reached for a cigarette.

"Here, let me," Toni said, offering her a light.

Jill accidently knocked the pack off the wall counter with her elbow, but, before Toni could move, she was bending down to pick it up. Toni noticed a rather large, strange-looking mark on Jill's shoulder. *A scar from a burn, or maybe a birthmark.* She made a mental note of it.

Taking a long drag on her cigarette, Jill blew the smoke in Toni's face. "Who the hell are you?" She asked, in a thin voice. She was obviously not pleased about having company.

"I told you, my name is Toni. I'm a friend of T.J.'s from out of town. She tells me you were once close with Nicky Clark. Is that correct?" Toni was pushing her luck now.

Jill's eyes grew wide. Behind the glassy stare Toni sensed an inner terror. "That's no one's business but mine." Her lips were pressed tightly together; they barely moved as she spoke. Without another word, Jill got up, turned, and left the bar.

Toni noticed a slight stagger to her walk.

Two more women had come in, and T.J. was busy mixing drinks. She looked up just as Toni reached the door. Toni waved, and mouthed, "I'll see you later."

Toni quickly removed her jacket and tossed it into the back seat. It was suffocatingly hot in the car. Her white cotton shirt was already beginning to stick to her skin. Putting the key into the ignition, she started the engine, and turned the air on full blast.

Then she pulled down the visor, searching. *Let's see, I know I left my notebook in here somewhere.* She opened the glove compartment. *Ah, there you are.*

Pulling out her pen, Toni quickly drew a picture of the mark she'd observed on Jill Collins' shoulder.

It was 7:30 p.m. when Toni pulled in her driveway. The sun was beginning to dip low in the sky, but the temperature was still 116.

Boy, Toni thought, opening the front door, *I can hardly wait to jump in the pool.*

She started unbuttoning her blouse as she headed for the bedroom. Soft music came from the radio beside the bed. Toni froze. She reached for her gun, pulling it quickly from her belt holster.

Reaching back to the small of her back with her left hand, she checked to make sure the flap of her handcuff holder was open. Then, with both hands on her Smith and Wesson .45, she entered the bedroom carefully.

The sliding glass door was slightly open. Water was running in the bathroom. Toni inched her way along the wall to the bathroom door. *Who the hell is that?* She could hear someone humming softly. She took a deep breath. Raising her gun, and lifting her right leg, she gave one swift kick. The door flew open.

"Jesus Christ, Megan!" Toni could barely speak; her heart was pounding in her throat.

Megan was standing in the middle of the bathroom clutching a towel to her chest. They stood, frozen, staring at one another.

Finally, Megan spoke. "My God, Toni, you could have killed me."

"Megan, what in the hell are you doing here, and how the hell did you get in? I wasn't expecting you." Toni was screaming at her.

Composing herself, Megan quietly said, "Honey, just put the gun down, and I'll explain everything, okay?"

Toni blinked; she hadn't realized she was still holding the gun on Megan. Slowly, she lowered her weapon and walked to the bed.

"Do you know how close I came to shooting you?" Toni whispered, tears in her eyes.

"It's my fault, honey." She took Toni's trembling hand. "I should have called and told you I was coming. I requested a week's vacation and it was approved yesterday. And since I only wanted to surprise you, *not scare you to death,* I got a spare key from Carla Perry."

Tears were slowly trickling down Toni's face. "Please don't ever surprise me this way again. I think I've already made a bad enemy here, so I'm pretty tense."

Megan leaned over and gently kissed Toni's mouth. "Never again, honey, I promise."

They lay back on the bed holding each other, kissing each other tenderly. Toni looked deep into Megan's bright eyes. "I love you so much, babe, even if you did scare the holy shit out of me, you twit."

Hitting Toni on the arm, Megan jumped to her feet.

"Let's go for a swim." Abandoning her towel, she ran out the door and dove into the crystal clear water. Toni laughed, undressed, and dove in after her.

"God, this is wonderful," Megan said. "Good thing this house and backyard wall are surrounded by those, tall oleander bushes, or we might find ourselves *exposed* in one of the gossip magazines." She smiled broadly and gave Toni a sly wink.

She wrapped her long legs around Toni's waist. They laughed and played in the cool water for over an hour.

Finally, Toni said. "Come on, honey, I'm starving." Then her voice grew loud and deep. "Get me some dinner, woman."

Toni was putting on one of her best *macho* impressions. She pushed Megan toward the steps in the shallow end of the pool.

"I been workin' my ass off all day while you've laid around watchin' soap operas. Now get me some supper, and a beer, and make it quick."

"Oh yes, oh lord and master," Megan squealed. "Please, oh please, don't beat me."

"That's more like it, bitch," Toni roared.

"Oh, one more thing, oh, lord and master," Megan said sweetly.

"Yeah, what is it?" Toni replied stepping out of the pool.

"You can kiss my ass!" And with that, Megan reached for the bucket she had filled with ice and poured it over Toni's head, then pushed her back into the pool.

The shocked expression on Toni's face caused Megan to laugh until her sides ached. Toni came up spitting water.

"I'm gonna get you for this."

Toni's teeth were clenched as she started up the steps out of the pool. She hunched her back and curled her fingers as she stretched her arms out toward Megan. Her eyes were open wide and wild. Her hair was sticking out in all directions. She looked like a mad fiend.

Megan began backing up. "Toni, now stop it. You know how I hate it when you scare me. You win. Please don't make that face."

With a loud, hideous laugh Toni lunged for her. "Too late, my pretty. Revenge will be mine."

Toni grabbed Megan up in her arms and carried her to the edge of the pool. Kicking her legs wildly and beating on Toni's back, Megan screamed. "God damn it, Toni put me down. This isn't funny any more. I...."

Suddenly, Megan decided to try another tack. She didn't finish her sentence. Instead, she stopped kicking and hitting Toni and went limp in her arms. Closing her eyes, she softly moaned.

In a flash, Toni's mouth covered Megan's nipple, sucking it in. Her tongue began licking the tip, as she bit gently. And Megan's anger and fear were quickly erased by the sudden arousal she felt.

Carefully, Toni placed her on the edge of the pool, her legs dangled in the water up to the knee. Climbing into the pool she pulled herself between Megan's thighs.

Her face drew close as Megan opened herself to her lover. Without a moment's hesitation, Toni began licking and teasing Megan's clit with her tongue. Megan leaned back with pleasure, pushing her hips even more forward. Toni drew her in as she felt the clit grow hard.

Moments later, Megan's stomach muscles twitched as her climax gushed forth. Toni gently pulled her into the cool water and held her close, kissing her.

"I think I like this game after all." She whispered in Toni's ear.

Their breasts were touching; nipples hard against each other's. Megan's hand went under the water. Toni happily spread her legs as Megan's fingers rubbed against her. It didn't take much to get her over the peak of her passion, for she was already inflamed. She moaned; her legs felt like rubber as she came quick and hard.

They smiled at each other and dove under the water to cool their hot bodies.

After dressing in shorts and tee shirts, the two women began preparing dinner. There were steaks, potatoes, and lettuce in the refrigerator, and the bar was well stocked. They had everything needed for a glorious late night feast.

After dinner, Toni poured brandy, and they went outside. The moon was bright; it seemed they could see every star in the sky.

"Where's your car, honey?" Toni asked, realizing she hadn't seen it when she drove in.

Megan lowered her eyes. "It's in the garage. I hid it so you wouldn't know I was here."

"Hell, no wonder I didn't know who was in the house."

"Let's not bring that up again, okay? Tell me what's happening with the case?" She snuggled against Toni, wanting to change the subject before Toni got worked up all over again.

They sat sipping their drinks for two hours while Toni filled Megan in on all the information she and Sally had gathered so far.

Megan sat back taking a deep breath. "Sounds like this Nicky character may be a key player in all of this."

"Yeah, she's a piece of work all right. I can't really pin anything on her yet, but I know this all has something to do with her, and her god damn ranch. The one thing I have managed to do, is make her hate my guts. Maybe if I rag on her long enough, she'll make a mistake." Toni took a sip of brandy.

Megan listened thoughtfully. "Sounds like what you really need is someone on the inside. Someone who might be able to get close to her. Someone with big ears, and a nose for trouble, someone no one here knows." She poured Toni another drink.

"Yeah, that would be great."

Megan sat silently staring at Toni. She had one eyebrow raised, and a sly smile on her face. All of a sudden, it hit Toni like a slap in the face.

"OH, NO YOU DON'T!" Toni jumped to her feet. "DON'T EVEN TRY TO TALK ME INTO THIS; I WON'T HEAR OF IT!" She turned and stormed into the house.

"But, honey..." Megan was right on Toni's heels. "It's perfect, don't you see? No one knows who I am, or that I'm even here. Besides, I've done it before when I was still a uniformed cop, don't you remember?"

She kept following Toni from room to room. When Toni came to a sudden dead stop, Megan walked into her, almost knocking her down. Whirling around, Toni took Megan by the shoulders.

"Come with me." Toni led her into the living room and pushed her onto the couch. "Now listen to me. First of all, when you went undercover before, it was a mugger we were after. You were covered at all times. There was no real danger. Remember? *THIS* time we're after a psychopath who loves to beat and kill women. And we don't know who it is.

"Nicky Clark is not simply a women who runs a guest ranch. There's something mean about her. Her body language, her beady little eyes, her aura. The way she threatened T.J. at the bar this afternoon. Chalk it up to experience, but I feel it in my bones; she could be viciously dangerous."

Toni paused thoughtfully weighing her next words. "You'd be alone, no back-up. You'd be out on that fucking ranch alone. The answer is, NO! And that's final, honey." Toni sat down next to Megan, out of breath. Her thickly lashed eyelids blinked rapidly as she stared at Megan.

Megan turned and looked into Toni's clear blue eyes. "Honey, I know this idea scares you, but if you think about it, it's the only real chance you have of getting the inside line on what Nicky Clark has to do with this mess. I did work vice for two years before becoming a criminologist, you know. Just because I'm not in the field any more, doesn't mean I'm not a cop."

The blue, green, and brown flecks flashed in Megan's eyes as she continued excitedly. "A fake I.D., some phony background, a different name, and I'm sure no one would ever even question what I'm doing out at that ranch. I'm not stupid, and I sure don't want to die. Besides, it might only take two or three days at the most." Megan was on her feet now, pacing back and forth rapidly as she spoke.

"If we work together, maybe we can get this thing over with and you can concentrate on the future. I know you've thought a lot about leaving the force. This could be the last case for you. Let's finish it. I want the old Toni back and I want to see a smile on that wonderful face more often. Please let me help." Suddenly, she sat back down next to Toni, and silently stared into her eyes.

The look Toni gave her was hard as steel. But she had listened, and had to admit Megan's idea was a good one.

"If anything happened to you, I don't know what I'd do." Toni's voice was a whisper. She gently placed her hand on Megan's tanned face.

"Honey, nothing is going to happen to me, and even if it did, and of course it won't, you couldn't blame yourself. I insist on doing this, okay?" Megan smiled, and kissed her.

"I hate this. I hate it when you're right and I have no more arguments left to fight you with." Toni was on her feet pacing. Then she went to the phone.

"Who are you calling? It's one o'clock in the morning."

Without responding, she growled into the phone, "Murphy? Yeah, this is Toni. Get dressed, and get over to my place right now! Please."

Within thirty minutes Sally was knocking on the door. Toni opened it, her face grey.

"What the hell's up, Toni? You look like death warmed over." Sally looked concerned as she stepped into the living room. She had thrown on a tee shirt, jeans, and an old pair of sneakers. Her hair had been hastily pulled back into a pony tail, and she looked half asleep.

Megan approached Sally with her hand out. "Hi, you must be Sally. I've heard so much about you from Toni, I feel as if I already know you."

"And you're Megan. Toni's told me all about you, too." Sally smiled as she shook Megan's hand. Then she turned toward Toni. "So, what's going on?"

They all sat at the kitchen table while Toni filled Sally in on the plan. Sally didn't say a word through the whole conversation, and just listened intently while sipping the black coffee Megan had freshly brewed.

She watched as Toni smoked one cigarette after another and drank more brandy than she should. Sally knew Toni was not happy about this decision. Megan seemed relaxed, except for the slight shaking of her hands.

Finally, Sally sat back, taking a deep breath. "Wow! Some idea you came up with, Megan. I really have to hand it to you. It's great, but I still can't believe Toni's going to let you do it."

"The only way she's going to do it, is to have a gun with her at all times." Megan opened her mouth to speak. "Don't say a word." Toni continued, "No gun, no do. Got it?"

"But..."

Sally interrupted Megan. "That's really no big problem. You probably have your own gun, but I feel we should use a piece that a private citizen might carry. You know, a *lady's* gun. We can get a phony gun permit, and make up a cover story regarding the gun. A lot of women carry them nowadays."

With a resigned sigh, Toni said, "Okay, Sal, tomorrow, it's up to you to get all the stuff we need to make a new person out of Megan. But absolutely no one is to know what's going on. Do you understand? No one. This is between the three of us, and that's it."

Raising her eyebrows in a questioning manner, Megan asked, "Toni, don't you want to inform Captain Morris of our plan?"

"All in good time, honey. But until we get an idea of how this is going to play out, I want to keep this just between the three of us. Okay?"

Toni stood up and walked Sally to the door.

"See you both tomorrow." Sally waved, as the door closed behind her.

"She's okay," Megan said, getting into bed.

"Yeah, she is, babe. Now, let's see how smart she is."

Toni turned out the light. They held each other very close. Megan could feel Toni's heart beating; it seemed as though it would break through her chest.

"I love you, Toni Underwood," Megan whispered.

"You're my life, Megan," Toni responded softly.

Their lovemaking was long, and sweet, and gentle this night. There was a tenderness between them that hadn't been there for a long time, since the beginning, since when they were just getting to know each other.

Toni lay awake all night holding Megan to her. She wished tomorrow would never come. For the first time in her life, Toni truly wanted time to stand still.

7

"**I'll** get it," Toni called from the bedroom as she answered the phone. "Right. Okay. Got it," was all Toni said, and then she hung up.

"Who was it, honey?"

"It was Murphy. She'll have everything we need by one o'clock this afternoon. She'll come here and brief us then."

Toni went to the kitchen. Sitting down, she sipped her coffee. Megan sat across from her, staring into her coffee cup. Toni didn't say a word.

"Are you all right, honey?" Megan broke the silence.

"No, I'm not all right, and I won't be until this is over."

Megan took Toni's hand. "I love you, baby. Please don't worry. I know everything will be all right."

"Yeah, I know. But if anything, and I mean *anything*, seems weird, I want you to get out immediately. Do you understand? Don't try and outsmart Nicky Clark, or anyone else. *Promise me!*" Toni's face was tense and tight.

"I understand, and you have my word, I'll get out at the first sign of trouble."

They spent the morning by the pool, sunning, and swimming, and waiting for Sally. Toni watched Megan dozing on the lounge.

God, she really is beautiful, Toni thought. To this day, the sight of her thick auburn hair and hazel eyes still caused Toni's heart to skip a beat. The doorbell rang. Toni jumped.

"Hi, Sal, come on in," Toni said as she opened the door.

"Hi, Sally," Megan called from poolside.

"Come in here." Toni led Sally to the kitchen. "Pour yourself some iced tea and relax for a minute while Megan and I change."

"A cold drink sounds good." Sally looked tired.

Megan and Toni returned within ten minutes. Sally had already laid out all the papers on the table.

"Okay, this is everything you need to become Megan Marshall, Chief Executive Officer at Kendell Pharmaceuticals, Inc. in Portland, Oregon. A high-paying, prestigious position. Eight hundred grand a year, if anyone asks." Sally began her briefing.

"Now, I want you both to know I did the best I could to cover all the bases here, but if by chance I missed something, Megan's going to have to play it by ear.

"I've arranged a rental car for you, a Mercedes 450 SL. Credit cards, driver's license, Social Security card. Here's a wallet with family pictures, etc. We'll go over this in a minute, so you know who's who.

"I have a set of luggage with your name tags on it, and cancelled airline tickets. You'll find five hundred dollars, in cash, in the wallet. You're a little younger than the murdered women, but I upped your age five years to thirty nine, that should do. Now, are there any questions so far?" Sally looked at Toni and Megan.

"What about the gun?" Toni asked.

"You have a phony gun permit in your wallet, and the gun is in the purse. It's a .22 caliber. Very fancy. After all, you're a woman of some means now, you know," Sally answered, a slight smile on her face.

"A peashooter," Toni grumbled.

Sally paused for a moment, taking a sip of her iced tea. Megan's eyes sparkled as she watched Sally drink the tea. Little pangs of apprehension jabbed at her insides, but they were quickly replaced by feelings of excitement at the prospect of helping to solve these horrendous murders.

Toni sat stony-faced through the whole briefing.

"Your name is Megan Marshall, you've been divorced two years. Your ex-husband died a year ago of cancer; you have no children. In fact, you have no living relatives; it's easier that way.

"The pictures in the wallet are of your mother and father, Mary and Stewart Walsh, who were killed in an automobile accident four years ago. You've worked for Kendell Pharmaceuticals for twelve years.

"I want the two of you to go over this information for the rest of the day, until you've got it down. I'm going out to purchase enough clothes to get you by for now. You, of course, will go on a shopping spree later. There is a ten o'clock American Airlines flight due in from Portland tonight. Megan, you will arrive on that flight. Your luggage will be waiting for you at the Palm Springs airport, and so will your rental car, at the Desert Car Rentals. Their office is in the terminal. You'll drive to the ranch and check in. Here's a map.

"Since it's the off season here in Palm Springs, I had no trouble in making your reservation at the Lazy Q."

"How do I get to the airport?" Megan asked.

"I'll pick you up at 9:00 p.m.. Just make sure no one sees you leave the house. I'll be driving a dark blue Ford Escort and I'll take you to the airport, okay?" Sally sat back and took a deep breath.

Toni was impressed. "God damn, Sal, you're something else. I can't believe you managed all this so quickly. It sounds perfect."

"You big city cops aren't the only ones with brains, you know?" Sally replied, a smug look on her face. But her expression changed as she looked at Megan. "Remember, Megan, you're the one who has to convince Nicky Clark you're who you say you are. Once you get to the ranch, all Toni and I can do is pray our plan works."

"You have to play it cool, and keep your wits about you at all times. Don't ever let your guard down," Toni added.

Sally got up. "Oh, one more thing. Every two days we will meet you in Indio at the shopping mall pet shop. A friend of mine, Carol, owns the shop. I'll be dressed as if I work there. Toni, you'll be in the backroom. I thought it best to set up our meetings outside of the Palm Springs area. That way we're less likely to run into someone who may recognize me.

"Megan, if you ever feel this thing is going up in smoke and you need us, call the number on this card, and tell them you wish to leave a message for Mr. Bunker. It doesn't matter what you say after that...that's our signal to move."

"Sounds just fine, Sally," Megan said, giving her a big hug. "Thanks."

"Don't thank me yet, Megan; thank me when it's over, okay?" Sally returned the hug.

"Do you feel better, honey?" Megan asked Toni.

"I guess so, but I won't sleep until you're back here with me. Now let's not waste time. Sit down and start telling me about yourself, Mrs. Marshall."

It was 8:00 p.m. when Toni picked up the phone and called Captain Morris at home. "Hi, Harvey, how the hell are you?"

"What's up, Toni?"

"Have you received all my reports so far on the case?"

"Sure have, Toni. Sounds like you're making a little progress, but the Chief is still on my ass everyday. The detectives on your Highway 60 Murders task force will be faxing their reports to you tomorrow."

"Great! Sure hope they've come up with some new information. This whole case is like a maze, and it's starting to scramble my brain." Toni expelled a deep sigh. Then wearily she said, "I'll talk to you later Harvey. Just wanted to touch base."

"You know, Toni, I tried to keep you off this case, but the Chief insisted it be you. I can try one more time to get you replaced, if that's what *you* want, of course."

"Thanks for telling me that, Harvey. I knew you understood how I've been feeling lately about this job, and I appreciate your trying to ease my stress, but this case is mine now, and I have to see it through to the end, *no matter what*."

"Okay, Toni, but I just hope this whole thing doesn't bring you more grief than you can handle," Harvey warned in a deep, steady voice.

After hanging up the phone, Toni smiled slightly. *He really does worry about me,* she thought. Then, she turned to Megan. With a tightening in her voice she said, "It's just about time to *Play Ball!*"

At nine o'clock Megan was ready to go. Toni kissed her and held her close. Finally, pulling away gently, Megan looked into Toni's face.

"See you soon, honey. Please try not to worry too much. You're always with me. Sweet dreams until we meet again."

With that, Megan turned and stepped through the door into the fast approaching darkness of night. A sudden numbness spread through Toni's body as she watched Megan disappear down the street.

An elegant Megan Marshall stepped into the lobby of the Thunderbird Lodge at 11:00 p.m., wearing an Armani powder-blue linen pants suit. Shoes by Cole Haan. A white kidskin handbag designed by Gucci hung from her shoulder.

The gold jewelry, on loan from the property section of the police department, glistened against her tanned skin. Her long auburn hair was swept up on the sides and back from her face, then fell in wavy cascades down to her shoulders. The clerk gave her a big welcoming smile.

"Mrs. Marshall, I presume." The clerk continued smiling.

"Why, yes," Megan answered. She signed the register, and looked up at the well-endowed clerk. "Is your dining room still serving?"

"I'm sorry, Mrs. Marshall, the dining room stops serving dinner at 10:30, but if you'd like to have a drink in the bar while you wait, I can have the cook make you a nice ham or roast beef sandwich."

"I'll have the roast beef, and please make sure it's rare and lean," Megan answered casually. "I'd like some fresh fruit, also."

"Let me have someone take your bags to your villa. It's number three, near the pool." She motioned to a muscular young woman who had just come out of Nicky's office. Megan handed her the car keys.

"My name is Kelly," the clerk said. "If you need anything else, I will be happy to do what I can."

"Thank you, Kelly." Megan smiled slightly, and headed for the bar.

Nicky Clark had been standing in the shadows by the door of her office. Her square jaw was set tight and her dark eyes watched as Megan disappeared through the doorway into the lounge. She walked up to the counter and turned the registration book around.

"Megan Marshall, huh. Not bad, not bad at all." Nicky took long confident strides as she walked toward the bar.

"Here we go again," Kelly said softly, shaking her head. "Please God, no trouble this time, please." She turned the book back to its proper position.

Megan picked a stool at the far end of the bar and ordered a gin and tonic.

The cocktail lounge was spacious and elegantly appointed. The back bar was mirrored, with hidden lights reflecting off bottles and glasses. The bar itself was long, the stools well-padded and comfortable. A postage-stamp size dance floor took up a small space at the far end of the room. The jukebox played softly in the background. It was very nice.

Two women sat together at a small table near the dance floor. Their faces almost touched as they whispered over their drinks. They were oblivious to everything but each other.

Megan sighed and took a sip of her drink. It had been a hard day. Leaving Toni almost tore her apart inside.

Nicky entered the bar quietly and took a seat four stools down from where Megan was sitting. She signalled the bartender to give Megan another drink.

As the bartender set the drink down in front of her, Megan looked up with a questioning expression. She hadn't noticed Nicky; she had been so absorbed in her thoughts of Toni. The bartender pointed at Nicky. "Compliments," the tall woman said. With that, she turned away and walked to the other end of the bar.

Giving Nicky a small smile, Megan nodded her head in thanks. Almost immediately she knew this was Nicky Clark; the description given to her by Toni and Sally fit to a tee. Her features were strong and heavy, almost masculine. Megan hadn't expected to run into her so soon.

"Hello, Mrs. Marshall. Welcome to the Lazy Q." Nicky's voice was deep and velvety, full of self-assurance. Smoothly, she moved to the stool next to Megan. Her black silk shirt was opened to the top of her breasts, allowing a bit of the cleavage to show. Megan couldn't place Nicky's cologne, but it was very clean and fresh-smelling.

"Good evening. I'm afraid you have me at a disadvantage. You are..." Megan replied, not smiling.

"Well, I'm Nicky Clark, your host here. I own the Lazy Q, and personally take care of our special guests, such as yourself." Nicky was as smooth as silk. "Is there anything you need, or want?"

"Not at the moment, Ms. Clark; your clerk was kind enough to order me a sandwich, which I'm waiting for. But if I think of anything I need, I'll come to you right away." She gave Nicky a warm smile.

Nicky called to the bartender, "Karen, buzz the kitchen, and see what's holding up Mrs. Marshall's food."

"Thank you, Ms. Clark."

"Please, call me Nicky." She looked wantonly into Megan's eyes.

Great! She's already trying to make a move on me. Toni was right, I really have to keep my wits about me.

"On second thought, could you have that sent to my villa? I'm suddenly quite tired. I'd like to get out of these clothes and into something more comfortable." With that, Megan stood up, shook

Nicky's hand daintily, and left the room, leaving the drink Nicky had ordered for her untouched.

"Playing hard to get. I like that," Nicky muttered as she watched Megan disappear around the corner. "I love taking these high-tone types down a couple of notches. They come here for fun and games, to let their hair down, and do some mingling with the common folk. Well, I'll give her fun and games, *my kind of fun and games!* And I thought the week ahead would be dull." Nicky Clark had a wide grin on her face. Her dark eyes gleamed in the reflected light coming from behind the bar.

"That woman gives me the creeps, for sure," Megan said out loud, as she began unpacking. "I can see, though, how someone out for a fling might find her appealing."

There was a light tap on her door. Kelly was standing there, a tray in hand.

"Sorry it took so long, Mrs. Marshall," Kelly said, setting the tray down on the table.

"Oh, no problem, Kelly. Thank you for all your trouble." Megan handed Kelly a ten dollar bill.

"I can't take this, Mrs. Marshall. Orders from Ms. Clark." Kelly seemed nervous when talking about her boss. "No one can take anything from you. The whole staff is at your disposal at anytime."

"I'm sure you've had to go out of your way to do this, and it's only fair to reward your kindness in some way." Megan shoved the bill at Kelly once more.

"I'm sorry, Mrs. Marshall, I just can't. You don't want me to lose my job, do you?" Kelly was getting tense now; Megan could sense it.

"All right then, but when I leave, I'll make sure you get something, and no one has to know about it." Megan patted Kelly on the back as she left.

Megan tossed and turned most of the night. Her thoughts were filled with Toni. Not having Toni's long, muscular body lying next to her felt strange and lonely. She knew Toni wasn't sleeping either. Megan wasn't afraid, but Toni's warnings about Nicky kept going through her mind over and over again. Just from her brief meeting with the woman she knew this would not be a piece of cake. For the first time in many years she truly felt alone.

The morning sun worked its way through a small crack in the drapes, hitting Megan directly in the eye. She squinted, got up and pulled the curtains shut. The heat was already coming through the glass. The blistering desert summer was in full swing.

"What time is it?" she mumbled, looking at her clock. "I'd better get my act together, it's already 8:30. I should be seen as much as possible. And be sure I'm available for Ms. Nicky Clark."

The needle-sharp spray of the shower felt good, and seemed to clear away some of the cobwebs lack of sleep had left in her brain. *Must stay alert,* she thought. *Can't let my guard down for a minute.* Toni's words echoed through her mind.

After drying herself, Megan put on a pair of white silk shorts and a blue tank top, then slipped into a pair of tan leather sandals by Gucci. She smiled at herself in the mirror. *This outfit should get Nicky's attention.* She slung a straw purse over her shoulder and left her villa.

There were two couples in the dining room. The two from last night, still smiling and whispering secret things to each other, and an older pair, clearly comfortable with one another after years of sharing a life.

This scene brought a smile to Megan's face and she was lost in her own thoughts of Toni.

"And a wonderful, good Monday morning to you," Nicky Clark said. Megan was startled. "I'm sorry. Did I intrude on some deep personal thoughts?" Nicky smiled winningly. Her thin lips parted revealing very white teeth.

"I was just planning my day," Megan answered, smiling up at Nicky from her chair.

"Did you sleep well?"

"Just fine, thank you," she lied. "This is certainly a lovely spot. I looked around before coming in for breakfast."

"Later on, perhaps you'll allow me the pleasure of taking you on a tour?" Nicky paused, waiting for a response.

"That would be nice." Megan smiled once more, giving Nicky one of her sweetest looks.

"How about three o'clock?"

"That's perfect; it will give me time to get some sunbathing in. Even during the summer in Oregon the weather is so unpredictable that the opportunity for sunbathing is limited." Megan continued smiling.

"Oh, Ms. Clark," Kelly called softly from the doorway. "There's a call for you on line one. Sounds important."

"See you then." Nicky turned to leave. "Oh, and don't forget to wear a hat; the sun out here can be murderous."

"Right, see you later." Megan picked up the menu.

On the phone in her office Nicky screamed into the receiver. "I don't give a flying fuck what you say. This stuff has to be moved, and soon. I've got a plane coming in tomorrow with another shipment. This shit is backing up on me; it's costing me money, and the risk increases the longer I keep it on my property. Now, I expect to see someone out here tonight at the usual time, understand?" She slammed the phone down.

She sat down angrily, and attempted to catch up on some paper work, still fuming over the phone conversation.

Nicky had lunch brought in at noon. As morning wore on into afternoon, her mood didn't change much. *God damn bunch of assholes. They just better not give me any more trouble. I got too much on all of 'em. I don't have to take this shit.*

Glancing at her watch, she realized it was almost three o'clock and time for her to take Megan on a tour of the ranch. *Better change my attitude real quick, 'Little Miss Cutie' needs to see the charming Nicky Clark. For now, anyway.*

Megan was waiting in the lobby reading a book. She wore a large straw hat, purchased from the gift shop, and a new pair of Ralph Lauren sunglasses.

"All set, I see." Nicky smiled as she approached.

"Hi, you bet. This was a great idea." Megan rose to her feet.

Nicky's denim cut-offs revealed her muscular thighs.

A bright red Jeep waited outside at the bottom of the steps. Nicky gallantly helped Megan in, then slid behind the wheel. Dust rose behind them as they headed for the stables.

"I just love horses," Megan bubbled as the jeep bumped along the road. "I have two thoroughbred Appaloosas back home in Portland. And I've been looking at some Arabians. Guess that's why I chose a ranch as the place to spend my vacation; just can't seem to do without the dear, sweet things." Megan looked at Nicky and batted her eyelashes a few times.

"That's great. Seems we have something in common, because horses are my favorite animal." Nicky looked at her briefly and smiled.

Outside the stables a short Mexican man was raking around the palm trees and plants, while the other, a tall gray-haired man, brushed down a pinto pony.

Stopping the jeep at the stable door, Nicky jumped out and moved to the passenger side. "Come on," she said, holding out her hand to Megan. "We've got some beauties in the stables that I'd like to show you."

As Megan's foot touched the ground, loud thunderous sounds began exploding from inside the building. Plumes of dust billowed out from under the door. A high, shrill, almost human screaming resounded through the air. Stable boards creaked and snapped; the building itself seemed to shake.

A look of total shock shot across Nicky's face. She ran for the stables. Megan was right behind her, with both ranch hands on her heels.

"Stay out," Nicky screamed at Megan. The two men ran past her.

The sounds coming from inside were terrifying. An animal was suffering some great agony, locked in an uncontrollable frenzy. Megan ran over to a nearby window and peered inside. Nicky and the two men were running from one side of the stable to the other.

Each had a halter and rope in hand. A large black mare was bucking and kicking frantically at anything in her path. Foam bubbled from her nose and mouth. Her tongue was black and hanging out.

The mare's eyes were open wide, almost popping out of her skull. Her legs were covered with deep cuts; blood was splattered everywhere.

Too late, Nicky yelled for the two men to get out of the way. A hind hoof caught one in the stomach, hurling him into the wall, where he lay moaning.

Blood began pouring from the horse's mouth. Suddenly, it stopped in mid-stride, threw its head back, and with one final scream, fell over with a loud thud.

No one moved. Then, carefully, Nicky approached the huge form. "She's dead." Nicky's voice was a whisper. And as she touched the mare, the animal's blood covered her hand.

"John, go see if Mario's all right." Nicky pointed to the man slumped against the wall. The other horses were kicking at their stalls, panic filled their eyes. Two women came running in. "Get the others calmed down," Nicky shouted at them.

Megan could restrain herself no longer. She entered the stables. Hay and dust were still swirling through the air. The horse lay there, blood still seeping from its mouth and nose.

Nicky was shaking so hard she had to grab the railing of the stall to keep from falling. The man named John was helping Mario to his feet. Mario was coughing and spitting, while holding his stomach.

Slowly, sanity returned to the scene. Nicky looked at Megan with glassy eyes. Pieces of straw were clinging to her short black hair. Sweat poured down her face.

"Take Mrs. Marshall back to the lodge," Nicky barked to a small brown-haired woman.

Megan walked up to Nicky. "Can I be of any help?" she asked, gently putting her hand on Nicky's shoulder.

"No, but thank you," Nicky responded. Her voice was shaking. "I have to take care of this, and then I'll see you back at the Thunderbird. Now, please just go with Cookie." Megan almost felt sorry for Nicky.

Still shaking, Megan decided a shower and change of clothes might help calm her down. But she couldn't erase from her mind the vision of what she had just witnessed. Her deep love for animals only added to her depression.

She dressed in a clean pair of shorts and tee shirt, then walked to the Thunderbird Lodge. The hot Santa Ana winds had begun to blow, and she was thankful it was not too far a walk.

What would cause an animal to do that, she kept asking herself over and over again. *Nicky was sincerely shaken by it. In complete shock, I'd say. By now, I'll bet she knows just what did happen to that poor animal. Something is really wrong with this picture.*

8

AT the same time Megan was going through the trauma of watching Nicky's mare die, Toni and Sally were hard at work reviewing Nicky Clark's transcribed statement.

"Have *you* got anything that sounds interesting?" Toni asked, looking up from her latest report.

"I don't know, Toni, maybe we should compare our impressions of what Nicky said." Sally continued, "Nicky repeats over and over again that all of these encounters were just one-night stands which meant nothing to her. She goes on to say the women were only out for a good time, and she provided it. She also said nothing out of the ordinary happened with, or to, any of them."

"She's feeding us a crock of shit. If everything was so sweet and easy, why did she threaten T.J. after learning she'd spoken with us?"

"You're right, Toni, but how do we prove these murders are connected to Nicky? These women aren't alive to give their version of the story." Sally had a deep frown on her forehead as she studied the board.

"I don't know, Sal. We just have to keep digging."

Toni got up and pinned the drawing she'd made of Jill Collins' scar on the board.

"What's this?" Sally asked, looking at the crude sketch.

"It's something...a mark...I saw on this gal's back. Someone who used to be involved with Nicky; it intrigued me."

"Hmm." Sally examined it, turning her head to one side and then the other. "There's something about this, something that rings a bell. Something I've read or seen, but *where*?"

Sally began pacing back and forth, her mind searching. She stopped abruptly. "That's it!" She rushed to her desk.

"That's what?" Toni asked, following her.

Sally began pushing papers and pictures around on the desk, picking some up, then tossing them back down. She moved to Toni's desk, and began the same frantic search.

Confused by this sudden outburst, Toni asked, "What the hell are you doing?"

"Here they are," Sally said, out of breath.

In her hand, Sally held pictures of the dead women taken by the police photographer. She sorted through them, selecting one of each woman. Handing them to Toni, she said, "Take a look at these."

Toni studied each picture and its corresponding report. Grabbing a magnifying glass, Sally handed it to Toni. "Take a *good* look. Especially the pictures of Martha Parker and Anita Lewis."

"Well, I'll be damned, Sal. I think you've got something." Toni put the magnifying glass down and said, "You're talking about he marks the coroner noted after he autopsied the first three victims."

"Right.Where did you see the mark you sketched?"

"Remember, I mentioned speaking to a young woman at the Pussy Willow...a Jill Collins? Well, her scar wasn't exactly like the victims' scars, but we sure should check it out."

"Looks like we've got a live body to question now, doesn't it?" Sally smiled triumphantly at Toni. Her bright blue eyes were shining.

Toni again studied the photographs one by one. Then, one by one, she pinned them on the board. "That's sure as hell IT." She stepped back.

"Hello, Jill Collins," Toni exclaimed, smiling with satisfaction.

"I'll go down and run a DMV check on Jill Collins. Once we have her address, we're on our way," Sally said, closing the door behind her.

Toni's mind wandered as she waited for Sally's return. Her thoughts had been on Megan all night; she hadn't slept. Now, there was nothing she wanted as much as to drive to the Lazy Q, bust Nicky Clark in the mouth, and bring Megan home. But she knew she couldn't blow it.

"Got it." Sally burst into the office. "She lives in Cathedral City."

Sally's voice brought Toni back from her thoughts.

"Let's go, time's a wastin'!" Sally shoved Toni toward the door.

Grabbing her windbreaker, Toni asked, "Cathedral City? Where the hell is Cathedral City?"

"It's not far from Palm Springs; it's an older town. Runs along either side of Palm Canyon Drive. East of Palm Springs. You must have passed through it at one time or another. Most of the people who work at the resorts live there because it's cheap. It's got some bad areas, but I can't tell by this address if Jill Collins lives in one of them or not."

Sally watched for Eighth St. as the car sped down Palm Canyon Drive.

"How come you know so much about all the towns around here?" Toni questioned.

"I was born and raised in Palm Springs, guess I'd better know something about the area. My parents are retired and live in Palm Desert," Sally answered, flashing her dazzling smile.

"Bet you were a cheerleader in high school, and prom queen. Right?"

Sally laughed. "You think you know everything, don't you?"

"Well?" Toni responded with a smirk.

"All right, yes.... I was all those things, but it's what's up here that counts," she said pointing to her head. "I love my job, and plan to make police work my lifetime career. So...what do you think about that?"

Suddenly, Sally realized her tone had become coy and flirta-
tious, and she blushed. This confused her and she felt uncomfortable.
What am I doing? Am I flirting with Toni? she thought.

Unaware of the feelings Sally was experiencing, Toni paused
before she answered. "I hope it all works out for you, Sal, but life
has a way of throwing us some unexpected curves, so stay alert."
Toni glanced down at Sally's large purse. "Isn't it kind of a pain to
always have to carry that thing just to hold your gun and cuffs?" Toni
nodded her head toward the black leather shoulder bag.

"Better than having to take a jacket off and on all day like
you do to conceal yours. And besides, what makes you think that's
all I carry in there?" Sally gave her a sly look. *Damn, I'm doing it
again!* "Here we are," Sally blurted out. She felt relieved they had
reached their destination.

The two-story apartment building was set back away from
the street about fifteen feet. The fence surrounding it was rotting,
and part of what was once the gate lay on the ground. The building's
exterior paint had peeled off in large sections, exposing the chipped
and cracking stucco.

A torn canvas sign hung from the roof and beat against the
side of the building as gusts of hot wind slapped it. "Apartments for
Rent," it read. The lettering had almost been obliterated by blowing
sand and the dry desert weather. Waves of heat rose from the sandy
dirt surrounding the building. Dust covered their shoes as Toni and
Sally approached the apartment house.

They scanned the mail boxes located on the wall next to the
front steps. Jill Collins, Apt. 2A. The faded name was written on a
piece of old tape.

"Here we go." Sally took a deep breath.

They headed upstairs.

Approaching Jill's door, they could hear the TV. A game show
was on and people were laughing. The light in the hallway was dim,
the air hot and musty. Sweat began trickling down the back of Toni's
neck and onto the collar of her windbreaker. She knocked on the door.

They waited. No answer.

Sally put her ear to the door. "Someone's in there; I can hear them moving around."

Again Toni knocked, with more force this time. No answer.

"Miss Collins, please open the door. It's Toni, Toni Underwood. I spoke to you at the Pussy Willow, remember? I'm a police officer. It's most urgent I talk with you," Toni yelled through the crack. Again, no answer.

Toni was becoming impatient. "Miss Collins, I'm investigating four murders and I feel you might have information that can be of help to us in that investigation. There could be more women's lives at stake here, do you understand?" Still no answer.

"Well," Sally said, "if she doesn't want to help us, we have no choice but to leave."

They turned to go. "Wait!" Toni said, grabbing Sally's arm. Slowly, the door opened a bit. The watery blue eyes of Jill Collins looked up into theirs.

"May we come in, Miss Collins?" Sally asked, showing her badge to Jill through the crack in the door. She quietly slid her foot inside the doorway. Jill nodded and stepped back, allowing them to enter.

She walked to the center of the room, turned and faced Sally and Toni. Jill's drab blonde hair looked uncombed. She had on a faded cotton robe with the hem drooping on one side. Her feet were bare. She stood staring, her arms hanging loosely at her sides. There was a weary, fragile look about her. A small air-conditioning unit sat in the window of the small apartment.

"What do you want?" Jill asked, in her thin high-pitched voice.

"May we sit down, Miss Collins?" Sally asked, motioning to the worn couch.

Toni showed her badge.

Jill's eyes widened. "What do you want?" she repeated.

"Please, Miss Collins, relax, we just have a few simple questions to ask, and then we'll be on our way." Sally smiled, trying to soothe Jill.

"All right," Jill responded, "but I have to get ready for work soon."

Sally sat down and took out her notebook. Toni slowly walked around studying the apartment, what there was of it.

There was a small kitchenette off the living room. Dirty dishes were piled high in the sink. At least a week's worth, Toni thought. A tiny bathroom with tub and shower was to the left of the front door. Underwear hung over the shower curtain rod, and a towel lay on the floor.

The one window in the room was covered with faded blue drapes. Even with the small AC on, the air in the apartment was stifling. A dirty fish tank sat on a table in front of the window. It was a sad, depressing place.

Jill was becoming visibly nervous, as Sally began her questioning. "Please, sit down, Miss Collins," Sally said soothingly. "We understand, Miss Collins, you at one time had some kind of relationship with Nicky Clark. Is that correct?"

No answer. Jill sat stiffly in the wooden chair.

Patiently, Sally repeated her question. "Is that correct, Miss Collins?"

"Yes," Jill finally said, looking down at her hands.

Sally pushed on. "How long did this relationship last?"

"About six months, I guess." Jill still didn't look up.

"During that period, did you actually live on the ranch with Ms. Clark?"

"Part of the time." Jill was beginning to fidget in her seat.

"Look, Jill..." Toni decided to get to some of the heavy questions. *Cut the bullshit, and take your chances,* that's how she felt. "I've met Nicky Clark, and she is not a nice person; that's obvious. Now, did she at any time mistreat you, or physically harm you?"

Jill's hands were shaking; she looked up at Toni. Toni saw the same look of terror in her eyes that she had seen the first time she had met her. There was a slight twitch to Jill's lower lip. Tears formed in her eyes and spilled over onto her thin, pale face.

"I can't say any more," she said, getting to her feet and walking to the window, her back to Sally and Toni.

They looked at each other. Sally shrugged her shoulders as if to say, "What do we do now?" Toni got up, went over to Jill, and put her arm around her shoulder.

"Jill, we need your help," Toni began gently. "We are faced with four horrible murders. The victims were all lesbians. I'm not going to lie to you—we think Nicky Clark is involved in some way. And we need you to tell us everything you know about her. We want to nail the bastard who's mutilating and murdering these women... before there's a fifth victim. If you're afraid she might hurt you if you talk to us, we'll give you protection. Around the clock, if necessary. You have my word, nothing will happen to you. I know this isn't easy, but please help us stop these murders."

Turning around, Jill stared at Toni, and then Sally. She walked back to her chair. Tears were streaming down her face now. Sally pulled a Kleenex out of her bag, and handed it to her.

"Would you like a drink of water?" Sally asked. Jill nodded yes.

After moving some dirty dishes around and rinsing out a glass, Toni filled it and handed it to Jill. She took a long drink, closed her eyes for a moment, and in a trembling voice began her story.

"About seven months ago, I moved from my home in Seattle, Washington. I was tired of the weather; it rained all the time. I saw pictures a friend of mine took while on vacation here, and I fell in love with the place. I got a job at The Inland Empire Bank, and began a new life. I've been out since I was eighteen, and of course looked for the local lesbian bar as soon as I got settled. I wanted to connect up and make some friends. I didn't know where else to go to meet women. Know what I mean?" she said looking up first at Toni and then Sally.

"The first time I went into the Pussy Willow, I felt comfortable. T.J. was friendly. She introduced me to some of the other women, and all in all, everything was going great—until my third week here—that's when I met Nicky. She'd just come back from a trip to Mexico. She was in the bar with some other women, having a wild time.

"She was loud, and sure of herself. Had a certain charisma that made everyone sit up and take notice. I think they were all just a little afraid of Nicky. I'd never met anyone like her. She fascinated me. I begged T.J. to introduce me to her. T.J. told me to let well enough alone, but I wouldn't listen. Finally, one day, to get me off her back, T.J. gave in and introduced us.

"At the time, I looked pretty good with my tan and all. Right away, Nicky looked me up and down and gave me a sly smile when she sat down next to me at the bar. Guess she sensed right away I wasn't very experienced or sure of myself...just the type she liked.

"She began buying me drinks. I've never been a heavy drinker, so it didn't take much to get a buzz on. Know what I mean? I got sloshed and more talkative as the night wore on. Nicky asked all about my family and friends. Things like that. I told her I'd never been close with them, and I had no real friends to speak of...." Jill picked at a rough cuticle as she continued to tell her story.

"'Sounds like you need a *Daddy* to take care of you, darlin',' Nicky said. And then she kissed me.

"That was the first real attention anyone had paid me in a long time and I just lapped it up. God, was I a jerk! That night she drove me home, walked me to my door, and left after making a date for Saturday night. She was smooth, all right. She didn't want to scare me off, I know that now." Jill sighed deeply, and then continued.

"I was impressed. After all, Nicky was a big shot in town, and rich. Just having her pay attention to me made me feel important. She seemed kind and understanding. Wasn't just after one thing, like others I'd met.

"That Saturday night—our first date—at exactly 7:30, a long black Mercedes limo pulled up in front of my apartment house. Can you believe it? A limo and a uniformed driver stood at my door as I opened it.

"I was floored. 'Yes,' I said, 'can I help you?'"

"'Are you Miss Jill Collins?' the driver asked me, with a nice smile.

"'Why, yes I am.' I said, still puzzled."

"'Ms. Clark sent me to pick you up, and drive you to the Lazy Q Ranch.'"

"'You gotta be kidding! I must be dreaming,' I'd blurted out like some dumb teenager.

"'I assure you, Miss Collins, you are not dreaming. Please, come with me.'

"The limo...it was like something out of the movies. The driver opened the door and I slid in across the white leather. There was beautiful soft music, too.

"The chauffeur told me to help myself to the champagne in the bar. It was unreal. Know what I mean—ahh—Lieutenant?" she said, looking directly at Toni.

Jill stopped for a moment to take another sip of water, then continued. "Nothing like this had ever happened to me—ever. I was, like, overwhelmed, especially when the limo pulled up in front of Nicky's house.

"Nicky's home was about a quarter of a mile from the lodge. It was gorgeous—trees all around, hidden from view. Upstairs, you could see the entire ranch and the whole valley.

"A wide grin spread across Nicky's face as she opened the front door. I could tell she was real glad to see me.

"We had a fab dinner, served by a maid. Candlelight, soft music, the works. Like in the movies—know what I mean? Nicky was charming, she couldn't do enough for me. We danced on the veranda.

"'It's getting late.' Nicky finally whispered in my ear. 'Please stay the night. I promise, you won't be sorry, darlin.'

"I looked into Nicky's eyes and told her there was nowhere else I'd rather be.

"She led me upstairs, to a huge bedroom. Flower petals were everywhere—on the black satin sheets and this thick maroon carpeting. Candles everywhere. And "Bolero," I think it's called, was playing on this outrageous stereo. The whole scene was like a fairy tale, know what I mean, Lieutenant?

And then Jill got a faraway look on her face as her thoughts drifted back to every detail of what happened next. Toni could see that these intimate events were too personal for her ever to reveal to anyone. Jill closed her eyes, and paused, as she became lost in the memory of her first night with Nicky.

Nicky began kissing her eyes, forehead, cheeks, then mouth. She was completely swept away and responded to Nicky's every touch with eager abandonment. They swayed together in the center of the room, as Nicky's hands explored her body.

Gently, Nicky laid her down upon the bed. With relish, she undressed Jill, revealing her young tanned body. The satin sheets felt cool, yet their bodies burned with desire, and beads of perspiration covered their flesh. Nicky's mouth found Jill's breast; her tongue teased the nipple until it became hard.

Jill moaned softly as Nicky's hand slid between her thighs. She opened her legs as Nicky's hand touched her clit, stroking and massaging, until her body began twitching with every caress.

Jill's sudden silence seemed strange to Toni and Sally, for she had stopped relating her story in mid-sentence. Her eyes were closed and she seemed far away, as if she had drifted off somewhere. Jill's mind continued to clutch at her memories.

Reaching under the pillow next to her head, Nicky pulled out a dildo and strapped it on. She rubbed it up and down against Jill's throbbing wetness. Then gently, she entered her with the dildo. Jill thrust her hips forward, moving them with a sensuous, lustful rhythm. All the while, Nicky's lips teased her breast, gently biting and licking.

Nicky suddenly whispered. "Turn around and get on your knees."

As if in a trance, she did as instructed, kneeling on the bed, her buttocks toward Nicky. Nicky pulled Jill to the edge of the bed so she could stand behind her, and began thrusting the dildo in and out at an ever-increasing pace, while the fingers of her other hand continued massaging Jill's wet pussy.

Eyes closed, her mouth open, Jill reached the peak of her passion. She shuddered and screamed as the ecstasy raced through her body, then lay back limp and exhausted. Her breathing was heavy. She had never experienced such a complete climax before.

Slowly she opened her eyes, forcing herself back from the abyss of passion.

Nicky smiled down into Jill's face. "Are you all right?" she whispered.

"I'm wonderful," Jill answered, still out of breath, "but what about you?"

"I'm fine," Nicky whispered. "I get my pleasure from watching. That's all I really need, and watching you was especially wonderful." She kissed Jill. "I have to leave for just a while, but I'll be back before you know it."

With her eyes already closing, Jill smiled weakly. Nicky covered her and quietly left the room. It was midnight.

"Jill, are you okay?" Sally was shaking her gently.

Jill blinked several times as she fought to clear away the images flashing through her mind. Then she looked at Toni and Sally. Taking a long, deep breath, she continued her story.

"I moved in with Nicky soon after that. Things were fine for about a week, then she wanted me to try some drugs. Said I didn't know what I was missing; it made sex even better to be a little high. I was completely hooked on her, totally in love; I would have done anything to make her happy. And then she wanted me to quit my job at the bank. Swore I'd never have to work again, that she was going to take care of me. What a jerk I was." Jill rolled her eyes heavenward and laughed, self deprecatingly. "I can't believe how naive I was. I really believed everything Nicky told me.

"Soon I was using cocaine, and then heroin. Hate to admit this, but at first I really enjoyed the high—never felt anything like it before. Before I knew it, I was hooked. Got hooked real fast—within a few months. I lost weight. God, did I lose weight. And didn't care about anything, except Nicky, and my next fix. Funny thing—Nicky never took drugs of any kind. At the time, I couldn't understand why she never wanted to get high with me. Stupid, right?" Shaking her head, she looked at Sally.

Toni and Sally looked at each other quickly, then back at Jill.

"Nicky's lovemaking became hard and nasty. I was usually in a stupor, so it made it easy for her to handle me any way she wanted. I'd wake up with welts and bruises all over my body. Some things I could vaguely remember, and others I might have imagined. Most of them are too sick to repeat.

"Sometimes I remember seeing, as if through a haze, some men surrounding the bed. I can almost smell their stinking bodies and feel the weight of them on top of me. But what really hurt was hearing Nicky, somewhere in the background, laughing and shouting, 'Enjoy, boys!'" Jill paused, shaking her head, tears quietly rolling down her cheeks. "Their hands poked and grabbed at my body. Pain...pain...everywhere. I usually drifted in and out of consciousness. Always woke to pain.

"One night, when I wasn't totally out of it, Nicky came into my room.

"'Sit up, cunt. I have something to show you.' She grabbed me by the hair and jerked my head up. 'I've made a star out of you, you drugged-up bitch.'

"Then she pushed a button and a panel opened on the far wall. There was this big screen TV. She put a videotape in the VCR.

"'You're gonna love this, bitch,' she hissed in my ear. I was so doped up I could hardly keep my eyes focused. As the light came on the screen, I could see these guys surrounding a bed. They were naked. One hairy fat guy was dancing in front of the camera. Three others were leaning over the bed, laughing. A woman's voice was screaming. A hand raised up with a riding crop clenched in the fist. It came down with a loud crack. The woman screamed again.

"'Keep those bloodshot eyes open now, whore, this is your big close-up,' Nicky said. Her dark eyes were gleaming. And then I realized it was me! They were all over ME!"

Suddenly Jill became silent. It was as though her mind would not allow her voice to continue speaking of the horror. Hand shaking, she took another drink of water. She closed her eyes, and with tears running down her face, forced herself to continue.

"After about six months, my looks were gone. I was sick, and ashamed of myself. That's when Nicky threw me in the car, drove me back to Palm Springs, and dumped me on T.J.'s doorstep. Before she left, she took out a pocket-knife. 'Here's something to always remember me by, darlin'.' She ripped open my blouse, grabbed my shoulder and carved the letter "N" into my shoulder. Here, you can see for yourself," she said, as she pulled her robe aside, and off her shoulder."

Toni had grown increasingly incensed as she listened, and fought hard not to interrupt Jill's painful revelations.

"I'm working real hard to clean up my habit now, and with T.J.'s help, I think maybe, just maybe, I can make it. I'm still sick as hell from the withdrawal effects, but that's getting better, too. When I met you, Lieutenant, I was scared you were one of Nicky's people checking to be sure I hadn't blabbed to anyone about this. She threatened to kill me if I did." Jill's whole body was shaking.

"Oh, God," Sally whispered. Her face was ashen.

"Please," Jill begged, wiping the tears from her eyes. "Please, whatever you do, don't let her hurt me anymore."

Toni's jaw was set tight and the muscle twitched as she moved to Jill's side. "She'll never hurt anyone again, Jill. You must believe that." Toni's voice shook with anger as she spoke.

Sally had regained her composure, and took the pathetic young woman's hand. It was ice cold.

"Jill, we want you to pack a bag, bring everything you think you need. Toni and I are going to take you to a safe place. We don't want you to contact anyone. When we get you to the safe house, call your boss and tell him you have a family emergency and have to leave town for a few days. I'll square it with him when this is over so you won't lose your job. We will be the only ones who know where you are."

After Jill left the room to get some tissues and pack a few things, Toni whispered, "Where the hell are we going to stash her?"

"We'll figure something out. Wait a minute, didn't T.J. say she had helped Jill before?" Sally answered.

"Yeah, that's right. Maybe she'll be willing to help one more time. I think she hates Nicky about as much as I do." Toni picked up the phone.

"I'm ready," Jill said simply as she came back into the room carrying a small, worn suitcase.

"Good," Toni said as she dialed the bar. "Hi, T.J., this is Toni Underwood. I'm fine, but right now I need a big favor from you."

She proceeded to explain as quickly as possible what the situation was, and how desperately Jill needed her help.

"Shit. I knew most of the story, but now that I've heard all of it, I could kill that bitch, Nicky, myself," T.J. said, angrily. "Of course I'll take Jill in. Bring her to my place right away. I'll meet you there." She gave Toni the address and directions to her apartment, then added, "I'll make sure no one gets to her. You have my word."

"Thanks, T.J., we're on our way." Toni hung up.

"What about your fish?" Sally asked.

"I don't have them anymore," Jill replied. "They died last week. Just haven't gotten myself together enough to clean out the tank."

"All right then," Toni said with a shrug. She looked around the apartment and closed the door behind them. "Let's do it."

After getting Jill settled in, Sally and Toni returned to police headquarters.

"I think we should put a tail on Clark and stake out her place," Toni said, pouring herself a cup of coffee.

"That's going to be hard, Toni. We can't have anyone just sitting outside the Lazy Q in the parking lot, and there's really no cover for miles around, nowhere for a car to park out of sight."

"Yeah, you're right, Sal, guess we'll just have to count on Megan for whatever information we get on Nicky's activities. Damn, I hope we can get some concrete evidence to link that sick bitch with the Highway 60 Murders."

"Don't worry, Toni, I'm sure she's up to her neck in something, we just have to find out what it is. And we will," Sally answered, patting Toni on the back reassuringly. "But one thing bothers me. If Nicky is our killer, how come Jill's still alive?"

"I don't know, Sally. Maybe she wasn't in the killing mood when she carved her initial into Jill's shoulder. Who the hell knows how the mind of a sadist really works?"

Then leaning back in her chair, Toni said urgently, "I think we should get Megan the hell out of that place today. After hearing Jill's story, I'm scared to death for her."

"Look, Toni, I know how you feel, but we're scheduled to see Megan tomorrow. We still don't really have enough to hang anything on Nicky. When we do nail her, lets make it stick."

Toni didn't answer, her thoughts were of Megan. "If that stinking bitch touches Megan, she'll beg to die before I'm through with her." Toni's fists were clenched, her knuckles white. "Tomorrow, and that's IT!" Her fist came down hard on the desk.

9

MEGAN walked into the lobby at 3:25 p.m.. She still felt queasy, but was determined to put on a good front.

"Oh, Mrs. Marshall," Kelly called as she approached Megan.

"Yes, Kelly, what is it?"

"Ms. Clark asked that you wait in her office, she'll be here soon. We all heard what happened at the stable. Just a shame...a rotten shame. Can I get you anything while you wait?"

"Yes, Kelly, a large glass of iced tea, please. I'm quite parched." Megan sighed dramatically, and dabbed at her forehead with the dainty white linen handkerchief she had pulled out of her straw shoulder bag.

"I'll get it right away, Mrs. Marshall." Kelly rushed off toward the dining room.

Megan slowly opened the door to Nicky's office. *This is great. Maybe I can do a little snooping.* She laid her handbag on the large mahogany desk, and slowly began walking around the room. All of the furniture was very masculine in appearance. Heavy and bold.

A few moments later there was a soft rap on the door. It opened and Kelly entered. "Here's your iced tea, Mrs. Marshall," she said setting down a tray.

When Kelly was gone, Megan opened the door a crack and looked out, making sure Nicky wasn't coming.

Then she sat down behind the desk and began quickly flipping through the papers in each drawer. *Damn, nothing but invoices, bills, supply lists.*

She stopped suddenly as her eyes fell on the .38 caliber snub-nosed revolver lying in the center of the top drawer. She left the weapon where it was and shut the drawer.

As she looked up, her eyes scanned the top of the desk. "What's this?" she whispered, as she got up and moved around to the front of the desk.

Lying on the corner of the desk, with some folders, was a manila envelope marked: Birth Certificate, Photos, Passport, Immunization Records. As she reached for it, the door suddenly flew open, and there stood Nicky. She hadn't changed her clothes. Her blue tee shirt was torn and spotted with dried blood. Her hair was wild looking and streaks of dirt ran down her face.

Startled, Megan's hand hit the stack of folders and they fell, scattering all over the floor. The two women stared at each other, not moving.

With her heart pounding, Megan placed the palms of both hands on her chest and said, "Why, Nicky, you startled me." Glancing down at the manila envelope which was scattered amongst the other folders on the floor, she continued, "You look awful, are you all right?"

Nicky walked toward her, silently, her dark, close-set eyes never leaving Megan's. Then she bent down and began picking up the papers and folders.

"Here, let me help you," Megan offered.

Nicky held her hand up. "No, I'll do it," she responded in a gruff tone. After quickly gathering up the papers, Nicky placed them on the wet bar across the room.

Megan hadn't moved, but as Nicky turned to look at her, she casually picked up the frosted glass from the tray and took a sip of iced tea.

With her eyes still on Megan, Nicky reached behind the wet bar and pulled out a bottle of Canadian Club and a shot-glass. She poured the glass full and downed the drink in one gulp. She appeared deep in thought, as she picked up the bottle and shot-glass, walked to the desk, and sat down.

"What happened to that poor animal?" Megan asked quietly.

"I'm not sure," Nicky answered. "It could have been a stroke, or heart attack." She tipped the glass to her lips once more.

"What did you do with the body?"

"We had to leave it. It's too large to move. I'll call tomorrow and have the vet take care of it. I'm sorry you had to see this. I wanted everything to be perfect for you."

"Don't worry about me," Megan answered. She could feel Nicky becoming more relaxed. She stood next to her and took her hand. "I'm fine. It's you I'm worried about. You look exhausted."

"I'm beat," Nicky replied, downing her third whiskey.

"Look, why don't you go take a shower and lie down for a couple of hours. It's still early. Then, if you still feel like doing something, let me know," Megan offered.

"You're sure you don't mind?"

"Not at all. I'll just do some exploring on my own, or maybe lie out by the pool. No problem." The truth was, Megan wanted to go back to the stables and take a look at the mare without anyone around.

"Good idea." Nicky smiled weakly. Setting her glass down on the desk, she got up, held the door open for Megan, and then locked it behind them as they left.

Megan stood in the center of the lobby for a moment watching Nicky as she disappeared out the front door. *That was close. I need to find out what her birth certificate was doing on her desk. Obviously, she didn't want me to see it. Damn, I wish I'd gotten a look at it.*

Megan returned to her villa, an idea taking shape in her head. She went through her bags looking for a container. "Anything will do," she said aloud. "Ah, this will be perfect." In her hand she held a bottle of aspirins.

After emptying the bottle, she washed it thoroughly, and put it in her pocket, along with a nail file.

Outside, the afternoon sun was hot and the winds were picking up. No one was by the pool; in fact, the ranch looked deserted. Sand was blowing and the trees and bushes were bending from the force of the ever-growing wind.

Megan pulled her straw hat down tighter, put her head down, then hurried toward the stables. It was farther away than she thought. By the time she reached the double door she was out of breath; particles of sand filled her eyes and nose. Before stepping inside, she took a quick look around.

Once inside, she took out a Kleenex, and wiped the sand from her eyes, then checked the rest of the stable. *No one's here, great.*

The huge form of the mare was lying where it had fallen. Blankets covered the body. Dried blood was everywhere. Megan carefully approached the dead horse. She knelt down beside it, slowly raising a corner of the blanket.

Suddenly, a loud thud froze her. She dropped the blanket. Then another, louder thud, seemed to originate above her head. Heart pounding, she slowly looked up, not knowing what to expect. A weak smile crossed her lips. The force of the wind had blown open a pair of loading doors in the loft.

With a great sigh of relief, she picked up the corner of the blanket once more. Again she looked around, making sure no one had followed her in. She took the bottle and nail file out of her pocket.

Cautiously, she touched the body, then began moving her fingers over the skin. Suddenly she stopped. Her fingertips found a deep cut in the animal's flesh. The blood was still sticky; she wanted to pull away and run from this place, but forced herself to continue. *Hang on, you've got to do this.*

Oblivious to the sound of the stable door opening behind her, she held the bottle close to the wound, and with the file, began scraping coagulated blood into the bottle. "Won't need much," she whispered. "That should do it." Finally, she dropped the bottle file into her shoulder bag.

"What the hell are you doing?" an angry voice suddenly rang out.

Megan leapt to her feet. She whirled around and found herself face to face with John, the ranch hand she'd seen in the morning. Her heart jumped out of her chest. All she could do was stare at him...at a loss for words.

"I said what the hell are you doing in here, lady?" He moved closer, menacingly.

Her mouth was dry; her tongue stuck to the roof of her mouth. "I...I...I just had to come and see this poor animal one more time." Megan's voice was raspy and strained. "I couldn't get it out of my mind. You know how it is. I wanted to make sure it was dead, and not lying here suffering."

John looked at her for what seemed an eternity, his lean six-foot body not moving. His weather-beaten face was like stone. And his icy blue eyes never left hers. Then, without warning, he moved toward her. She readied herself for an attack. But John just stepped past her, bent down, and pulled the blanket back over the mare's body.

Harshly, he said, "Believe me, she's dead. No doubt about it."

"Yes, I know that now, but I just felt so bad, I had to see for myself. Did Ms. Clark say anything to you about the mare?"

"Like what?" he responded in a flat voice.

"Oh, I don't know, maybe why it died, or what might have caused this terrible thing to happen."

"Never said a word 'bout nothin' like that. Just told us to cover her up and get out."

Megan paused, studying his face. "Well, I'll be going now, John. And thanks for not being mad at a *silly* woman." She reached out and shook his hand, smiled sweetly, then turned and walked out the door. When safely outside the stables, she let out a sigh. All right! John had bought the Megan Marshall persona.

The wind was still blowing; the hot air and sand assaulted her face. Megan leaned against the building; she felt sick. Bending over, she vomited until she thought her insides would come up, too.

She leaned her body into the gusting wind and began walking. Her legs felt like pieces of lead, each step was agony. Everything was blurred and spinning, and then she sank into blackness.

"Mrs. Marshall...Mrs. Marshall, are you all right?"

Megan opened her eyes. She was on her bed and Kelly was standing over her, holding a cool, wet washcloth.

"What happened?"

"I found you on your knees out by the pool," Kelly answered, placing the washcloth on Megan's forehead. "Should I call Ms. Clark?"

"No! No, that isn't necessary, Kelly. I guess between the heat and wind, I just got dizzy. Not used to this type of climate. I was stupid to even go outside." Megan tried to get up. The sickening dizziness hit her again.

"You just lie back now and take it easy. I've seen this before. Heat exhaustion, that's what it is. Best thing to do is drink plenty of water and relax." Kelly fluffed the pillows behind Megan's head as she lay back on the king-sized brass bed.

"Thank you, Kelly. Thank you very much," she mumbled, as she drifted off to sleep.

The ringing of the phone startled Megan back from her dreams of Toni. "Hello." She sounded confused, her voice husky with sleep.

"Good evening, Megan, it's Nicky. I believe we have a date." Nicky's voice sounded bright and cheerful.

"Oh, yes...Nicky. How are you?" Megan managed, in a soft even voice.

"I'm fine, slept awhile, showered, dressed, and now I'm ready to have a fantastic evening with you, darlin'" Nicky sounded so chipper, Megan wanted to vomit again!

She knew by the sound of Nicky's voice that she wasn't aware of her trip to the stables, or her fainting episode.

"Oh, wonderful. Ahh...I just woke up myself, Nicky. So I'll need at *least* an hour to shower and dress. Should I meet you in the bar?" She glanced at the diamond and gold Rolex watch lying on the nightstand. "It's seven o'clock, shall we say eightish?"

"That's fine. I have a wonderful evening planned for us. First, we'll hit the Pussy Willow, and after I show you off a bit, I have a big surprise waiting for you back here. How's that sound?"

"Sounds exciting, and I do love surprises, Nicky. Now you have my curiosity piqued. See you soon." Megan put the phone down..

Going to the large closet, she began looking through her wardrobe. *Ah, this is great.* She pulled out an Armani silk tuxedo shirt, and silky pin-striped trousers by Norma Kamali. *Hmm, very nice...very nice, indeed. I could really get used to this kind of life. Sally's got great taste. This should knock "Nicky The Hun's" socks off!*

After a quick shower, Megan smiled to herself as she slipped into the outfit, making sure the shirt was unbuttoned just enough to show some cleavage. Then she hid the sample bottle of blood inside one of her tennis shoes and stuffed a sock in after it. A few dabs of Opium in just the right places and she was ready. She glanced once more in the mirror, gave the room a quick check, locked the door, and headed for the bar.

"Wow!" Nicky whistled. "Man, those dykes at the Pussy Willow are gonna light up when they see you comin'."

"Why, thank you, Ms. Clark," Megan replied, as she batted her eyelashes just a bit.

Nicky's right eye twitched a few times. "I thought perhaps you might be hungry, so I took the liberty of ordering some hors d'oeuvres, and a bottle of champagne."

"Why, thank you, Nicky, how thoughtful. I am hungry, now that you mention it." Calculatingly, Megan thought, *Shouldn't act too snobbish, might scare her off.* She smiled sweetly as they moved to a booth near the tiny dance floor.

Karen, the bartender, brought over the champagne and a beautifully arranged platter filled with artichoke hearts, goose liver paté, sweet shrimp, and a variety of crackers and cheeses.

After their champagne toast, Megan rotated her glass in her hands thoughtfully, looked at Nicky and said, "I believe you're going to think I'm just awful to ask you this, but I've been so curious since this afternoon in your office, I just can't help but blurt it out."

"Oh, and what do you want to ask?" Nicky frowned, looking confused.

Megan took Nicky's hand, giving it a little squeeze. "That envelope on your desk that was marked, birth certificate, photos, passport...oh, you know the one."

"Yeah, what about it?" Nicky's eyes narrowed a bit.

"Well, I have to confess, I almost opened it to look at your birth certificate."

"What? Why would you do that?" Nicky's voice grew louder and she stiffened in her seat.

"Now you're really going to think I'm silly, but you look so young, I wanted to see how old you really are. Asking would have been rude, but I guess looking in private papers is even worse, right?" Megan lowered her gaze to the table.

Nicky's head went back, her mouth opened wide and she let out a roar of laughter. Then she looked at Megan. "Is that all? Well, I'm thirty-two. Now are you happy...or disappointed? I had that file on my desk because I am getting ready to bring my passport up to date. Never know when I may have to make a quick getaway, right?" Nicky said jokingly.

They both laughed heartily. Then, getting up, Nicky held out her hand gallantly, "Shall we?"

"What is the name of this place you're taking me to?" Megan asked, as they walked out the door.

Nicky opened the car door for Megan and said, "I'm taking you to the Pussy Willow. It's the nicest lesbian bar in town. I think you'll enjoy the experience. You can let your hair down and relax there." Nicky stepped on the gas, and the black Jag took off with a roar.

It was close to 9:30 by the time they reached the Pussy Willow. The parking lot was full. Nicky pulled her car up to the front door where two women were standing and talking. Getting out of the car, Nicky called to a chunky, hard-looking dyke. "Hey Dobie, park my car."

Megan knew what was expected of her so she waited for Nicky to come around and open her door. As Nicky helped her out of the Jag, Megan smiled coquettishly, and took her date's arm as they entered the Pussy Willow.

Even though it was a Monday night, there were two birthday parties in full swing. The music was loud and the bar was packed. A pool tournament was in progress near the back of the room, in the alcove off the dance floor.

"Do you want to sit at the bar, or at a table?" Nicky yelled in Megan's ear.

"I don't see anywhere to sit at all."

"No problem," she said as she glanced around the crowded room. "Just tell me where you want to sit."

"At the bar," Megan replied. "Where I can see the action, of course."

"Move it, you two," Nicky snapped at two women sitting at the horse-shoe shaped bar.

Both women turned around at the sound of Nicky's bark. When they saw who it was, they quickly got up without a word and disappeared into the crowd.

"I love a woman who takes charge and gets what she wants." Megan smiled coyly as she sat down. *Arrogant Bitch!*

T.J. was busy working the far end of the crowded bar when Nicky caught her eye. Nicky motioned to her to come down to where she and Megan were sitting. Reluctantly, T.J. made her way toward them.

"T.J., this is Megan Marshall. She's a guest of mine, so make sure she gets anything she wants, understand?" Nicky ordered drinks in spite of the dirty look she got from T.J..

"Nice to meet you, Megan." T.J. smiled.

God, is everyone in this town afraid of this woman? Megan thought.

Ten minutes later, Nicky had ordered her another drink. She was only half through with the first one. Megan quickly realized that Nicky intended to get to her drunk. She continued to sip her first drink slowly. *This dyke has another think coming if she thinks she's going to get me drunk.*

At 10:15, Megan turned just in time to see Toni walk in the door. Her heart skipped a beat, and momentarily, their eyes locked on each other. In her multicolored silk shirt and dark blue cotton Dockers, Toni looked like a million bucks to Megan.

Oh God, please don't let me blow it now. I've got to act like I've never seen her before. She held her breath as Toni approached.

Toni's jaw was set tight. She walked straight up to Nicky.

"Well, Clark, which rock did you climb out from under tonight?" A sneering smile spread across Toni's lips. She didn't look at Megan. Nicky whirled around, but didn't say a word.

"Having a good time, I hope. Better enjoy yourself while you can, I always say," Toni hissed in Nicky's face.

Small beads of sweat broke out on Nicky's upper lip. "Look, Lieutenant, I don't know what you have against me, but as far as I know, you have no reason to harass me the way you do. So why don't you just go about your business and give out some parking tickets." Nicky was trying real hard not to appear nervous in front of Megan.

Toni pushed up against Nicky, forcing her back up against the bar, their faces inches apart. She kept her voice low enough so only Nicky could hear. "Look, you piece of shit, you're something people scrape off the bottom of their shoes. Consider yourself lucky I carry a badge, because if I didn't, they'd be scraping your body parts off of every wall in this place." Jill Collins' story was still fresh in Toni's mind and she would have loved to tear Nicky apart. The images of the eyeless, beaten, murdered women flashed before her eyes. Toni's rage was growing. *Thank God I don't wear my .45 when I'm off duty, or I might just blow this bitch's head off.*

Nicky's eyes grew wide; a vein in her forehead began to throb. Toni continued to push against her.

Turning her head toward Megan, Nicky said, "Come on, let's get out of this dump." The strains of "Happy Birthday To You" broke out and everyone began singing at the top of their lungs. Megan barely heard what Nicky said.

"Don't leave on my account," Toni mocked as she suddenly stepped back. Then she turned abruptly and left, disappearing into the crowd.

"Fuckin' bitch," Nicky yelled, downing her whiskey. The corner of her right eye twitched and her black Western-style tuxedo jacket was beginning to wrinkle from perspiration.

"Who was that rude woman?" Megan asked solicitously, as she gently patted the sweat from Nicky's forehead with her dainty, linen handkerchief.

"Just a god damn stupid cop who thinks she's Rambo, that's all. Now let's get the hell outta here."

"Can you wait just one minute, Nicky? I really do have to go to the ladies' room." Megan slurred her words slightly, for effect.

Nicky's manner softened. "Sure, babe, it's okay. I'll wait for you here."

Megan pushed her way across the smoke filled barroom, and through the crowd on the dance floor. The restrooms were to the back, near the exit. There was a long line of people standing outside the bathroom door. She stood, looking around, searching for Toni. Someone touched her arm. Everyone in line was talking and laughing, and most of them were drunk; no one noticed the look on Megan's face as her eyes met Toni's.

"Follow me," Toni whispered urgently. She turned and slipped out the back door.

Megan paused for a moment, taking a quick look at the bar to make sure Nicky was still there. Being true to form, Nicky was busy downing another whiskey and talking to the woman next to her. And T.J. had just set another full shot glass in front of her. *That should keep her busy for a few minutes.*

She quickly followed Toni outside. It was pitch black except for the bare light bulb over the back door. Large trash dumpsters lined the wall behind the bar. Megan took several steps into the darkness when a hand grabbed her and jerked her into the narrow space between two dumpsters.

Before she could open her mouth, Toni was kissing her lips. They kissed each other hungrily, drinking in the love and warmth between them.

Toni held her tight around the waist with one arm, while her other hand gently stroked Megan's face. "God, I miss you. I'm worried sick." Toni was out of breath.

"Honey, it's okay, I'm all right. But this is really dangerous; Nicky's no dummy; I can't be gone long." She kissed Toni deeply.

Toni pulled away. "Listen, we only have a minute. We've found out some things, some very nasty things about Nicky Clark. I'll tell you all about it tomorrow, but for now, just take my word, and be on your guard every minute you're with her. Your life may depend on it."

Suddenly, the back door opened; light flooded the area, along with the sound of Whitney Houston's voice. Toni and Megan froze. They barely breathed as footsteps approached them. Frantically, Toni pulled Megan further back into the shadows. They heard a creaking and then the crash of glass hitting metal. A lid slammed shut. Eventually, the back door closed, and they were alone again.

Relieved, Megan kissed Toni once more and quickly turned to walk away.

"Remember what I said," Toni whispered. Megan nodded, then vanished back into the bar. Toni felt more alone and helpless than she had ever felt before in her life.

A few minutes later, Megan was back at Nicky's side smiling seductively, taking Nicky's arm. "I'm ready." Nicky downed the last of her drink and swivelled around to face Megan.

"Well, hi, darlin'. Back so soon?" Her speech was beginning to slur.

Actually, too soon, Megan thought.

The ride home with Nicky at the wheel was a white-knuckle affair all the way. She was all over the road.

"You seem quite tired. Would you like me to drive?" Megan asked just as Nicky's eyes closed.

"Nah, I'm fine. I been drivin' this road for years," Nicky replied, her head bobbing up and down.

Thank God, we're out in the boondocks so I don't have to worry about being killed in a head-on collision. Sooner than she expected, Nicky skidded to a stop. *Where the hell are we?*

With a little difficulty Nicky stepped out of the car, and slowly, with carefully measured steps, she walked around to the passenger side, where she attempted to help Megan out.

"Come on," Nicky mumbled.

As they reached the steps, Megan looked back over her shoulder. Her eyes grew wide. *Oh Lord, that's the Thunderbird Lodge back there. This must be Nicky's private residence. I never thought of that.*

"Look, Nicky, we've both had a rough day. Why don't we just call it a night, okay?"

Swaying back and forth, Nicky looked at her with glazed eyes. Her face turned hard and mean. As she straightened her black jacket, she said, "I had a fine, fuckin' dinner prepared for you, god damn it. Wanted this to be a special night for both of us."

Megan knew she had to be careful. "I want that special dinner too, baby," she crooned. "But, I want us both to be ready for it, if you know what I mean. You've had a very upsetting day, and so have I. It's really sweet of you to want to do nice things for me, but let's do them tomorrow, okay? I want you strong and feeling good for what I have in mind for us." She took a step forward, and then holding her breath, kissed Nicky on the mouth, as she brushed against her seductively.

Nicky paused briefly, then said, "Well, okay, you sweet thing. You're right, I have had a rough day. It's hell running this place sometimes. Here, take the car keys and drive yourself back to your villa. I gotta get up at 4:00 a.m. anyway. What the hell time is it now?" Nicky's eyes wouldn't focus as she looked at her watch.

Glancing at her Rolex, Megan answered, "It's late, especially if you have to be up by four. It's after 1:00 a.m.."

Woozily, Nicky tried to kiss Megan again. It didn't take much to push her away.

"Go on, sweetie, get yourself to bed, now. See you tomorrow." Megan waved as she walked away. She slipped behind the wheel of the Jag and drove off, leaving Nicky staggering up the steps of her front porch.

✦ ✦ ✦ ✦ ✦

Megan's dreams were troubled, filled with visions of the mare writhing in pain. Nicky's drunken face kept looming up in front of her.

Not sure of what had awakened her, Megan found herself rubbing her eyes. Was it the dreams or the sound of a motor? She got out of bed and went to the window at the rear of her villa. Moving the curtains aside and lifting the window shade, she strained to see past a nearby stand of pines. A large flatbed truck had pulled up in front of the stables. It was still dark, but the moon was bright. Megan checked the clock on the bureau. It was 4:00 a.m..

Quickly, she put on her light cotton robe and quietly slipped out the door. Staying close to the villa wall, in the shadows, she made her way past the Thunderbird Lodge and stopped about 500 yards from the stable. She was afraid to go any closer for fear of discovery.

She could make out several figures moving about. The light coming from inside the stables flooded the area around the truck. A forklift slowly advanced from behind the doors. Its cargo was loaded onto the truck and tied down. Megan strained her eyes.

"What the hell are they loading at this hour?" she whispered out loud. Then her face suddenly filled with the recognition of what she was seeing. "It's hay! Why are they loading bales of hay at four o'clock in the morning?"

It didn't take long. The door to the stables was soon closed, and the truck's engine roared. Everything had been done quickly and efficiently, without a word. The truck disappeared back down the driveway.

Megan quickly returned to her villa. Once inside, she stood staring out the window, a confused frown on her forehead. *Got to tell Toni and Sally about this.*

By 9:30 a.m. Megan was dressed and ready to go. She left a note at the desk for Nicky. "Gone shopping in Rancho Mirage. I'll call when I get back. Megan."

Forty-five minutes later she was parking outside the entrance to the Indio Mall.

Toni and Sally wouldn't be arriving until 11:00 a.m., so she had time to get some breakfast. Megan quickly found a coffee shop inside the mall. She dropped fifty cents in the newspaper machine and pulled out *The Daily Sun Times*. The Tuesday morning headline hit her in the face.

WOMAN FOUND MURDERED NEAR PALM SPRINGS
By Susan Abbot, staff writer
Shirley Coleman, owner of Coleman Interior Designs of Newport Beach, found dead along Highway 60. Her new BMW was not located until early this morning in downtown Palm Springs. The Police are baffled by the twenty-five mile distance between where the body was found and the location of the murdered victim's abandoned vehicle

Megan took a sip of her coffee, and continued reading.

This latest murder has the same earmarks as four other murders of women reported in the area over the last four months. The police provided no further details. They have, however, admitted this is almost surely the work of a serial killer.

Toni must be going out of her mind, Megan thought. After finishing her breakfast and the paper, she walked to the pet shop where they were to rendezvous.

Sally, posing as an employee, looked busy as she cleaned out a hamster cage. Megan walked around the shop looking at the merchandise and various animals and fish. She stopped to talk to a large, brightly colored parrot.

"Hello. Polly want a cracker?" she chirped in a high voice.

"Not very original," Sally softly said out of the corner of her mouth.

"Best I can do on short notice." Megan smiled.

"Is there anything I can help you with?" Sally said loudly, in a businesslike manner, playing her role as an employee.

"No, thanks, not right now; I'm just looking." Megan was slowly working her way back toward the storeroom.

There were only two people in the store, a woman and her little girl. Sally diverted their attention long enough for Megan to slip through the storeroom door. Toni was standing in the corner, close to some boxes. She looked beat.

"Hi, honey," Megan whispered. She put her arms around Toni.

Toni held her so tight Megan could hardly breathe. She felt like crying. They held each other for a long time. Finally, she cupped Toni's face in her hands and kissed her gently. Toni looked exhausted. "You've been up all night, haven't you?"

Then, stepping back, Megan said, "I read the paper this morning, honey. Any details yet?" Toni shook her head in disgust. "Are we any closer to finding the bastard?"

"Actually, we are. But it's not happening fast enough for me."

There was a small table and two chairs in the storeroom. Toni sat down, as did Megan.

"It's the same as the others, babe. Same MO...everything. I got the faxes from the detectives in Riverside, but since this last murder, I haven't had a real chance to go over the reports yet. Toni sighed deeply. She reached into the pocket of her white cotton shirt and pulled out a pack of Marlboros, and lit up.

Megan coughed and waved her hand futilely at the cigarette smoke. "Toni, you really have to give up those things. Promise me you'll try. Will you? "

Toni just smiled and shrugged her shoulders. "Okay, babe, okay. Now, tell me what's been going on at the ranch."

"Okay. I know we don't have long, honey, so let me fill you in." Megan handed her the bottle containing the horse's dried blood.

"What's this?" Toni asked, frowning.

Megan explained what had happened to the mare, and how strange she thought it was.

"I've just got this feeling the blood will tell us something." Then she continued by telling Toni about the truck loaded with hay at four o'clock that morning. "One other thing—I was in Nicky's office alone yesterday, and made a quick check of the drawers in her desk."

"Did you find anything interesting?" Toni leaned forward listening intently.

"Not really, but she does have a gun. And one other thing— it may mean nothing, but I saw an envelope on her desk which contained her birth certificate. I couldn't get a look at it, but Nicky seemed disturbed when I mentioned the birth certificate to her."

Toni took a last puff from her cigarette and then rubbed her chin. "Hmm, bales of hay and her birth certificate. Well, I don't know the importance of those things right now, but you can bet I'm going to find out. Now, I've got some things to tell you." Toni began relating Jill Collins' horror story to Megan.

When she finished, Megan looked ill. "Oh, my God. Nicky must be insane. What kind of person could do that to someone?"

"A very sick one," Toni answered bitterly.

Megan rose to her feet, her face suddenly turned white. "She had a dinner ready for *me* last night at her house."

"She WHAT?" Toni shouted.

"If you hadn't upset her so bad that she had to get drunk, she might have tried to pull the same thing on me that she did on Jill." Megan paused and shuddered.

"That does it!" Toni's voice was getting loud. "You're not going back."

"Shush," Megan said nervously. "Someone will hear us."

Toni lowered her voice and stepped close to Megan. "If we don't have enough evidence to get Nicky, we'll just have to approach this from another angle. I'm not letting you go near the mother-fucker again, and that's all there is to it."

"I don't want to go back, honey, but if I don't, more women will die. I know what to watch for now, and I'm sure I can handle Ms. Nicky Clark just fine. Just give me one more night. Okay, babe?" Megan took Toni's hand and kissed it.

"She's right, you know." Sally had been standing in the doorway long enough to hear most of their conversation.

"Who asked you, god damn it?" Toni barked at Sally.

Unfazed, Sally continued. "Look, Toni, so far, it doesn't sound like Nicky even suspects anything. Megan's not stupid. She'll get out at the first sign of danger."

Toni paced back and forth, her jaw set tight. At last she growled, "I'm giving you until tomorrow morning, and then I'm coming to get you. Don't say a word, that's it."

"Thanks, honey. You won't be sorry."

"Yeah, right! I'm already sorry." Toni huffed.

"Okay you two, better get on with it. Megan has to do some shopping. I'll go back out front and make sure the coast is clear."

Toni handed Sally the bottle. "Here, get this to the lab as soon as possible. I want it checked for everything, and I mean EVERYTHING. And I want the results on my desk by this afternoon...."

She kissed Megan and held her tightly. "I'll see you tomorrow. Be packed and ready to leave by noon."

"Okay, honey, sweet dreams." Megan patted Toni gently on the cheek, and slipped out the door.

Toni stood motionless, staring at the empty doorway. "Until we meet again," she whispered fervently.

10

AFTER Toni returned to the house, she grabbed some lunch while reading over the data they had on Nicky Clark. She decided to let Harvey in on the undercover work Megan was doing at the ranch. *Harvey may be able to come up with some new tack for us to follow now that Megan is in place*, she thought, as she dialed the phone.

The briefing with Captain Morris resulted in getting his full backing for the undercover operation. Toni was pleased with how it had all gone and returned to the police station around 4 p.m..

The desk sergeant motioned to her. "Captain Powers would like to see you, Lieutenant," he said.

"Thanks, Harry."

She knocked on the Captain's door. "Come in."

"Good afternoon, Captain. You wanted to see me?"

"Yeah, Toni. We just received all the information available on the new murder." He didn't stand, but reached across his desk and handed Toni a folder.

"Thanks, Captain." She opened the folder.

"Are you getting any closer to solving these murders, Lieutenant?"

Not looking up from the pages of the report she answered, "I have a couple of new leads to check out, and the reports from my Highway 60 Murders task force in Riverside to go over. Maybe between all of that, something will click." Then she closed the manila folder and looked at Powers.

"Is there anything you want to discuss with me?" he asked.

"Not at this time, sir. But if I do, I'll let you know." Toni shook his well manicured-hand, turned and left the office.

Powers watched until the door shut behind her. *If they'd let a man handle this investigation instead of this dyke, things would move a lot faster. Of course, it gives the killer time to knock off a few more of these god damn bitches!* Captain Powers smiled to himself. Then he picked up his private telephone and began to dial.

Sally was sitting at her desk, already going over the lab report on the bottle containing the horse's blood, when Toni walked in.

"Got that back fast, didn't you," Toni said approvingly, briefly reading over Sally's shoulder.

"Better sit down, Toni." Sally rose to her feet.

"Why?" Toni asked, moving to her desk. She lit a cigarette and took a long drag as she hung her jacket over the back of the chair. "What's up, Sal? What's in the report that makes you say that?" she asked with raised eyebrows.

Sally stood in front of Toni's desk looking down at her, a deep frown creased her forehead. She held the report papers in one hand and nervously fidgeted with the button on her Levis with the other. "I think you're going to find this report quite interesting, Toni. So, I'm going to cut through all the details and get right to the point."

"Please do, oh comrade of mine," Toni answered, smartly.

"The horse OD'd!" She leaned over Toni's desk as she spoke.

"The horse what?"

"I'm telling you the horse died of an overdose of drugs. Cocaine, to be exact." Sally laid the report down in front of Toni.

"What the...?" Toni grabbed the papers, and began reading. "How? Why? I don't understand." Utter shock was written all over her face.

"I don't know how or why. I just know that's how the mare died."

"We gotta figure this out, and quick." Toni was on her feet, pacing around the room, hands shoved deep into the pockets of her white Dockers.

"Okay," Toni began, "We know about the horse dying in front of Nicky, and we know Nicky was stunned. That means at the time, she had no idea what happened to it. We also know that later that night she seemed rested and calm. Blamed the death on a heart attack or stroke. Let's assume by this time she'd figured it out.

"Then, later, at the Pussy Willow bar, I ruined her whole evening, and plans for Megan." A chill ran through Toni at the thought of what might have happened to Megan. "Nicky made a remark to Megan that she had to be up at 4:00 a.m. that morning, and then, Megan was awakened by the noise of a truck at 4:00 a.m.. The truck was being loaded with bales of hay." Toni and Sally stared at each other.

"Jesus Christ, it's the hay! Nicky's stashing drugs in the bales of hay for shipment out to the dealers. Somehow, the horse got into one of the bales which contained the uncut cocaine, and ingested enough to kill it. Nicky discovered this, figured the dope would be gone that night, and no one would be the wiser."

Toni sat down taking a deep breath. "Gotcha, bitch!" She smiled as she leaned back in her chair.

"Not so fast," Sally said. "The drugs were shipped out at 4:00 in the morning, and we don't know when Nicky will be getting more. By now the horse is gone, too."

"Shit, you're right. We have to find out how the coke is shipped to her, and when her next shipment is due. Then we can catch her red-handed with the goods. Another thing, this doesn't prove she had anything to do with the murders. We can put her away for a long time on a drug charge, that's true, but how do we prove she killed those women?" Toni flopped forward in her chair and expelled a big sigh.

Sally took up the thread of Toni's thoughts. "We can sure put some fire under her, though. I think we can scare the hell out of her if we really try. Once we nail her on the drug charge, we can put the pressure on her regarding the murders. Dealing drugs is one thing, but murder is a whole new ball game." Sally smiled as she sat down on the corner of Toni's desk.

"You're right, Sal. If we can figure out when the next shipment is arriving, we got that sick bitch right where we want her. Let's see what a bad ass she is then." Toni returned Sally's smile.

"We better go over the reports your Highway 60 Murders task force sent us."

After two hours of poring over the notes and information, Toni stood up. She walked to the blackboard, picked up a piece of chalk, and began to write.

"What are you doing?" Sally asked as she rubbed her eyes and stretched.

"I'm going to briefly list everything these murders have in common. Then, we're going to pick out anything new or different from what we already know in this information." Toni finished her list and stepped back. "Now, if I've missed anything let me know."

Sally got up and walked to the board. Scanning over it, she said, "I think everything's there. Oh, don't forget, we think they all knew the killer."

Thoughtfully, they both sat down at the conference table with their note pads.

Toni began, "Okay, here goes." She began to read from the blackboard. "Divorced, highly-paid executives, stayed at the Lazy Q, knew Nicky Clark. Here's something new—they were all active in promoting passage of the ERA." Toni paused, taking a deep breath. Then, she continued, "All resided in various parts of California from San Francisco to San Diego...out of towners. Except for Lana Washington, who lived in Riverside. They were all killed in Riverside County, cars all found in Palm Springs, same MO as to cause of death. No drugs in system, no signs of a struggle. Three of the victims had rented cars. Hold on, this is new information." Toni pointed to the list of organizations.

Getting to her feet, Toni picked up the chalk and wrote on the blackboard...Professional Women Against Abuse. She began pacing, as she clicked her ball point furiously.

Sally sat frozen, studying the blackboard.

Suddenly, Toni whirled around toward Sally. "Well. Do you see or feel anything?" She sounded tense, almost desperate.

"Yes, I think I do," Sally replied quietly.

"Go on." Toni quickly sat down next to her, waiting.

"Look at this." She pointed to the reports on the table. "These women were not randomly picked." Sally quickly got to her feet and underlined the words Professional Women Against Abuse, which Toni had written on the blackboard.

Toni's eyes grew wide. She jumped up and began pacing once more. "Yeah, I know that group. It was formed about four years ago right here in California. I remember reading about it in the newspaper. Highly paid professional women were getting together to fight against abuse. The members had all been either sexually or physically abused during childhood or marriage, and were in the process of coming out of the closet. Supposedly, this year they were going to name names, and probably ruin some pretty important men."

Sally began to talk excitedly. "These murders were carefully planned. We assumed the women were killed because they were lesbians..."

Toni interrupted and continued the train of thought. "But maybe that's NOT why. Maybe they were killed because of their affiliation with this organization...and the potential power it had! And maybe Nicky wasn't the killer. Maybe Nicky Clark's ranch just happened to be a vacation spot for the murdered women. A place where they could go and let their hair down and relax."

Toni stopped in mid-stride, the look on her face suddenly blank.

"Don't stop now. Keep going," Sally said, encouraging her to continue.

"If Nicky Clark isn't our killer, then it has to be someone who has access to her guest and reservation information," Toni said, trying not to lose the momentum. "Our killer leaves the cars in Palm Springs because he knows Nicky, and may have even called her to pick him up somewhere near the victims' abandoned automobiles.

"Maybe Nicky doesn't even know what's going on, Sally offered."

"Give me a break, Sal. She's an A-Number-One ass-hole and purely mean. I think she knows what's going on and is capable of just about anything," Toni blurted out. "But I think we're on to something here, Sal. I want a couple of your guys on the Palm Springs force to start checking out Nicky Clark's employees. Someone, if not Nicky herself, who either works on the ranch, or has access to the place, could be the perp. Another thing, are we assuming that if it wasn't Nicky killing these women, it was a man? Maybe we should re-think that idea."

Both women felt suddenly exhausted. Pouring two cups of stale coffee from the automatic coffee maker, Sally sat back down at the conference table and motioned for Toni to join her. Silently they drank, each lost in her own thoughts.

Finally, Sally looked up to the clock on the wall. "Look, Toni, it's close to 7:30 p.m. Why don't we call it a day? We'll be fresh tomorrow and we can get started on this theory again."

Toni stood up and stretched her long frame. "You're right, Sal. New day, fresh start, that's what we need. See ya bright and early. Don't forget we're going to get Megan off that damn ranch tomorrow." She patted Sally on the back, slipped on her jacket and left.

Sally walked to the window and watched as Toni sped off into the night. *Some kind of special woman you are, Toni Underwood. If I could meet a man with half your smarts and good looks, I'd marry him tomorrow.* She turned and walked to the door, flipping off the lights before leaving.

After eating a TV dinner that tasted like cardboard, Toni sat at the kitchen table drinking her coffee and smoking a cigarette, the smoke drifting up to the lonely overhead light. The air conditioning hummed in the background as she studied the reports on the latest murder. It must have been close to 1:00 a.m. when she heard an unfamiliar noise.

She looked up sharply, straining to hear. She waited, every muscle alert. *There it is again.*

The sound was coming from near the garage by the side of the house. Cautiously, Toni got up, and removed her gun from its holster.

Slowly, with her gun held firmly in two hands, she walked over to the light switch, turned off the kitchen light, and slipped out the back door. The moon was bright, but the street light didn't afford much in the way of illumination.

Toni worked her way up the side of the house farthest from the garage side. Cautiously, she stuck her head around the corner. *Shit. I forgot to put the car in the garage.*

She could make out the dark form of a large man by the driver's side of her car, his back to her. He was kneeling and appeared to be plunging a knife into the front tire. Toni could hear the steady hissing of the escaping air. She inched her way across the front of the house, keeping low to the ground.

When she got within six feet of him she shouted, "Police, freeze! Now turn around slowly, and keep your hands up where I can see them." He was holding a five inch switch-blade in his right hand. "Drop it," Toni ordered, her gun held straight out in front of her, both hands clasped firmly around the butt. The man smiled at her. "I said, POLICE DROP IT!"

Without warning, a crowbar smashed down across her wrists. Searing pain shot up her arms as her gun fell to the ground. "Are you having a problem, senorita?" A voice snarled in her ear.

"You son of a bitch," Toni screamed.

"That ain't a nice way for a lady to talk. I think my friend and me'll have to teach ya some manners," the man said as he let go of the crowbar and bent down to grab Toni's gun.

Instantly, without deliberation, Toni's booted foot kicked into the side of the thug's face. He fell sideways, holding his head. But before she could finish him off, the man with the switch blade lunged at her. Toni blocked his thrust with her left arm, and delivered a stunning blow with her fist to his throat. As he gasped for air, he clutched at his throat, and the knife dropped from his hand

In one fluid motion, she turned back to the second man, who was on the ground, still holding his head. Again she brought her foot up swiftly, into his nose and mouth. For a brief moment, a look of surprise crossed his face, as he fell backwards—out cold.

Next, her attention centered on the big blond still clutching his throat. Although obviously in pain, he started to move toward her. Toni spun around on one leg, and with her other foot kicked his testicles into the next county. His hands now clutched his crotch. In a blur of motion, she grabbed his head with both hands, bringing his head down and her knee up sharply. She caught him square in the face, flattening his nose. When she stepped back from him, he fell, face first, onto the dirt and gravel, blood spurting freely from his nose and mouth.

As she leaned against the car, Toni fought to catch her breath. She bent down and picked up her gun. "Fucking idiots," she said. "I think they made me rip my pants." She went in the house and called the police.

Toni had already cuffed the two men and was standing outside having a cigarette when the police unit pulled up.

"Are you all right, Lieutenant Underwood?" The officer asked as he approached her.

"Oh, I'm fine, but you better get these two perps to a hospital. I have a feeling they may need some medical attention," Toni said, grinning. Her wrist ached, but she'd had worse pain.

"Jesus Christ, what did these two run into, a Mack truck?" The young officer asked.

"Just little ole me!" Toni smiled.

"Did you use a bat on 'em, Lieutenant? the tall officer asked with awe.

Still smiling, Toni looked at him smugly. "After you get 'em some medical attention, take 'em to the station and book 'em for assault. I'll make out a full report in the morning." She turned and walked inside, went to the phone, and called Sally.

"That's right, Sal, two of 'em. I'm fine, just a sore wrist and some bruises. I think our friend Nicky sent these two bastards to get me. Now I've got another reason to get that bitch. Right...see you in the morning, Sal."

Then Toni dialed the police station. "Lieutenant Underwood here. Let me speak to the officer in charge." While waiting, cordless phone in hand, she went from room to room, securing the windows and doors.

Finally someone answered. "Hello, this is Detective Vince Goodman. May I help you?"

"Detective Goodman, this is Lieutenant Underwood. I think we've met."

"Yes, Lieutenant, what can I do for you?"

"Shortly there will be two men brought in. They attacked me and tried to steal my car. I want you to question them. If it's possible, I want to know if they picked me randomly, or if they were hired by someone to target me."

"I'll do my best, Lieutenant. How much pressure do you want put on 'em?"

Toni smiled. "As much as legally possible, Vince. Get the picture? Hold them as long as you can before you ship 'em off to county. Book 'em on attempted auto theft, resisting arrest, assaulting a police officer, and anything else you can think of."

"Gotcha, Lieutenant. My report will be on your desk in the morning."

"Thanks, Goodman. Good night." Toni hung up and headed for the bathroom.

She turned on the shower, took off her clothes, stepped into the steaming water and began singing, "I AM WOMAN." The hot water felt good and she stood there a long time. Thoughts of Megan and their last shower together flooded her mind.

A half hour later, Toni fell into bed exhausted. "Sweet dreams, my love, until we meet again," she mumbled, just before welcome sleep enveloped her.

✦ ✦ ✦ ✦ ✦

At the ranch, around 4:15 p.m., about the same time Toni had returned to the police station that same day, Nicky was at her desk doing paperwork. Her head still ached from last night's drinking spree and her mood was dark.

Suddenly, her private telephone rang, causing her to jump. She grabbed the receiver and answered gruffly, "Yeah." Nicky closed her eyes while she listened to the voice on the other end of the line.

After a few moments, she spoke, "There's no one here that would interest you. The place is nearly deserted." Her hands trembled a bit as she talked. Then she listened once more.

Nicky's eyes suddenly flew open. "Megan, Megan Marshall? How do you know about her?" Another pause while she listened, unblinking. "You have your ways? What the fuck does that mean?"

"She's a WHAT?" Nicky jumped to her feet. "Yeah, I've been out with the bitch," she replied to the question posed to her. "The only thing that you might call suspicious was when she asked me about my birth certificate. She saw an envelope on my desk and the certificate was inside."

Nicky's upper lip began to twitch as she waited for the next question. "No, god damn it, she didn't see it. At least I don't think she did. Anyway, she explained why she was curious." Taking a deep breath and holding it, she waited.

"What do you mean she has to go? I'm not going near the bitch again!" Nicky was sweating profusely now, her shorts and tee shirt were sticking to her body. "I'm not stupid...." Tears welled up in her eyes, panic had set in. "I'm getting my passport updated, that's all." Another pause.

Nicky sat back in her high-backed office chair. Suddenly, her face turned white and she began trembling. "Yes, I know what you'll do to me if I don't." Her voice was a whisper. She paused to listen. "All right, I'll call her and act as though everything's okay." Nicky slammed the phone down and headed for the reservation desk.

She walked briskly to the counter. "Cookie, I want you to monitor all calls from, or to, Mrs. Marshall's villa. And keep your mouth shut about this, understand?" she said quietly, her eyes narrowing. "I'll be at the house."

"Yes, Ms. Clark."

She picked up a piece of paper and pen. Quickly jotting down a short note, she handed it to Cookie. "This is what I want you to tell Mrs. Marshall, if you see her." Then she turned and angrily stomped out of the building.

After meeting Toni at the pet shop, and then doing some shopping in Rancho Mirage, Megan had returned to the ranch. To impress Nicky, she had purchased a stunning outfit—a Giorgio Armani white silk crepe tuxedo with satin lapels, plus earrings, necklace, gold pumps and a Gucci handbag. *Have to look the part,* she thought, as she hung up the outfit, feeling only a little guilty over the extravagance.

As she walked into the lobby of the Thunderbird Lodge, Megan inquired, "Any messages for me?"

"Yes, Mrs. Marshall. Ms. Clark said to tell you she won't be able to see you until later tonight. Some important business came up that has to be handled this afternoon."

"Thank you," Megan replied.

As she headed back to her villa, the sound of an airplane drew her attention skyward. "What's that plane doing?" Megan said out loud. A twin engine private plane zoomed past overhead. "Wonder why it keeps circling? I don't remember seeing an airfield anywhere near here."

Then the plane straightened out its pattern and began to descend rapidly. "Oh, my God, it's going to crash!"

It disappeared just over a small cluster of hills about a mile away. Megan waited to hear an explosion. But nothing happened. She turned and rushed toward the stables.

"John, would you please saddle up one of the horses for me? I feel like taking a ride."

"Well, I don't know. Ms. Clark only allows the horses to be ridden in the early mornings in the summer. Heat's too hard on 'em."

"Didn't she tell everyone *I* was to have the *run* of the ranch?"

"Yeah, I suppose so, but you ain't even dressed for ridin', wearin' those shorts and that halter thing ya got on up top." John gave her a disdainful look.

"That's my business...not a ranch hand's. Now, if you please, get me a horse, or do I have to bring this incident to Ms. Clark's attention?" Megan placed her hands on her hips, and struck a challenging pose.

John turned and walked toward the stables. "I'll get ya a horse, ya damn spoiled bitch," he mumbled under his breath.

"Hurry, John, hurry," Megan whispered to herself.

Within minutes John brought out a gray mare. She was beautiful.

"She's very gentle, and easy to handle," the stable hand said, with his deadpan expression, as Megan mounted the mare. "Don't get her overheated, now, and don't go too far." She barely caught his last words, for the mare took off like the wind.

Once she was well out of John's view, Megan circled back around toward the hills. She slowed the mare down to a trot. *Don't want to raise any dust,* she thought.

When she reached the bottom of the hill, she dismounted, tied the horse to a withered old tree, and carefully climbed to the top of the rocky dune. The last few feet, she pulled herself along on her stomach. Rocks and gravel tore tiny cuts in her bare legs and hands. A scorpion ran past, inches from her fingers. She shuddered.

The sun was hot and taking its toll on her. Out of breath, she finally reached the top. She could see down into the small valley below. And then her mouth dropped open. A rough air strip, cut out of the desert floor, stretched out below her.

And there, at the end of the crude runway was a twin engine Cessna. A truck was parked next to it, and two men were going in and out of the open door handing down square packages, which appeared to be wrapped in brown paper. Two men on the ground were then placing them in cardboard boxes which, when full, were quickly loaded into the back of the truck.

Squinting, she tried to block out the glaring sun, but even her expensive sunglasses couldn't shield her eyes from its harsh rays.

The truck and plane seemed to waver as the scorching heat waves danced across the air strip.

She lay there not moving for twenty minutes. *Five cartons full, no six. This is really weird. Why make a delivery out here in the middle of nowhere, at a hidden airfield? It's got to be drugs. I've seen those types of packages before. Must get this information to Toni right away, somehow.*

Again, Megan shielded her eyes from the glare of the sun. Moments later a woman emerged from the cab of the truck holding a briefcase, and approached the pilot.

"Christ! It's Nicky!" Megan said aloud.

Nicky handed the case to the pilot, shook his hand, and climbed back into the truck. One man got into the truck with her. It was Mario, the small Mexican man who worked at the ranch. The other two men entered the plane.

The engine kicked over and Nicky's truck pulled away. Megan slid back down the hill as quickly as possible. She jumped on her horse, kicked the mare and took off toward the ranch. *Got to get back before Nicky.* She slapped the mare across the rump. After a short, hard ride, they reached the barn in a cloud of dust. The horse was wet and foam was coming out of its mouth.

John came running out. "God damn it, I told you not to run her. If this horse gets sick, Ms. Clark will have my hide." Angrily, he jerked the reins out of Megan's hand.

"I'm sorry, John," she replied, out of breath, trying to look contrite. "Something must have scared her. She took off with me, and wouldn't stop until she got back here. But if you're smart, you won't mention this to Ms. Clark. It might just get you fired."

John just stared at her, then turned and led the horse away.

As she ran back toward the lodge, Megan kept glancing over her shoulder. She didn't see Nicky, and her truck still hadn't arrived at the stables. Relieved, she slowed her pace as she walked past the Thunderbird Lodge.

Don't want to attract attention, she kept saying to herself. Finally, she reached the door to her villa.

As she turned the knob a voice close behind her said, "Mrs. Marshall, what happened to you? You look like you've been in a fight or something."

Megan's heart stopped. She turned. It was Kelly. "Oh, Kelly, it's nothing. I fell off my horse, that's all, I'm really fine. Just my ego seems to be hurt." She managed a weak smile.

"Are you sure, Mrs. Marshall? Maybe I should get Ms. Clark."

"No, Kelly, really, I'm just fine. Please don't embarrass me by telling Ms. Clark. Let's keep this our secret, okay?" She flashed her winning smile.

"Well, all right, Mrs. Marshall, but if you need anything, please call me," Kelly replied, a worried look on her face.

"Thank you, I will." Megan stepped inside the door, closing it behind her as quickly as possible. She leaned against it and released a loud sigh. *Now, how am I going to get a message to Toni?*

After a cool shower, she put on her pink cotton robe. She felt totally exhausted. The ringing of the phone startled her. "Hello."

"Hi, it's Nicky. Miss me?" Nicky's voice sounded cheerful, yet restrained.

"Yes, as a matter of fact, I have." Megan sat down on the soft couch in her sitting room. "Where have you been?"

Nicky was silent for a moment. "Well, sweetheart, believe it or not, even *I* have to work around here once in a while. Had a problem no one but me could handle."

"Let's see..." Megan was stalling for time, "it's 5:30. I have to have time to get dressed, so why don't you pick me up at my villa by...let's say 7:30."

"That's perfect. Gives me time to set up a very special evening for a very special lady. See you later." Nicky hung up. *Yeah, I got a special evening planned for you all right, you stinkin' cop.*

Megan thought, *she's going to make me throw up yet. Now, I've got to figure out a way to get a message to Toni. If I call the number Sally gave me in case of an emergency and ask for Mr. Bunker, she'll think I'm in trouble, and rush over here with sirens blaring. I can't call the Police Department. And the phone may be bugged. What am I going to do?* She paced back and forth. Suddenly, it hit her. *The pet shop! I'll call, and say I need to get a message to Ms. Murphy. Sally said the owner's a friend of hers. Have to take the chance. It's the only way.*

Megan looked up the number in the Riverside County phone book and quickly dialed it.

"Village Pets. May I help you?"

"Yes, I hope so," she said to the young voice on the other end of the line. "I need to get a message to Ms. Murphy, she's a clerk there I believe."

Megan heard a click on the line. She knew someone was monitoring the call.

"I don't know anyone here by that name," the girl answered.

"Well, I believe she's new. I spoke with her earlier today. Maybe she only works part-time, or something."

"Ma'am, I'm telling you I don't know anyone here by that name."

"Is the owner there?" A feeling of panic swept over Megan. *I must get this information to Toni without blowing my cover to whoever may be listening in.*

"The owner won't be back until tomorrow morning. Is there anything else I can do for you?" It sounded like the clerk was about to hang up.

"Please wait. Write this down, and give it to her first thing in the morning. It's very important." There was a long silence.

"All right, what's the message?" the girl replied, with an annoyed sigh.

Megan's mind was racing as she mentally composed the message. "Now please copy this down word for word."

"Okay, okay!" The girl was losing patience.

Megan began, "Ms. Murphy, I have decided on the plain, straw-colored, hand woven horse blanket. You told me it would be in later this afternoon. Please save it for me. It's a gift for Ms. Clark. Thank you, Megan Marshall."

"Is that all?" the clerk asked.

"Yes, thank you. Remember, as soon as your manager gets in..."

"Yeah, I know, give her the note."

"Now, all I can do is pray." Megan whispered out loud as she hung up. *Now my second problem. How to get out of being trapped alone with Nicky tonight.*

Her hand was still resting on the phone when it rang. She jumped. "It's only six o'clock. Why is that idiot Nicky calling me again?" Megan picked up the phone, "I'm not ready yet, sweetie.... Oh, I'm sorry, I thought you were someone else."

She listened while the voice on the other end of the line spoke. Her eyes grew wide with panic and fear.

"When did this happen? Early this evening? Yes, I know where that is. All right, I'll meet you there as soon as possible. I'm on my way."

Throwing on a pair of jeans, a tee shirt, and sandals, she grabbed her purse and ran to her car.

Nicky was just approaching the entrance of the lodge when she spied Megan running for the Mercedes. "Now where the hell is she going?" Nicky watched as Megan's car sped off down the road toward Palm Springs.

11

TONI was in high spirits and felt good. Her wrist ached a bit, but other than that, it was a fine day. She and Sal had come up with some new and very interesting theories, and she was going to get Megan back today.

Captain Powers was standing in the parking lot of the Palm Springs Police Department when Toni pulled her white Honda Prelude in and parked. His back was turned to her, and he hadn't noticed she was within earshot of his conversation. Powers was smiling and talking to two detectives.

"Well, boys, how's our project going?"

The short stocky detective smiled at Powers. "So far, so good. We been buggin' the hell out of 'em."

"Yeah, Bud, here, really enjoys his work. We caught one of 'em alone the other night. He was in the parking lot of that club near Desert Hot Springs. You know, the one that's painted pink, and has all the pictures of half naked men stuck up on the billboard." The buck-toothed detective leered as he spoke.

"Cliff noticed this creep's license plate was past due for renewal. When the kid tried to explain, Cliff accused him of getting belligerent with a police officer, and don't you just know, the next thing we knew, he took a swing at *poor* Cliff," Bud said, winking.

"So, what did the *fag* do after you hit him in the mouth?" Powers asked, a wide grin on his face.

Returning the grin, Bud answered, "He cried, what else?" Powers roared with laughter. They were all oblivious to Toni's presence behind them.

What the hell? Toni was stunned. She stood motionless as their conversation continued; she couldn't believe the words coming out of Captain Powers' mouth, but she couldn't stop listening.

"Good work, guys. If we can discourage these *queer* bastards from thinking they can live a peaceful life here, then as far as I'm concerned, we're doing the citizens of Palm Springs a big favor." Powers put his arm around one of the men's shoulder as they all went inside.

Gotta make a note of this. She pulled a small pad out of the back pocket of her Levis and began to write.

9:00 a.m., Thurs. July 2nd., Conversation in parking lot of P.S. Police Dept. between Capt. Jerry Powers and two detectives...*I'll have to get their last names later,* she thought. Toni wrote for another minute or two, and then put the pad back into her hip pocket.

She paced around the parking lot trying to regain her composure. After about ten minutes, she took a deep breath, pulled her shoulders back and started for the door. *Now's not the time to bring this out; let the bastards alone for now. It might come in handy having this information.*

As she passed by the front desk Captain Powers turned to greet her. "Good morning, Lieutenant Underwood. How's everything going?"

Without acknowledging him she continued down the hall to her office. "Fucking son of a bitch," she mumbled under her breath.

Toni noted that she was the first one in this morning. She slipped her jacket over the back of her chair, then walked over to Sally's desk. There was a note lying on it: "Please call Carol at the Village Pet Shop as soon as possible."

What the hell does this mean? Toni picked up the phone and dialed the number written on the piece of paper, drumming her fingers on the desk while she waited.

"Hello, Village Pet Shop?"

"Yes, may I speak with Carol, please?"

"Speaking."

"Hi, Carol, this is Toni Underwood. Sally Murphy asked me to call. I understand you have a message for her."

"Well, I guess it's okay to give it to you. I don't understand it, but maybe Sally will." Carol read the message slowly, while Toni wrote it down.

"Thank you, Carol. Thank you very much." Toni hung up just as Sally came in.

"Sal, we got a message from Megan. I don't know what it means yet, but I have a feeling it's important." Toni handed the paper to Sally, while she walked over to the coffee maker to pour herself a cup of coffee. *Good ole Harry, always has a fresh pot ready for us,* she thought.

Returning to where Sally was standing, she took the note back. "Plain straw horse blanket? Does that ring a bell?" Toni asked, with a confused look on her face.

"No, she didn't look at any horse blankets yesterday," Sally answered.

"Okay, we have to assume there's a hidden meaning to this message. She couldn't talk freely on the phone, so she coded it in some way." Toni picked up a piece of yellow chalk and wrote out the words on the blackboard.

"Plain...straw...horse...this afternoon. Get anything from that, Sal?" Toni's hand was on her chin.

"Nothing." Sally stood back away from the blackboard, scratching her head and frowning.

"Okay, straw, what is straw?" Toni tried another approach.

"Straw is light in color, they use it to stuff scarecrows, it's used to fill wagons for hay rides, it's what's left over after farmers bale their hay...HAY! That's it...hay." Sally's voice showed her excitement.

"Okay, let's figure this means bales of hay." Toni wrote the words on the board. "This afternoon—that's pretty clear, she must have meant yesterday afternoon. She wrote "This Afternoon" on the board. "Now, I think we just about got it," Toni said stepping back.

"Plain, plain. There's plain Jane, the plain truth, plain as day, airplane."

"That's it, Sal, airplane. There it is!" Bales of hay, this afternoon, airplane." Toni and Sally hugged each other.

"That other half of yours is some smart cookie." Sally smiled appreciatively.

"She sure is. Okay, Nicky got a shipment in by plane yesterday afternoon. I doubt if she's had time to move it, so it's got to be stuffed in some bales of hay on the ranch. Sally, I want you to make out a Declaration in Support of Arrest Warrant, and a search warrant, A.S.A.P. I'll arrange for backup."

"We can't get either of those without probable cause," Sally said glumly.

"Right, I'll make out a Statement of Probable Cause." Toni opened her desk drawer and began searching for the form.

"Do we have sufficient cause?" Sally asked, frowning.

"Look, Sal, we can't wait any longer. Nicky will get rid of the drugs and we'll be standing here with nothing. We have a horse that OD'd on Nicky's ranch, we have an eyewitness in Megan to the fact of the delivery. Yeah, I know that's weak, she didn't actually see the cocaine, but she *is* an experienced officer. God damn, Sal, even if we have to get down on our knees and beg, we have to get these warrants. This has to be done now!" Toni banged her fist on the desk.

Sally stared at Toni thoughtfully. There was a long silence. Finally, she spoke. "Judge Mitchell is an old friend of my father's; he's also my godfather. Give me some time and I'll see what I can do."

Hurriedly, the two women filled out the necessary paperwork. Toni handed her finished forms to Sally and wished her luck. "Oh, one minute, Sal," Toni said just before Sally reached the door. "What about Harry? Is he trustworthy? I mean, can he keep his mouth shut? I may need to confide in him when this all comes down."

"He's okay, Toni. He worked with my dad when he was on the force and my dad would have trusted him with his life." Then Sally dashed out the door.

You can do it Sal, you can do it, Toni repeated over and over again to herself.

Picking up her phone, Toni pushed the intercom button. The desk sergeant answered. "Harry, I want three units, two men each, plus four detectives. I'm counting on you to pick out the best men you've got. I want them in my office within twenty minutes for a briefing. Make sure two detectives called Bud and Cliff are *not* included." She didn't want the two detectives she'd overheard talking to Captain Powers in the parking lot earlier to know what was going down. Toni hung up and began working out a game plan.

Within twenty minutes, all the officers were gathered in Toni's office. She stood up and looked each of them squarely in the eyes. "Good morning, gentlemen. We are about to conduct a surprise raid on what Sergeant Murphy and I believe is an extremely large cocaine operation working out of this area.

"I've drawn a rough sketch of our target on the blackboard. To the left, set off from the rest of the buildings, you see a house. This is the prime suspect's home. When we go in, I want two units to go immediately to this sector. One in front, and one in back. Haggart and Green front, Wilson and Simpler rear. You will wait only long enough to let everyone get in position, and then enter from both directions. Don't let anyone get away. We will be communicating by walkie-talkie during this operation."

Toni paused for a moment. "I want four detectives to hit the stable; the same mode of operation will apply here. No one is to leave. I want each unit to carry a shotgun. Sergeant Murphy and I will take the Thunderbird Lodge. The third unit will act as our backup. After you have secured your sectors, wait for further instructions from me. I want this whole place sealed up. I'm going to arrange for several more backup units to follow us in as soon as we've secured the premises. They will not be informed as to the purpose of this operation until they arrive. You are to discuss this operation with no one, and I mean no one. Is that clear?"

The detectives and uniformed officers were all silent. "If there are no questions, you are dismissed. But I want all of you ready to move on a moment's notice. You will follow Sergeant Murphy and me. Harry is running off copies of the map right now. Each unit will receive a copy before you leave."

Picking up the phone, she buzzed the front desk. "Harry, after I leave, I want all available units to follow fifteen minutes later. They are to go to the Lazy Q Dude Ranch. Don't tell any of them where they're headed until it's time to leave and they get a map, understand?"

"Yes, Lieutenant," Harry answered.

"Oh, Harry, is Captain Powers around?"

"Why, no, Lieutenant, he left to attend a brunch in his honor, for twenty years of service to the community."

"That's good, Harry. No need to bother him. Please come in here. I have the map I want you to copy. And have my special units outside my office at noon."

"Yes, Lieutenant."

No one is going to screw this up. After what I heard in the parking lot this morning, I wouldn't trust Powers, or his two "boys" as far as I could throw them.

When Sally returned close to an hour later, she found Toni was pacing up and down like a caged animal.

"Jesus Christ, where have you been?" Toni asked, her voice tense.

"I got these damn warrants as quickly as possible. Judge Mitchell wasn't happy about our probable cause...or should I say *lack* of it? But I convinced him this was a situation of "Exigent Circumstances" and time was of the essence."

"Thanks, Sal; he won't regret it. I can hardly wait to see the look on Nicky Clark's face when we bust her," Toni said with a contemptuous smile on her lips.

During the next ten minutes, the two policewomen doublechecked their weapons, making sure they carried extra ammo.They slipped their .45 Smith and Wessons into their belt holsters, checked their handcuffs, sliding the holders onto their belts. Finally, they clipped their I.D. tags onto the pockets of their shirts.

Satisfied that they were ready, Toni glanced at her watch. "Noon, exactly," she said, "Let's hit it, Sal, this is our big day." Both women put on green nylon jackets with the word POLICE printed in big white letters across the back.

They were smiling as they stepped out the door. Harry walked up to Toni and handed her the copies of the map with the diagram of Nicky's ranch. "Okay, all you men assigned to me, here are your maps."

The policemen lined up and each unit took a copy. "Now, follow me. No sirens, and no lights." As the group left the building a murmur of surprise swept through the office as the other officers were caught off guard by this sudden rush of activity.

Toni's car turned slowly down the road leading to the ranch. "There it is, Sal. Only a half a mile now before we nail this creep." Toni sounded excited. Her heart hammered in her chest and every nerve and muscle in her body was ready for action. She was always this way when a big bust was about to go down, but today was really special for her. One of her own had turned rotten, destroying her own community. This was totally unforgivable, and Nicky Clark was about to pay dearly for it.

At the end of the long driveway, the five cars split, each quickly moving to its designated area.

Weapons drawn, Toni and Sally ran up the front steps of the Thunderbird Lodge. They burst through the doors and sprinted toward Nicky's office. Each was on guard against any threatening moves. Kelly and two guests were standing at the reservation desk. Their mouths dropped open when they saw Sally and Toni. The three startled women froze in place.

Abruptly, the policewomen stopped outside Nicky's office door. Toni announced in a thunderous voice, "POLICE, SEARCH WARRANT, open the door!" Sally tried the doorknob. The door was locked. Toni braced herself and repeated, "POLICE, SEARCH WARRANT," and then kicked the door open with her foot. Sally dropped to one knee, weapon held in both hands, and aimed at the center of the room. Toni followed her in. Nicky looked up in total shock.

"Freeze!" Toni yelled, leveling her weapon at Nicky.

Great, the surprise had worked. No one had warned Nicky. Toni smiled.

"What the hell?" Nicky yelled.

"Don't move," Toni shouted, approaching the desk. "These are for you." She handed the warrants to Nicky. Nicky's close-set eyes flashed across the documents.

"Put your hands on top of the desk, palms up, NOW! Cuff her, Sal," Toni ordered.

Sally stepped behind Nicky. "Stand up," she ordered. Nicky hesitated. Then with prodding from Sally's gun, she rose slowly to her feet. Taking one arm and then the other, Sally snapped the handcuffs on Nicky Clark's shaking wrists.

"What the fuck do you think you're doing?" Nicky was screaming, her face red with anger.

"Shut up, you piece of shit," Toni screamed back. "See this, it's a search warrant. Get the picture, *Sweetie*. Read her her rights, Sal."

Nicky was outraged. "You can't do this. I know people in high places in this town. I'll have your badges for this. I want my lawyer." While Nicky raved on, Sally calmly read her her rights.

"Can it, shit breath," Toni said, as she turned to leave. "Bring her along, Sal. I think it's time to take a roll in the *hay*, what do you think?"

"Sounds like great fun to me. What about you, Nicky?" Sally answered as she pushed Nicky toward the door.

Meanwhile, the other four units had pulled up in front, and the officers were now entering the lobby.

"Nobody move," Toni said in a loud voice to the confused, babbling crowd that had now gathered in the lobby. She motioned to a sergeant. "I want everyone here to stay put," Toni instructed him. "Get all their names, addresses, etc. Keep them here until I get back. Now, I want three men to remain here. Another three come with me, and the rest go up to Clark's house. I want the house searched from top to bottom."

"What are we looking for, Lieutenant?" the Sergeant asked.

"You'll know it when you see it," Toni replied. "Send a couple of men through the rooms and villas. I want all the guests gathered here by the time I get back." With that, Toni whirled around toward Nicky. "After you, bitch."

Nicky's face was almost purple by the time they walked through the stable doorway. John and Mario were standing in the middle of the room, hands on their heads.

"Okay, Nicky, do you want to make this easy, or are we going to have to spend the day tearing this place apart?" Toni sneered in Nicky's face.

"Fuck you!" she spat out.

"What about you two?" Toni turned to John and Mario.

"I...I...swear, ma'am, I don't know what's goin' on here," John stammered.

"Me, too," Mario whined. Toni zeroed in on Mario.

"Look, mister, why don't you make it easy on yourself. If you cooperate, I can put in a good word for you. Otherwise, they will put you away for a long time." Toni could see the fear forming in his eyes.

"Keep your mouth shut!" Nicky screamed at Mario. He jumped at the sound of her voice.

"Don't pay any attention to her, Mario," Toni continued soothingly. "Look at her. She's nothing now. She can't hurt you, or anyone else. She's finished."

Mario looked at Toni, and then Nicky, and back again. Sweat was trickling down his round, weathered face. "I will tell you what you want to know," he whispered to Toni.

"You little son of a bitch," Nicky screamed, taking a step toward him.

"Whoa there, *pard*," Toni said, holding up her hand to Nicky. "Take one more step, and you might just trip and fall on your face, know what I mean?" Toni turned back to Mario. "Okay, Mario, show me."

He led her, Sally, Nicky, and two policemen to the wall at the very back of the stables. He pointed to the bales of hay stacked there.

"Behind these. The ones with the red tags. That is what you want." Mario hung his head.

"Cuff him," Toni said.

The two officers pulled down the first row of bales. There they were, bright red tags hanging from six bales of hay.

"Pull them apart," Toni said stepping closer. Her heart beat faster.

Carefully, they began pulling at the straw. One bale after another gave up its secret. Sealed brown paper packages of pure cocaine fell to the ground.

"Wow!" Sally whistled. "This is big time. Must be millions in coke here."

"You got it, Sal, and our *friend* is going to do big time for dealing." Toni glared at Nicky.

"Okay, men," Toni said, "I want pictures of all this. When you're through, tag and count the bags. I want your reports on my desk by five this afternoon. Come on, Sal, let's get up to the house and see what they've come up with there."

As Toni, Sally, and Nicky walked through the front door of Nicky's home, an officer called to Toni from the stairs. "Lieutenant Underwood, up here. I think I may have something you'll be interested in."

Nicky was looking pale; she had become extremely quiet. They followed the officer up to the bedroom.

As she looked around the large room, Toni gave a long whistle. "I'm impressed, Clark. This doesn't look like a cage at all. I thought animals like you slept in cages."

The officer motioned to her. "Over here, Lieutenant."

They stopped in front of a wide screen TV. Next to it was a shelf filled with videotapes.

Toni picked one up. "Jill Collins" was written on the label. She picked up another. The name "Anita Lewis" jumped out at her. She read them all, one by one. Each videotape was labeled with the name of one of the victims. There were more than just tapes of the murdered women here, but for now, those were the ones Toni zeroed in on. Just holding these tapes in her hand and imagining what was on them made her feel ill.

"She made tapes of all of them," Sally whispered.

"Yeah, we gotta get these back to the office and see what's here," Toni answered, her jaw set tight. "Officer, I want all these tapes marked, put in a box, and taken to my car." To the policeman standing beside her, Toni said, "Have any of you found anything else of interest?"

"We found a wall safe downstairs," Haggart answered. "The safe was behind a picture in the living room. Wanna take a look?"

"All right, Clark, are we going to play some more games, or will you open it?" Toni asked.

"Go fuck yourself," Nicky lashed out, but the punch had faded from her tone.

"My, my, Sal, I don't think she's having a good time." Toni smiled at Sally. She walked to the staircase and called down to an officer standing near the front door. "Go down to the stables and ask that guy named John if they have a blowtorch around anywhere. If they do, bring him, and it, back with you."

Then she walked back to Nicky's bedroom. While they waited, Toni took a look around. "This low-life did okay for herself while it lasted," she said to Sally.

Blowtorch in hand, the young officer came running in the front door and called up the stairs to Toni, "Lieutenant, we got the torch."

"Great. Give it to John, and tell him to get to work on the safe. We'll be down in a minute." Turning to Nicky, "It's just about over, Clark," she announced triumphantly.

John had already begun working on the safe by the time they reached the living room.

"Can you get it open, John?" Toni asked, standing next to him.

"I think so," he replied, just as the lock fell out onto the floor. "Easy as cuttin' a piece of pie," he said, stepping back.

Carefully, so as not to burn her hand, Toni wrapped a towel around it before she opened the safe door. Inside the safe was a large pile of cash. She guessed close to a million. Under it were two ledgers. Toni opened them.

"Hmm, looks like we hit the jackpot, Sal. Names, dates, times, places. Damn, we got everything here to close down this sleazy operation completely, and nail a few more people while we're at it. Tag and log these ledgers, and then put them in my car, please," Toni said, handing the ledgers to Haggart.

Toni picked up her walkie-talkie. "This is Lieutenant Underwood. I want all guests brought to the Thunderbird Lodge, on the double." Then she turned to Nicky. "Come on, Clark, I've got to find someone."

Back in the lodge, Toni began wandering among the people gathered there, her eyes frantically searching for Megan. She had a frown on her face when she turned to the sergeant in charge.

"Are you positive everyone is here? All the guests? You didn't miss anybody?" Toni asked, suddenly feeling a knife-like panic rip at her insides.

"Yes, Lieutenant Underwood, this is everyone."

Toni turned to Kelly. "What villa is Mrs. Marshall in?"

"Number three, down by the pool. Here's the key."

"Let's go, Sal." Toni was already halfway out the door, with fear consuming her, enveloping her in its clutches.

The room was dark and hot. *No one's been here all night.* Toni rushed through the living room area and into the large bedroom. The bed hadn't been slept in. Megan's pink cotton robe was lying in a heap on the floor.

"Her purse and car keys are gone," Sally said quietly, seeing the fear written on Toni's face.

"Megan! Megan!" Toni called out as she headed toward the bathroom.

"Toni." Sally put her hand on Toni's arm. "Toni...she's not here," Sally said, afraid to say what she really thought.

"What do you mean she's not here? That can't be. She knew we were coming to get her today; she wouldn't leave." Fear flooded Toni's face. "Where? Where would she go, Sally?"

Then her eyes narrowed; they were like daggers, her jaw set tight. She suddenly turned without a word, and ran out of the villa and toward the lodge.

"Toni, wait! Don't do anything stupid." Sally ran after her. Catching Toni by the arm, she spun her around and forced her up against the villa wall.

"Let me go, Sal." The look in Toni's eyes was terrifying. "That bitch Clark has her hidden away somewhere as a hostage. I'm gonna kill the mother-fucker if she doesn't tell me where Megan is, right now."

"Listen to me, please," Sally pleaded.

Toni was fighting to free herself. "I don't wanna hurt you, Sal, now let me go!" Toni was screaming, as tears filled her eyes. Fear and rage filled her heart. She knew she was out of control.

"All right, god damn it, go ahead and lose it. Lose the chance of putting Nicky away for good. Lose the chance of ever finding Megan. Go ahead, you damned hothead!" Sally released her grip and stepped back.

But Toni's sobbing was breaking her heart and she softened.

"Come back inside with me," Sally gently urged. She took Toni's arm and led her toward the villa. "Let's sit down for a minute and see if we can think clearly about this, okay?"

Perspiration and tears were streaming down Toni's face; she felt sick. Her shirt was drenched with sweat, her hair stuck to her forehead.

Back in the villa, Sally turned the air-conditioning on, went into the bathroom, got a glass of water and a wet towel. "Here," she said gently, handing them to Toni.

"What are we gonna do, Sal?" Toni sounded like a lost child. It took everything Sally had not to cry.

She sat down on the bed next to Toni and put her arm around her shoulder. "We're going to get Megan back. She's not stupid, you know. I'm sure she's okay. If Clark has her stashed somewhere, we *will* get it out of her, I promise." Sally was going all out in an effort to calm and comfort Toni. "We're going to conduct ourselves like professionals. We're NOT going to let Nicky get the best of us. No matter how hard it is, you are going to hang in there. For Megan's sake, you can't fall apart. You're a police officer, the best, and that's who Nicky Clark and the rest of the department are going to see."

Toni sat on the edge of the bed staring at the floor for a long time, not moving. Finally she sighed, and looked at Sally.

"Okay, Sal, we do it your way. I'll be okay, I promise. For Megan, I'll be okay." Toni took several deep breaths, then stood, pulling her tall body up straight. "Let's find Megan." Slipping on her Raybans, she walked to the door and stepped out into the bright desert sun.

12

WHEN Toni and Sally reentered the lodge, the detectives had just about finished collecting information from the eleven guests and twelve employees.

"I want everyone's attention," Toni said, addressing the crowd. "After you have finished your statements, you're free to go. The Lazy Q will be closed temporarily, since it is now involved in a criminal investigation. Guests will be given time to pack, and make arrangements with the assistant manager for refunds, transportation, etc. The same applies to employees. However, none of you will change your place of residence without notifying the department. Is that clear?" Toni's voice was controlled as she spoke.

Turning toward Nicky, Toni clenched her teeth and whispered, "You come with me." She took Nicky by the arm, squeezing it tight and pushing.

"Toni," Sally called after her in a cautioning tone.

"It's all right Sal, everything is all right."

Shoving Nicky into the passenger side of the squad car, Toni drove to Nicky's house. She pulled up in front, got out of the car and roughly dragged Nicky out. Neither of them said a word. The handcuffs on Nicky's wrist had tightened due to swelling caused by the heat, and were growing painful.

Once inside, Toni shoved and pushed Nicky upstairs. She opened the door to Nicky's bedroom and, grabbing her by the arm, threw Nicky inside. Nicky stumbled across the room, fighting to maintain her balance. Then Toni closed and locked the door behind them.

Nicky stood motionless in the center of the room, hate radiating from her. Beads of sweat began breaking out on her forehead. Toni slowly circled around her.

"What the fuck are we doin' here?" Nicky's lower lip and cheek were twitching.

"Why, Clark, ole buddy, I thought you and me, alone, would come up here and reminisce about some of the good old days. You know, when you had your *Parties!*" Toni's face was hard.

"I don't know what hell you're talkin' about." Nicky's voice was belligerent.

"How soon we forget." Toni roughly pushed her down onto the bed. "Have a seat, Clark, while I refresh your memory." Then she walked to the closet and opened the door.

Hanging inside on hooks were whips, chains, handcuffs, knives, and an assortment of other instruments of *"Pleasure."* Toni wanted to vomit, but she knew she had to play this scene out. She had to be cold and calculating.

Slowly, Toni took a riding crop down from one of the hooks, and held it up, studying it in the light. Her fingers slid down the oiled leather, caressing it.

Deliberately, she turned toward Nicky. Slapping the short whip against the palm of her hand, Toni walked slowly back to the bed.

"Hey! This really has a sting to it. Ever been hit with one of these, Clark?" She traced Nicky's face with the end of the riding crop, following the contours from forehead to chin.

"I'll just bet if you rapped someone across the face real hard with this, it might just leave a scar. What do you think, Clark?" Toni asked casually.

"What do ya want? You can't hurt me, you're a cop. If you touch me, it's police brutality. You'll lose your job." Nicky's voice had become a little high pitched.

"Why, what do you think I'm going to do to you, Clark? We're just reminiscing, remember?"

As she paced back and forth in front of Nicky, Toni continued slapping the riding crop against the palm of her hand. Then she stopped abruptly.

Facing Nicky, she placed the black leather handle of the riding crop under Nicky's chin, pushing her face up.

Toni leaned down until her face was inches from Nicky's. Then she smiled a strange, twisted smile. Toni's blue eyes were wild and glassy. "Listen real good, you heap of garbage." Spit flew out of Toni's mouth as she spoke. "You know Megan Marshall, don't you?"

"Yeah, I know her." A taunting grin crossed Nicky Clark's face. Yeah, I know her real well...if you *know* what I mean, Lieutenant." She laughed.

Without warning, Toni backhanded the grin off Nicky's face. A trickle of blood appeared on her upper lip and her eyes watered. Nicky Clark sat there stunned. And now, scared.

"Don't fuck with me, Clark. We're playing for keeps, here. Know what *I* mean?" She glowered as she grabbed Nick's chin hard.

"Now, listen real good. A *police officer* is missing, who also happens to be my lover, Clark. So, I'll make this perfectly clear. I *don't* give a fuck about this job. I *don't* give a fuck about police brutality. And I *don't* care what happens to me. All I care about is Megan Marshall. Do I make myself clear, Clark?" Toni knew she was about to lose it—tears filled her eyes. She stood up, slowly walked to the window, and stared out.

Moments later, Toni stood with the chair between her and Nicky. Thoughtfully, she ran her fingers along the frame. Though quiet, her voice held an ominous tone. She had made a decision. "I don't have any more time to waste with you, Clark. Time is running out. I'd just as soon blow your useless head off, and save the tax payers a lot of money. There is nothing in this whole god damn world as important to me as Megan. I have no reason to go on without her."

Toni straightened up, standing tall over Nicky. "Do you have the picture yet, you fucking bitch?" As she spoke, Toni was grappling with her own fears. Panic threatened to overwhelm her. Her rational mind knew she had to keep control, yet in her heart, she really wanted to kill this vile woman.

Toni stood stony-faced, staring down at her. Time seemed to stand still. Finally, she picked up the riding crop from the bed, and slapped it against the palm of her other hand—still deliberating. Nicky's face had grown suddenly pale. The silence in the room was deafening.

"D...D...Don't hit me." Nicky begged.

"I'll bet you've heard that plenty of times." There was a menacing calm in Toni's voice. "Get ahold of yourself, Clark. Our discussion is almost over." Toni moved the straight-backed chair out from between her and Nicky. She stood over Nicky, continuing to slap the leather crop against her palm.

Nicky looked up with watery eyes. "Could you loosen these handcuffs? They're cutting off the circulation in my hands," she pleaded meekly.

Roughly, Toni pulled Nicky's body forward so she could see behind Nicky's back. She grabbed the handcuffed wrists.

"Hmm, you know what, Clark, I'm glad you brought this to my attention. Because I don't think they're tight enough!" With that, she drew the cuffs up one more notch. Nicky cried out in pain. Toni ignored her.

"Now, here's what we're going to do. Are you listening, Ms. Clark?" She pushed the handle of the riding crop under Nicky's chin. "Because you only get one chance to get the right answer to my questions.... Ready?" Toni pulled the chair back over, and sat down in front of the shaken Nicky Clark. "Here we go."

"First question. Where is Megan Marshall?"

"I don't know." Nicky's voice was trembling so much Toni barely heard the answer.

"What was that, Clark? Did you say, 'I don't know'?" Toni raised the riding crop and smashed it down onNicky's collar bone.

Nicky jumped and winced with pain. She screamed, "You fuck. I *don't* know."

"Wrong answer, Clark," Toni responded, raising the riding crop once more, this time striking a blow to Nicky's knee cap.

Nicky howled in pain, "I swear on my life, I don't know."

"When was the last time you saw her? Quickly now, Clark."

Nicky hesitated for a moment. Toni suddenly jumped out of the chair, knocking it over. She threw the ridding crop down and grabbed the .45 from her holster. Toni was frantic for an answer. She had finally lost it.

Standing to the side of Nicky, she grabbed a handful of hair and yanked Nicky's head up. She placed the gun muzzle under Nicky's nose. "You're taking too long to answer, Clark. Maybe I'll just go ahead and blow your fucking head off," Toni hissed. "Open your mouth." For a brief moment Toni realized that she was enjoying the prospect of actually killing this lowlife. But the next moment she felt ashamed.

"Wha...What are you doing?" Nicky was crying, her voice a whisper.

"If you don't open that ugly mouth of yours, NOW, I'll knock your teeth out, one by one." Toni drew back her gun menacingly.

Reluctantly, Nicky opened her mouth, her eyes wide with fear. Toni shoved the muzzle of her .45 Smith & Wesson into it, and smiled. The steel gray, semi-automatic was cocked and locked. With her thumb, Toni released the safety.

"This gun has a hair trigger, so don't breathe too hard or move your head," Toni warned, staring into Nicky's tear-filled eyes. "I'm going to ask some more questions now, Clark, and I want you to blink once for yes, and twice for no. But, remember, be very careful. Your worthless life depends on it."

Nicky was beginning to gag, and sweat dripped down her face as she strained to keep her head from moving.

"Did you send those assholes to my house the other night? One blink, that's good Clark. You did it right the first time. Okay, try this one. Did you kidnap Megan Marshall? Two blinks. I don't know if I like that answer, Clark."

Relentless, Toni shoved the gun further into Nicky's mouth. Gagging sounds began to emit from deep inside Nicky's throat as she blinked her eyes frantically. Then, slowly, Toni eased the weapon out of her mouth. For the first time since she had closed the bedroom door, Toni believed that Nicky Clark truly did not know where Megan was.

Nicky coughed and choked wildly until her face was beet red.

Deciding to try a new tack, Toni continued her questioning without letup. "When was the last time you saw Megan Marshall?"

"Yesterday afternoon, about six o'clock. She was driving off toward Palm Springs," Nicky gasped.

"Go on, go on!"

"That's all. We had a date for 7:00 p.m.. I don't know why she left, but she was in a hurry." Nicky was close to collapsing.

Toni was holding the .45 at her side. The longer she looked at Nicky, the harder it became for her not to just blow her head off. She had never hated anyone so much. And it scared her. Her own hate scared her.

Toni raised her gun again to Nicky's tear-stained face. "Okay, Clark, one final question, and be real sure you get this one right. Your life depends on it. Because if I *think* you're lying, I'm going to kill you." Toni's voice was low and steady as she pulled Nicky to her feet. Her eyes were like ice, as she looked into Nicky's. Once again she placed the gun under Nicky's nose. "Did you, or anyone else, ever touch Megan Marshall?"

"*No!* No," Nicky cried, tears streaming down her face, her legs threatening to buckle under her. "I swear to you, no one touched her. Please, please, don't kill me, I'm telling you the truth."

She held Nicky up by the front of her shirt. Tears filled Toni's eyes as she felt her finger tighten on the trigger. Then, slowly she lowered the gun as Megan's sweet face flashed before her eyes. *Megan wouldn't want this.* She slowly placed the gun in her holster.

She studied Nicky's face for a long time, and then let her drop back down onto the bed.

"Please don't hurt me. Please don't hurt me," Nicky continued to whimper, oblivious to the fact that Toni had holstered her gun.

Toni went into the bathroom and threw cold water on her face, then ran a pocket comb through her hair. Leaning over the sink, she drank some cool water from her cupped hand. Numbly, she stared into the mirror, not sure if she recognized the woman who stared back at her.

Bringing back a wet towel, she pulled Nicky up into a sitting position and roughly wiped the sweat from her face. Confused at her own behavior, she then pulled her comb from her back pocket, and ran it quickly through Nicky's hair.

"Now, that's better," Toni said, as she took out a cigarette and lit it. Then she helped Nicky to her feet. "We wouldn't want anyone to get the idea this was anything more than just a friendly chat going on up here, now would we, Clark?" Toni slipped her arm through Nicky's, and led her out.

Back at the Thunderbird Lodge, Toni shoved Nicky into a chair. The frightened woman didn't look up. She simply sat with her head down, her body limp.

"Detective Grant," Toni said crisply. "Take Ms.Clark down to the station and book her on possession of narcotics for sale, and any other charges that seem appropriate."

Sally walked to Toni's side and whispered, "Well, anything?"

"Not a fucking clue," Toni sighed. "She doesn't know where Megan is."

Toni turned to the short detective standing near the door. "I'm leaving you in charge, Harris. After you get everything wrapped up here, I want to see all the statements and any other information you have. Sergeant Murphy and I are returning to the station."

Toni slammed her car door, started the engine, and screeched out of the parking lot, heading back to Palm Springs. Her knuckles were white as her grip on the steering wheel grew tighter. "We gotta get back and put an A.P.B. out on Megan," Toni whispered. The speedometer was hitting 90 when Sally broke the silence.

"Slow it down, Toni. We can't help Megan if we're both dead," she said, as she gripped the passenger door arm rest.

"Sorry, Sally," Toni answered. "I don't know what to do. I thought for sure Nicky would give us some answers, but she was just another dead end. Tell you the truth, Sal, I don't know how long I can keep it together. I came close to killing her. I feel like I'm going to explode." Tears ran down Toni's face from under her sunglasses.

"Hang in, Toni...just a while longer. I know we're going to get a break. You've got to keep a clear head." She squeezed Toni's arm, not knowing what else to say, or do.

Toni pulled her car to a screeching halt right in front of the station entrance. Jumping out of the car, the two women ran into the building. Toni approached Harry at the front desk.

"Harry, has a Megan Marshall or Megan Pollard called, or come by the office today while we were gone?"

"No, Lieutenant," Harry answered.

"I want an A.P.B. put out on her immediately. Megan Pollard is a police officer. She was working undercover at the Lazy Q Ranch, under the name Megan Marshall. She disappeared late yesterday afternoon. No one has heard from her since. Was last seen driving a 1992, yellow Mercedes 450 SL. Call Desert Car Rentals for the license number." A bitter taste of bile filled Toni's mouth as she spoke. Panic at the thought of losing Megan washed over her.

"Would you like to sit down, Lieutenant?" Harry asked, a concerned look on his ruddy face.

"No thanks, Harry, I'll be okay in a minute. Just give me a missing person form. After I complete it, I want you to transmit this to all agencies within a two hundred mile radius. "Let's see," she looked at her watch, "it's 4:30 p.m., there's still plenty of daylight. Get a helicopter up and scan the desert area for any signs of her car. I'll make sure all the information needed is on this report."

"Yes, Lieutenant."

Toni quickly filled in the details on the form provided for missing persons and gave it to Harry. "The minute you hear anything, I'm to be notified, no matter where I am. Is that clear?"

"Yes, Lieutenant," Harry replied looking at the report.

Then Toni and Sally headed for the conference room. They walked by Captain Powers office. The door was open but Powers wasn't there.

"Gee, I expected the Captain to meet us with a band playing," Sally commented.

Everyone else in the department had greeted them enthusiastically, shaking their hands, patting them on the back. "Great bust. Congratulations," they'd all said.

Toni was touched by their response, and as she opened the door to their office turned to Sally, "Boy, news travels fast around here, doesn't it?" She smiled weakly. Her legs felt like jelly.

"Well, at least our fellow officers are proud of us. To hell with Captain Powers," Sally responded angrily.

They removed their jackets and poured themselves a couple of cups of stale coffee. "Tell me about Captain Powers."

"What do you mean?" Sally asked.

"Oh, like how long has he been on the force, is he married, does he have children, you know, stuff like that."

"Well, let's see. He's been on the force for twenty-three years and from what I've heard, he's divorced. Gossip has it the divorce was nasty, he's paying big alimony. Caught cheating on his wife." Sally got up and poured herself another cup of coffee, then returned to the table.

"His friends managed to save his reputation and keep him in his position as Captain."

"Is he a high roller? How can he afford the life-style he seems to be enjoying if his wife is receiving a large alimony award?"

"I really don't know, but he does live the high life. As a matter of fact, he belongs to one of the most exclusive golf clubs in this area, has a beautiful home, and drives a new Corvette. I never thought about it before, but that IS strange."

"Does his ex-wife still live here?"

"I don't think so, I heard she moved to San Francisco. I don't think they have children, but even if they did, the kids would be grown by now."

"Do you know how he feels about gays and lesbians?"

"He hates homosexuals. He never has come right out and said it, but it's common knowledge around here. He always puts them down in little ways, but never says enough to get his ass in trouble."

"I think we may need to check out a few things concerning your Captain Powers. I heard a conversation he had with some other officers concerning gays, and his attitude was hostile, to put it mildly."

In spite of her worry and fear for Megan, Toni forced herself to continue the investigation. She believed Megan's disappearance had to be connected to Nicky Clark in some way. But how? Toni set the Lazy Q ledgers down on her desk, as Sally put the box of videotapes on the floor.

"Sal, call Harry out at the desk, and tell him to get us a TV and a videotape player right away."

Sitting down at her desk, Toni turned her attention to the ledgers.

"This is incredible," she said, looking up at Sally. "Every contact, supplier, and buyer is listed here. Every payoff, including amounts and names of people Nicky paid to keep their mouths shut."

After forty-five minutes of reading, she turned the last page. "Hello!" Toni said. Her eyes were fixed on one of the last entries in the book. Slowly, a wide grin spread across her face. She began to laugh. "This is wonderful. This is perfect."

"What is it? What's the joke?" Sally said, getting up and walking over to Toni's desk.

"Look." Toni pointed to the last entry.

Sally's eyes grew wide in disbelief. "I don't believe it."

"Believe it, babe. Believe it."

On the page, written in red ink, was the following: Jerry Powers, May 15,1992. $50,000.00. PD. (Informant police activities—drug cases.) The initials N.C. ended the line.

"Captain Powers. It's Captain Powers," Sally whispered, dumbstruck.

"The one and only, Sal. I knew something was wrong with that son of a bitch, and now we got him, too." Toni smiled at Sally. "That's why he's not here. He must have heard what went down today at the ranch."

Toni grabbed her phone. "Time to let the D.A. in on this. This could have far-reaching political ramifications."

Toni spent half an hour on the phone. "Yes sir, that's what I said, Captain Powers. Yes sir, I'll make out a complete report." Toni hung up, a broad grin on her face.

Sally was still in shock. "This is too much. Isn't there anyone left you can trust anymore?"

"Just you and me, Sal. Just you and me," Toni responded, patting Sally on the back.

"Do you think Powers could have something to do with the murders?"

"I don't know at this point, but I wouldn't rule it out. I do know we need to find the bastard, fast, because he may know something about Megan's disappearance."

Toni picked up her phone and pressed the intercom button. "Yeah, Harry. I want you to get out an A.P.B. on Captain Jerry Powers as soon as possible. He may be fleeing arrest." There was a long pause. "Yeah, Harry, that's right, Captain Powers." She hung up the phone and took a deep breath. "Okay, Sal, let's look at some of these tapes."

Neither one of them was fully prepared for what unfolded on the screen before their eyes.

"Enough!" Sally jumped to her feet halfway through the third tape. "That's enough. I can't watch anymore." Her face was ashen.

"I think we got all we need." Toni spoke in a soft voice. She was shaking as she ejected the tape from the machine. Not surprisingly, the dates on the tapes corresponded with the dates of deliveries and pick-ups of cocaine, which were noted in the ledgers.

"Nicky certainly provided entertainment for her *friends*." Toni threw the tapes back into the box. She almost wished she had blown the sick bitch's head off.

She sat down and lit a cigarette. "We still don't have the slightest idea where Megan could be. Why would she leave like that? She's sharp. She would have left us some kind of message. Damn it! Megan, where are you?"

"We'll stay here all night if we have to," Sally replied soothingly. "We'll go over each and every piece of information we've got, no matter how long it takes, Toni."

"Let's face it, Sal, the only solid piece of evidence we have so far is that fucking yellow feather they found near the body of Lana Washington, the Riverside mayor's niece. Finding the hat it came from will be like finding a needle in a haystack. Yeah, we got Nicky Clark on a drug charge, but that's it. We're just not getting anywhere connecting that to these Highway 60 Murders." Toni threw her pencil down on the table in disgust.

"We gotta keep trying Toni, come on," Sally prodded. Grumbling, Toni picked up a report and began to read. It was 6:30 p.m., and she felt as if Thursday had lasted a month.

At 8:40 p.m. Toni sat back and stretched. She rubbed her eyes. "I have to go to the can," she said, getting up.

"I'll make some fresh coffee," Sally offered. "We could both use a break," she said, smiling half-heartedly.

Toni's body ached, her head hurt, and her eyes felt as if they were lying on her cheeks.

She leaned over the sink and splashed cold water on her face. Then she looked up into the mirror. "Where are you, baby? Where are you?" Toni lowered her head, her body shook with sobs. "God, let her be all right. Please."

After making the coffee, Sally decided to go to the women's room and wash up. As she was about to enter, she could hear Toni sobbing. "Jesus, what can I say to her?" she whispered to herself. Feeling uncomfortable, Sally returned to the office.

As she opened the door leading to the office, she was startled to see a young man standing by Toni's desk.

"Excuse me." The timid voice broke the silence in the room. Sally snapped, "Who're you?"

"I'm really sorry if I frightened you. I'm here to see Lieutenant Underwood." He approached Sally as he reached in the back pocket of his bright blue cotton shorts for his I.D..

"Stop right there!" Sally said, holding up her hand. "I asked who the hell you are. Now are you going to answer me, or do I call for assistance?"

"Please, you don't have to do that. I'm a policeman, I work with Lieutenant Underwood in Riverside. I showed my I.D. to the officer at the desk outside, and he let me in. My name is Michael Hayward."

"Hayward? I haven't heard Lieutenant Underwood mention that name." Her eyes narrowed with suspicion. She picked up the phone without taking her eyes off him.

Just then, the door opened. Toni stood motionless, her hand still on the doorknob. She was clearly surprised. "Hayward! What the hell are you doing here?"

"You know him, Toni?" Sally asked, putting down the phone.

"Yeah, I know him," Toni sighed.

"Lieutenant, how are things?" Hayward asked, extending his hand hesitantly.

"Just bitchin', Hayward, just bitchin'." Toni shook Michael's hand. "Have a seat, Hayward," she said. *God is punishing me for something*, Toni thought, as she looked across her desk at him.

"Now, once more. What the hell are you doing here?" She repeated her original question.

"Well, Lieutenant, I took a couple of vacation days, and thought I'd come down here and see if I could be of any help to you." He smiled broadly, his boyish face glowing.

"I really appreciate it, Hayward, but between Sergeant Murphy here and me, we're doing just fine." Toni paused. "By the way, when did you arrive in town?"

"Why, yesterday afternoon, Lieutenant. I'll be here for two more days, though."

There was a long uncomfortable silence.

Toni got up. "Hayward, don't get the wrong idea, it's really been great seeing you, but Sergeant Murphy and I are really busy right now. You understand, don't you?" Toni's hand was on his back, gently urging him toward the door.

"Well...I guess so. I'm staying at Motel Six, if you need me."
The door slowly closed in his face.

Sally was cracking up. "What was that?" She laughed.

"That, my friend, is our new rookie at Riverside P.D." Toni
smiled wryly, shaking her head. "For some unknown reason, he wor-
ships the ground I walk on. Maybe he's made it his personal project
to save my soul or something. I've been rough on the kid, but he
needs to toughen up if he's going to make it on the police force." Toni
took a deep breath and sat down.

"He had quite a scratch on his cheek. Wonder where he got
that?" Sally remarked.

"Probably tripped over his own feet and into some bushes."
Toni shrugged her shoulders and walked back to her desk.

Sally laughed again.

At 10 p.m. a loud commotion outside the door brought Sally
and Toni to their feet.

"I'm telling you, you can't just go barging in there!" It was
Sam's voice.

The door flew open, and there stood Sam Spencer, the night
desk sergeant, pulling on the arm of a tall, extremely attractive blonde
female in her mid fifties. She shook her arm free, and looked into
Sam's face.

"I'll have you fired for these strong-arm tactics," she
screamed at him.

Sam made another grab at the woman.

"Hold on, hold on!" Toni yelled. "Let her go, Sam. What's
going on here?"

Still hanging on to the woman's arm, Sam said, "I'm really
sorry, Lieutenant Underwood. She was in the lobby demanding to
see the officer in charge of the Nicky Clark arrest. I told her to wait
and I'd call you out to speak with her." The tall blonde attempted
once more to pull free of Sam's grasp.

"Just let her go, Sam, and finish what you were saying," Toni
said, trying to be patient.

"I'm the only one working the front desk, and my attention was drawn away by the phone ringing. She must have walked over to the inner door, and when Officer Warren came out, she slipped through into the hall." Sam sounded out of breath. "I caught her just as she reached your office."

"Well, well," Toni said eyeing the woman suspiciously. "And how did you know which room I was in?" She was speaking directly to the blonde now.

"My daughter told me," the unknown intruder answered, in an indignant tone.

Toni looked at the frazzled Sam. "Go on, Sam, get back to your station, Sally and I can handle this. Don't worry about it."

"Thanks, Lieutenant," Sam answered, giving the woman a dirty look. Then he quietly left the room.

Sally had jumped to her feet when the commotion had begun and was still standing behind her desk, eyes glued on the classy-looking intruder.

"Won't you have a seat?" Toni said, motioning for the woman to sit down.

"Thank you, Miss..." She looked at Toni.

"Lieutenant Underwood, ma'am. Now what seems to be the problem here?" Toni walked to the water cooler and brought back a Dixie cup filled with water, and offered it to the woman.

"Thank you," she said, tipping the cup to her full red lips.

"You have us at a disadvantage, ma'am. Could we please have your name?" Toni was trying to maintain her cool.

"I am Susan Clark."

Toni stared at her. "And..."

"And...I'm Nicky Clark's lawyer."

Sally's mouth dropped open.

"I'm also Nicky Clark's mother."

"Oh, shit," Sally whispered under her breath.

"Well, I'll be damned. I remember someone telling me she had a mother," Toni responded. "Somehow I found that hard to believe, but then here you are, aren't you?"

Susan Clark stiffened in her chair. "Yes, I am here. And now I want a full explanation of what the charges are against my daughter. I want the reports now. Is that clear?" Leaning forward in her chair, she added, "And I want Nicky released— now."

UH, OH. Sally thought. *This babe's really pushing her luck.*

Toni leaned back in her chair studying Susan Clark, who was clearly fuming. She lit a Marlboro and took a deep drag..

"Did you hear what I said? Did you understand what I said? Do I need to get an interpreter, Lieutenant?" Susan Clark's voice was rising an octave, with every word.

Leaning across her desk, Toni spoke in a very soft and calm voice. "Mrs. Clark, I heard what you said, I understood what you said. Now I want you to listen very carefully to me, because I really do hate to repeat myself." Toni looked directly into Susan Clark's eyes. "Number one, the arraignment will take place tomorrow, at which time bail may, or may not, be set. Frankly, I hope the judge refuses to grant bail," Toni smiled. "So, your *Precious will* have to spend the night in jail. Number two, your daughter has been transferred to the county jail in Riverside. You can get copies of the arrest complaint and evidence reports from the District Attorney's office." Then she paused and took another long drag on her cigarette, blowing the smoke into Susan Clark's face.

Susan Clark coughed and covered her mouth and nose. "Must you smoke?" she said angrily.

Toni ignored the question. "Are you going to represent Nicky at her trial?"

"I don't know what business that is of yours, but no, I'm not. Criminal law is not my specialty." Susan Clark reached into her very expensive white leather purse and handed Toni her gold embossed business card.

Toni glanced at the gold lettering: Susan Clark and Associates, Attorneys-At-Law, 1216 Market St., San Francisco, Ca. The zip code and phone number followed.

"I intend to hire the best criminal lawyer in the state to defend my daughter." She shot a disdainful look in Sally's direction.

"And is Mr. Clark an attorney also?" Toni asked casually. She had decided to take a different tack with this woman.

"There is no Mr Clark...that is to say, he's no longer a part of Nicky's or my life. We've been divorced for many years." She took another drink of water, and seemed to fidget a bit as she spoke of her ex-husband.

"I'm sorry to hear that, Mrs. Clark. Sometimes a divorce can be quite traumatic in a young girl's life." Toni was trying to appear sympathetic, hoping to get whatever personal information she could about Nicky out of Susan Clark.

Susan straightened the skirt of her sleek black-and-white linen dress, and then looked at Toni. Softly, as though speaking to herself she said, "Yes, that's true. He was a brutal man; hated women." She sighed as her voice trailed off.

Then, suddenly, she realized what Toni was doing and stiffened in the chair. "I'm not here to tell you my life's story, Lieutenant, and I resent your attempt to pry into my personal affairs." With that, she rose to her feet, head held high in the air, and marched out of the room.

"Good night, now, and have a real fun time during your stay in Palm Springs." Toni said sweetly as the door slammed shut behind Susan Clark. "God, what a bitch. Like daughter, like mother."

Tony walked to the window and watched as Susan Clark got in her red Cadillac convertible and drove off. *Once I get Megan back and wrap this mess up, I'm outta this life for good.*

Toni and Sally returned to the tedious work of completing and reading reports.

By 1:00 a.m. there was still no word about Megan. Toni knew the department was doing all it could possibly do to find Megan, but a feeling of hopelessness washed over her. She tried not to think about what life without Megan would be like.

Finally, both women looked at each other, both bleary-eyed.

"I don't think I'd see a clue if it jumped in my face," Sally said, yawning.

"My eyes and brain have had it, too, Sal. Let's call it a night. I know I won't sleep, but at least I can get away from this place for awhile." Wearily, Toni turned off the light on her desk and grabbed her jacket from the back of her chair.

It was 1:45 a.m. when Toni walked in the house. Immediately, she took off all her clothes, opened the sliding glass door, and dove into the swimming pool. The water was cool and it felt silky on her skin. She swam for awhile, then went back inside.

After putting on her robe, she poured herself a straight shot of Canadian whiskey. Downing it in one swallow, she shuddered, and poured herself another. She took the bottle with her and sat down in the dark at the kitchen table, holding her head in her hands. She closed her eyes. Her head was splitting as visions of Megan filled her mind. Her worst fears bombarded her once again. "Oh Megan, dear, sweet Megan," she whispered. "I'll always love you." She poured another whiskey.

It's my fault she's missing, Toni thought. *I should have been stronger when she insisted on going undercover. I should have known better. I feel so alone. Damn, she's all I have to live for. They have to get a line on her soon...I can't make it without her. Tomorrow, I'm going to call in the Mounted Police and have them sweep the remote desert areas.* Toni poured another whiskey. The hum of the air conditioning kept her company.

Sally wandered aimlessly around her condo. The events of the day had taken their toll on her emotionally. The scenes on the videotapes and Nicky's leering smile kept flashing through her mind. And her heart ached for Megan and Toni. She realized she had never become so emotionally involved in a case before.

She flopped into a chair and put her head in her hands. *I should have backed Toni when she insisted Megan not return to the ranch. This is all my fault.*

Toni sat motionless, cradling her whiskey glass in her hands as her cigarette smoldered in the ashtray. Then, suddenly, her head jerked up. She turned her head, listening. *Yeah, someone's knocking at the door!*

The steady rapping on the door continued. She ran to answer it, her heartbeat drowning out her thoughts. *It has to be Megan.* She turned the doorknob and threw open the door. The light above the door shone on a woman who stood there smiling, her hands in her jeans pockets.

Toni blinked her eyes, surprise written all over her face. "Sal! Sally, what the hell are you doing here?" She looked at her watch. "It's 3:00 a.m."

"May I come in?" Sally asked sheepishly.

"Yeah, sure." Toni stepped back. The disappointment that it was not Megan clearly showed on her face.

She closed the door and followed Sally to the kitchen where they both sat down. There was a long silence. Toni tried to shake off her disappointment.

Then Sally began, "Toni, I'm sorry if I woke you. I couldn't sleep, and...well, to tell you the truth, I needed some company." Tears welled up in her eyes. "Damn," she said, her voice quivering. "I had all intentions of coming over here to comfort you, because I thought you might need a friend right now. And look at me. I'm just adding to the problem." Tears of frustration streamed down her face.

Toni reached across the table and took Sally's hand in hers. "Look, Sal, I do need a friend, and I don't mind you being here. I couldn't sleep either, and probably would have been completely out of my mind by dawn."She gently patted Sally's hand as she spoke.

Sally got up and went to the sink. She ran the cold water, splashed it on her face, then wiped it off with a paper towel. Taking a deep breath, she returned to the kitchen table.

"Okay, I think I have control of myself. Now, is there anything I can do to help you, right now?"

"Have a drink with me, Sal, I hate to drink alone," Toni answered in a low, flat tone.

The two women sat at the table silently downing several shots of whiskey. Sally wasn't used to drinking and the liquor hit her pretty fast. She didn't like the taste, but she stuck with Toni, shot for shot.

Toni finally realized what was happening to Sally. *Shit, I should have known better. Booze doesn't help, it only makes things worse.* She took the glass from Sally's hand.

"Come on, Sal, time to knock it off. I'm putting you in the spare bedroom. Not letting you drive home in this condition." She helped Sally to her feet.

With Toni's arm around her waist, Sally woozily walked toward the bedroom. When they had reached the center of the living room, she suddenly halted, and turned, looking into Toni's eyes.

"Did I help?" she mumbled, blinking her eyes at Toni.

"Yes, Sal, you helped a lot," Toni answered quietly.

Without warning, Sally pulled Toni's head down toward her and kissed her on the mouth. Toni jerked her head away, a shocked expression on her face.

An awkward silence hung in the room as the two women stood staring at each other.

"I'm sorry," Sally quietly apologized and stepped back. She looked as shocked as Toni.

Then Sally lowered her gaze to the floor. "Toni, I...."

"Shh, Sal, you don't have to say any more. I understand." As she spoke, Toni drew her close once more.

Sally buried her face in Toni's shoulder and began sobbing. They stood in the center of the room clinging to one another.

The two women remained in the embrace for several minutes before Sally stepped back once more and looked into Toni's drawn face.

Her lower lip quivered as she spoke. "You should see your face. It looks like a herd of cattle ran over it."

Toni smiled weakly. "Thanks a lot, that's just what I needed to hear." Then, "Come on, Sal, let's get you to bed."

Furious, he paced back and forth in the darkened room. The air-conditioning was on, yet he sweated profusely. His once neatly starched shirt clung to him. His eyes gleamed like pieces of shiny coal. Hate filled his very being.

"I'll get every one of those bitches," he mumbled. His voice was full of venom. "They can't just push us out of the way and take over man's place in the world. They won't get away with it. I won't let them."

He sat down at the small table, reached across and picked up the newspaper. The headline blared: "MAJOR DRUG BUST IN PALM SPRINGS."

He read on: "Lieutenant Toni Underwood and Sergeant Sally Murphy, pictured here, are being credited with breaking up one of the biggest drug operations in the history of Riverside County."

The article continued, but he wasn't interested in any further details. Instead, his eyes were fixed on the picture of Toni and Sally.

"They're getting too close," he whispered. "That stupid cunt Nicky might have given them just what they need to link me to the murders." He threw the newspaper down.

His hands were sweaty as he wrote two names on a piece of paper. "Toni Underwood & Sally Murphy." He sat staring at the names for a long time, running his fingertips over them, the dampness of his fingers smearing the ink.

"No two ways about it—they're next."

13

Toni and Sally arrived at the station about 8:00 a.m.. They fought their way through the throng of excited reporters, not saying a word. Quickly opening the door, they stepped inside the safety of their office. Toni immediately grabbed her phone and buzzed the front desk.

"Harry, is there anything on Megan Pollard?" She shakily lit a cigarette as she waited for an answer. Sally stood next to her nervously.

"No, Lieutenant. But we have two helicopters up."

"Harry, I want the Sheriff's Department brought in and the Mounted Police. Have them search every god damn inch of the Coachella Valley and the surrounding mountains, until they find Officer Pollard. This is on my authority, Harry, and I have it. So if anyone questions you, refer them to me. Understand?"

"Yes, Lieutenant Underwood."

Toni slammed down her phone. "I should be out there looking for her," she said in desperation. "She's out there—somewhere."

"Toni, I know how you feel, but with your being so personally involved, it's better if you leave the search up to cooler heads." Sally patted her on the back.

"You know, tomorrow is the Fourth of July. Megan loved the Fourth. Fireworks made her ooh and ah just like a kid." Tears filled her eyes as she remembered Megan's excitement.

The ringing of the phone startled Toni. Quickly she picked up the receiver. "Toni? Toni, it's Captain Morris. I heard about Megan.

My God, Toni, what happened?" His tone was concerned and confused.

"God, Harvey, this is a nightmare." She slumped into her chair. Hearing Harvey's kind voice touched her.

"Is there anything I can do?"

"Look, Harvey, just make sure the Riverside P.D. is covering all the bases on your end, and keep them on their toes. That's all I ask." Toni's head felt as though it was going to split open. "And Harvey, if you can manage it, call in the F.B.I."

"You got my word on that, Toni." Then there was a long painful pause before Morris spoke once more. "I hate to ask, but have you made any progress on the murders?"

"Fuck the murders! I don't give a shit about the murders. I don't give a shit about this job. All I want to do is get Megan back. Then I'm quitting, understand? I'm outta here for good." Toni continued ranting wildly for another few minutes.

Realizing how painful all of this was for Toni, Sally dropped what she was doing and rushed over to her side. "Give me the phone, Toni," she urged softly.

Toni didn't resist as Sally took it from her hand. "Hello, Captain Morris, this is Sergeant Murphy. I'm sorry, but Lieutenant Underwood was called away. We will keep you apprised of any new information regarding Megan Pollard or the murders. Is there anything else I can help you with?"

There was a long pause before Morris answered. "No thank you, Sergeant. Just tell Lieutenant Underwood I'll do whatever I can to find Megan."

"Thank you, sir, I will. Good-bye." Sally hung up and then turned her attention to Toni.

Toni had gotten up and was pacing around the room like a trapped animal. Sally took her by the shoulders, stopping her in mid-stride.

"Come over here and sit down," Sally insisted, leading her to the conference table. Toni's jaw was set tight. Her face was pale, chalk-like. Sally went to her purse and brought back a bottle of aspirin, then poured two coffees, handing a cup to Toni.

"I know about now you'd like something stronger, but this is the best I can do." She handed Toni four aspirin. "Go ahead, take them."

After swallowing them, Toni put her head back and looked up at the ceiling. She began taking deep breaths. Sally waited silently while Toni attempted to pull herself together.

Finally, Toni spoke as she lowered her gaze to meet Sally's. "I'm sorry, Sal. Big tough cop, that's me. Example for all the others, that's me. That's what I've believed all my life, and look at me now. Pretty sad, isn't it?"

"Shut up! Just shut up!" Sally yelled suddenly, her eyes flashing. "I can understand exactly how you feel and my heart breaks for you, but I *won't* listen to this feel sorry for myself bullshit. You *are* tough, you *are* an example for other policewomen to follow. But you're also a human being. Did you just happen to forget that over the years?" Sally was on her feet now, waving her arms in the air in frustration.

Toni sat, mouth agape, watching this petite woman roaring and swearing like a two-hundred-pound truck driver. She was shocked. She hadn't known Sally had it in her.

"Now, god damn it, we *are* going on with this job, and they *are* going to locate Megan. All we need is one break. Then you can crawl into a hole, or jump off a cliff, if it makes you happy." Finally, Sally stopped talking and fell, out of breath, into the chair across the table from Toni.

There was a long silence, as the two women sat motionless, staring at one another. Sally wasn't sure if Toni might not just punch her in the mouth for what she had said. But she had to try and pull her back, somehow.

"Well, what the hell do you want to do first?" Toni's voice boomed out at Sally.

Sally blinked a few times, and then smiled. Toni's sudden reply had startled her.

"Well, I've assigned two men to check out the backgrounds of Nicky's employees. I think we should also run a check on her mother's background and divorce. Then..." There was a soft knock on the door.

"Come in." Toni yelled out. *Oh, no!* In the doorway stood Michael Hayward.

"Hayward, what is it this time?" Toni asked with a sigh.

"Hi, Sergeant, hi, Lieutenant Underwood." Michael said shyly from under his newly acquired bright blue cap with the letters P.S. I LOVE YOU in bold gold print across the front.

"Hello, Officer Hayward," Sally said returning to her desk.

"Look, Hayward, like I said when you were here yesterday, we're really busy and..."

"Oh, I'm not here to bother you, Lieutenant. I just wanted to congratulate the two of you on the drug bust. And tell you how sorry I was to hear about Ms. Pollard." He was standing almost at attention as he spoke to Toni. "Sure wish I could have been there."

"How did you know about Megan's disappearance?" Toni asked immediately.

"Everyone knows, Lieutenant. It was in the morning papers."

"I see. Well thank you, Hayward." Toni couldn't help but notice the lettering on his cap. "By the way, Hayward, what the hell does P.S. I LOVE YOU, mean?"

"Why, 'Palm Springs, I love you.' Kinda neat, huh?"

"Yeah, real neat, Hayward, real neat." Toni got up and started for the door to urge him to leave.

"You know, it's Fourth of July tomorrow, the birthday of our nation." There was pride in his voice as he spoke. "You know, my sister was a real patriot. She died in the Gulf War."

"Oh, really, Hayward? I didn't know you had a sister." Toni was genuinely surprised.

"No one ever asked, Lieutenant," he answered sadly.

Toni put her arm around his shoulder. "I'm sure you were very proud of her," she said softly.

"Yes, I was, Lieutenant. You remind me a lot of her." He took a big gulp as though holding back some deep emotion.

"Look, Hayward, give me a couple of hours, maybe I can find something for you to do, okay?" She opened the door.

"Thanks, Lieutenant, thanks, you won't be sorry." Hayward smiled as he was leaving.

Toni walked to the window. The bright morning sun blinded her for a moment. She closed her eyes. *Birthday of our nation, huh. Man, there's nothin' to celebrate around this place.* Suddenly her eyes flew open. BIRTH! she shouted.

"What?" Sally looked up from the report she had been reading.

Toni was already at her desk, phone in hand. "Harry, is the evidence from the Clark bust still here?" She drummed her fingers on the desk. "Good. I want you to get a manila envelope taken from Nicky Clark's office. It's marked Passport, Photos, Immunization, etc. Make copies of everything in it and then bring the copies to my office, on the double!" She slammed down the phone and looked at Sally.

"What's going on?" Sally was taken aback by this sudden outburst.

"Megan had told me, or maybe it was both of us, about seeing an envelope in Nicky's office lying on her desk. And about Nicky's birth certificate being in it. And that Nicky seemed tense when Megan mentioned it." Toni was speaking rapidly.

"And we were going to look into it! Yeah, I remember. Then, Megan disappeared and we got sidetracked." Sally was excited now, too.

At 9:15 Harry knocked on the door. Toni rushed to open it, grabbing the manila envelope that was in his hand. She thanked him and sat down behind her desk.

She opened the envelope quickly, pulled out the contents, and began to read to herself. The tapping of Sally's pencil on her desk was the only sound in the room. Toni's eyes grew wide and staring. They were fixed on the document in front of her. Her mouth hung slightly open.

Just then, Harry buzzed Sally on the phone. "Sergeant Murphy, there's someone here wants to see you. Can you come out to the front desk?"

"I'm on my way, Harry."

Toni picked up her phone and grimly punched in a phone number. A voice on the other end announced, "Riverside Police Department. May I help you?"

"This is Lieutenant Toni Underwood, calling for Captain Morris." Toni was nervously fidgeting in her chair.

"I'm sorry, Lieutenant, Captain Morris just stepped out for a moment. Can I take a message?"

"Just tell him I'm on my way to Riverside, I need to talk with him. It's urgent."

She scribbled a note to Sally, then jumped to her feet, grabbed her jacket, and scooped the envelope up in one quick motion.

Outside, she literally ran into Hayward. He was walking up to the station door. "Oh, Lieutenant. I forgot to tell you..." The force of their contact knocked Hayward back three steps. "Lieutenant, what's wrong?" he said, trying to maintain his balance.

"Come on, Hayward, let's go for a ride." Toni grabbed his arm and pulled him toward her car. "You drive," she shouted, tossing him the keys. "And step on it!"

As he slid in behind the wheel of Toni's Prelude, he asked, "But where are we going?"

"Riverside P.D., Hayward, Riverside P.D.. Now get going. You said you wanted to help, right?" Her jaw was set tight, the muscles working.

"Yes, ma'am!" he answered with a wide grin. Tires squealing against the pavement, the car sped out of the driveway.

14

TONI leaned her head back against the seat, her eyes closed. Thoughts and images were racing through her mind. *Five women murdered, and for what? Because they were too powerful? Too rich?* Their dead faces flashed before her eyes.

The humming of the tires against the black asphalt highway was the only sound in the car.

Can't jump to conclusions. Have to have more information regarding this birth certificate. Gotta check it out.

"Did you ever wonder, Lieutenant, why I seem to be drawn to you so much?" The sudden sound of Hayward's voice startled her. Toni's eyes flew open.

"Did you say something, Hayward?"

"Yes, I was wondering if you realize how much I admire you, Lieutenant Underwood."

Toni looked at him, her eyes narrowing. She knew he was going to tell her, whether she cared or not.

"It's because of my sister. You know, I mentioned her earlier today."

"And..." she prompted.

"She was my hero, so to speak. After my father left us, she stepped in and took his place with me." His eyes never left the road as he spoke.

"That's nice, Hayward," Toni responded, trying to keep her mind on what he was saying.

"She was a...lesbian, Lieutenant, but it didn't matter. I loved her. She stood up for me, loved me, and always encouraged me. You understand what I'm trying to say, Lieutenant Underwood?" He swallowed hard.

Suddenly, Toni understood why this rookie was so eager to please and to work with her.

She turned and looked at him. "Yes, Michael, I do understand." Her voice was gentle and reassuring. Then, silence fell between them once more. Toni clutched the manila envelope in her hand.

Hayward pulled the car into the parking lot of the Riverside Police Department at 10:30 a.m.. As they entered the front door, they were greeted by the officers on duty.

"Hey, Lieutenant Underwood. Great job! Congratulations! Good to see you!"

Toni waved and shook a few hands as she headed toward the desk sergeant on duty. "Hi, Marv, is Captain Morris in?"

"He said he'd be back soon, Lieutenant, and you were to wait in his office."

Toni looked confused. "When did he leave?"

"Right after you called, Lieutenant. Said he had a meeting. He should be back any minute," Marv answered casually.

"I'll be right back, Lieutenant," Hayward said to Toni.

"Okay, Hayward, take your time. I'll be in the captain's office."

Toni walked briskly down the hall and went into Morris' office. She walked over to the window she stared out. *Same old view, same old smog.*

Then she turned around and walked over to Morris' desk, which was piled high with files and reports. As she lit a cigarette, she glanced down at the pile of forms. Her eyes fell on a piece of paper which was lying there. The words jumped out at her: Megan Marshall, Lazy Q Ranch, villa number three. *He shouldn't have left this lying around. I told him to be careful. This isn't like him.*

She wadded up the piece of paper and threw it angrily into the waste basket Desperate to keep her mind occupied while she waited, she began looking around the room.

Jesus, he's had those same pictures on the wall since before I came here; they've never been replaced. This place really needs a coat of paint. Damn, the chairs are even torn. Funny how you never really see things when they're right in front of your face every day.

Toni's eyes stopped moving. They became fixed on one object. One object she had never really noticed before, yet it had stood in the same corner for years. She blinked her eyes in disbelief and her jaw muscles tightened; she stood stiffly, frozen to the spot.

Her attention was fixed on a coat rack standing in the far corner of the office. Partially hidden by an old sweater, a small bright yellow feather could barely be seen protruding from behind the collar of the sweater.

Slowly, as though her legs were made of lead, she moved toward the coat rack. Her heart beat faster. It was as though she were moving in slow motion, each step taking an eternity. She reached out with her shaking hand and lifted the sweater off the coat rack. Her heart stopped. A black felt cowboy hat with white and yellow feathers decorating the brim silently hung before her wide, staring eyes. One feather was clearly missing!

Toni's knees almost gave way under her. She grabbed the coat rack for support. With every muscle in her body tense, she picked up the hat.

Unsteadily, she walked back to the desk, lowered herself into the chair, and put the hat down in front of her. Her mind was frozen. All she could do was stare at the black hat and the empty space where one of the feathers was missing. She felt ill, as her mind struggled to understand what she had just uncovered.

She reached for the hat, her hands still shaking. It felt as though it weighed a ton. She turned it, looking at every inch. The bright yellow and white feathers seemed to smile up at her.

Suddenly, Toni dropped it as though it were covered with a filth she could not endure. "Oh my God, I've got to clear my head and think this through," she said desperately.

Hands still shaking, she picked up the manila envelope and pulled out the birth certificate and began to reread it.

Place of birth: Riverside. Full name of child: Nicole Susan Clark Morris. Father: Harvey Alan Morris. Mother, full maiden name: Susan Mae Clark. She repeated the names over and over again.

There was a knock on the door. Toni jumped as though she was suddenly being awakened from a deep sleep.

Quickly, she slid the hat under the desk. "Come in," she called.

"Hi, Lieutenant." Detective Henderson smiled at Toni.

"What is it, Henderson?" Toni asked briskly.

"I have a message for you from Captain Morris. He gave it to me just before he stepped out, with orders that you get it as soon as you got here. He said you'd be in here." He handed Toni the sealed envelope. "Do you feel all right, Lieutenant? You're as white as a sheet."

"I'm just fine, Henderson, thank you."

Henderson quietly closed the door behind him as he left. She ripped open the envelope, and began to read.

"Dear Toni, Knowing you, you're probably sitting at my desk right now reading this. Also, because I know you so well, the major parts of your puzzle are beginning to fit. But just in case they haven't, take a look at my coat rack. There's a big surprise waiting there for you. The game begins. Catch me if you can, dyke! Harvey...P.S. I Love You."

Toni's face reddened, she pounded her fist down on the desk. She screamed inside. *"You fucking bastard! You piece of shit! I'll catch you, all right, and when I do, may God have mercy on you, because I won't!"*

Why didn't I see something? Jesus Christ, how could I have missed it? There were only three people who knew where Megan was, and what name she was using. I didn't tell Morris that Megan was in a villa, or its number. Damn...why didn't I ask Susan Clark who her husband was when I had the chance? Why didn't the bitch tell me her ex-husband was Harvey Morris? She and Nicky used the name Clark so no one would connect them with Morris. Megan wouldn't have left the ranch without a word unless she received a call from someone she trusted. Someone who probably told her something had happened to me. Toni paced up and down the office. A blind rage swept over her.

Tears welled up in Toni's eyes. It hit her like a sledgehammer—the full realization that Megan was more than likely dead. The blood drained from her face. She felt faint. Fighting to stay on her feet, she made her way back to the chair. Her body shook with deep sobs. She laid her head on the desk, tears falling onto the green ink blotter.

Hearing the sobbing from out in the hallway, Hayward quietly opened the door. He was surprised to see Toni crying. She looked delicate and helpless. For the first time, he saw the vulnerable side of Toni Underwood. It shocked him.

"Lieutenant, what is it? What's wrong? Can I help?" Hayward rattled off one question after the other.

He went to the water cooler and filled a cup. "Here, Lieutenant, drink this." His hand shook as he offered Toni a drink. She didn't respond. He gently touched her shoulder. She didn't feel it. "Please, Lieutenant, talk to me. I want to help." Hayward begged Toni to answer him. He was on his knees next to her. "Maybe I should find Captain Morris."

Toni's head jerked up. She looked Hayward in the eyes. "NO!" she growled.

Hayward pulled back. The look on Toni's face frightened him. Her blue eyes were like steel daggers. Finally, she straightened up and began taking long deep breaths. The passion and power of hate filled her. "Not yet, Harvey. The game isn't over yet!" she spat through her clenched teeth.

Getting to his feet, Hayward took a few steps backward. Fear was written all over his face. He couldn't decide whether to run or stay put. Toni stared at him.

She looked at the words on Hayward's baseball cap: "P.S. I Love You." Harvey had used the same postscript in his letter. *That's it! The son of a bitch is in Palm Springs!*

Toni grabbed the phone, and dialed the Palm Springs P.D.. "This is Lieutenant Underwood; I want to speak to Sergeant Murphy immediately!"

"She isn't here, Lieutenant," Harry answered.

"Where is she?"

"No one really knows, Lieutenant. She ran out of here about ten minutes ago without a word to anyone."

She slammed down the phone. "Come on, Hayward, we have to get back. Don't ask any questions, just follow me." Toni jumped to her feet grabbed him by the arm and ran out of the office It was 11:15 a.m.

At 11:05 a.m., Sally had picked up the phone in her office in Palm Springs.

"Hello. Yes, this is Sergeant Murphy, who is this?"

"This is Captain Morris, Sergeant, from Riverside. You know, Toni's boss."

"Oh, yes, Captain Morris, how may I help you? You know Toni's on her way to see you, Captain?"

"Why, no, I didn't. In fact, I called to talk with her."

"Where are you now, Captain?" Sally asked, as she picked up a pencil to jot down the number.

"I'm at the Pussy Willow bar, with Mrs. Richmond, the owner."

Sally was very surprised. "Oh...What are you doing there?"

"After hearing about Megan, and the troubles you and Toni are having with the Highway 60 Murders, I went over all the reports that Toni has faxed to me, trying to find something you might have missed." His voice was low and steady. Very businesslike.

"Toni will appreciate that, Captain. I know I certainly do. But why are you at the Pussy Willow bar?" Sally frowned.

"When I read over Mrs. Richmond's statement, I found something very interesting, so I thought I'd kill two birds with one stone, so to speak. I figured I'd drive up to Palm Springs so we could question her further, together."

"I see. Well, I don't know what to tell you, unless you want to come here and wait for Toni to return."

"I probably should have called first, but I was so anxious to investigate this new lead. Megan's disappearance has upset everyone here at headquarters." He hesitated a moment, and blew his nose. "Tell you what, why don't you come over to the bar, and you and I can question Mrs. Richmond. We may pick up something useful. Then we'll go back to the Palm Springs station and wait for Toni." His voice was less businesslike, and friendlier.

"That sounds good to me, Captain Morris. I'm on my way." Sally felt good about this. How wonderful to have a police captain go out of his way to help. *He really must like Toni a lot.* She glanced at her watch. *Hmm...11:07, I shouldn't be gone more than an hour. Maybe we're finally going to get a break.*

Sally picked up her purse, slipping it over her shoulder. *Damn, this thing gets heavier every day. Maybe I should get a smaller caliber gun.* Racing past the desk sergeant, she yelled, "Harry, I'll be back in an hour."

Harry, who was busy with a civilian, nodded, without looking up.

15

T.J. lay face down behind the bar. Blood ran from a deep wound in her head. The barroom was dark, except for the light coming from the back bar.

Harvey Morris idly flipped on the switch which turned on the big metallic ball hanging from the ceiling. The center of the dance floor was bathed in a rainbow of constantly changing colored lights. As the ball turned slowly, the lights danced across the floor and played on the walls. The sign on the front door still read "Closed."

"Beautiful," he said out loud, smiling. "Won't be long now."

Some music, we need some music. Something soft and sweet. He walked to the jukebox. *Good, lots of oldies. Let's see...* His eyes scanned the list of songs. His fingers pressed the buttons. Strains of "Mona Lisa" filled the room.

Morris returned to the bar and stepped behind it. He nudged T.J. with his foot. She didn't move. "Old dyke bitch," he muttered, walking toward the front door. Morris looked at his watch, 11:15 a.m. *Anytime now.*

A few moments later, a car pulled to a stop just outside. Morris' heartbeat quickened. He listened to the fast approaching footsteps. Anxiously, he hurried to the front door. Opening the door slightly, he peered through the crack.

"Captain Morris, is that you?" Sally asked from behind her sunglasses.

"Why, yes, Sergeant, won't you come in?" Morris smiled at her, his thin lips tight against his teeth.

She walked in a few paces past him, and stopped. "What is all this?" she asked, starting to turn back to face him.

The butt of his gun connected with the side of her jaw; Sally folded like a rag doll.

As her eyes slowly opened, a searing pain shot through her head. She couldn't move. "Where am I? What happened?" Sally raised her head. The pain in her temple was intense. She blinked her eyes, trying to focus them.

Quickly, she realized she was in the center of the dance floor, tied to a chair. She frantically attempted to work her arms free, but her head throbbed with the slightest motion.

"That won't do you any good, Sergeant," a voice said from the shadows.

"What do you want?" she yelled. The figure stepped out into the ever-changing, swirling colors of light. "Captain Morris?" Sally was totally confused.

"Yes, Sergeant, it's Captain Morris." His face looked distorted.

"My God, what are you doing?"

"I have a surprise for you, Sergeant," Morris sneered, coming closer. "You and that other bitch wanted the serial killer, didn't you? Well, I'm here to help you find him. He's very close now."

Morris' face was inches from Sally's. His breath was foul and smelled of stale beer.

Her mouth fell open in disbelief; her eyes grew wide. "You?" Sally cried out.

"Very good, Sergeant. How bright you are," Morris spat in her face.

She began struggling harder at the rope which held her tightly to the chair. Morris grabbed Sally's blonde hair and pulled her face up toward his.

"Now I told you it wouldn't do any good to struggle. Right?" And with that, he drew back his fist and smashed her in the jaw.

Blackness engulfed her. He let her head go; it dropped forward to her chest. "Now that's better, Sergeant. Must do as we're told."

Morris pulled out a long thin-bladed knife. He ran the razor-sharp edge along his fingertips. The colored lights caught the gleaming steel.

Smiling, he looked down at the unconscious woman. "Not yet, Sergeant, not yet. We have to wait for all the guests to arrive before I give you your surprise." Morris turned and walked to the bar, picking up his bottle of beer. "Beautiful music, just beautiful," he whispered.

Toni rushed in the station door at 12:35 p.m. Hayward was right behind her, still confused.

"Has anyone heard from Sergeant Murphy yet?" she yelled, as she opened the inner door to the hall.

"No, Lieutenant," they all responded.

Harry, the desk sergeant, caught up with her. "Is something wrong, Lieutenant?"

"I don't know, Harry, but I'm sure as hell going to find out!" She began to move down the hall again.

"Oh, Lieutenant," Harry called after Toni, "Mrs. Clark is waiting in your office."

Three more steps, and she was outside the door to her office. She grabbed the doorknob and threw open the door.

In one movement she reached Susan Clark, grabbed her by the front of her very expensive blouse, and pulled her to her feet. "What the hell kinda game did you think you were playing last night, you phoney bitch!"

Susan Clark was speechless; her mouth moved, but nothing came out.

"Answer me, dammit, before I break you in two!" Toni's nose was almost touching Susan's. Then, she whirled around to the stunned

Hayward. "Get outside that door, and no matter what happens, don't let anyone in. That's an order."

"Yes, ma'am, Lieutenant," he replied, his voice a whisper.

She threw Susan Clark into a chair. Toni's teeth clenched. Then in a low and steady voice, she spoke, "I want some answers, and I want 'em now. No more bullshit, do you understand me?" Susan nodded her head. "Why didn't you tell me Harvey Morris was your ex-husband?"

Susan swallowed hard, tears started running down her face. "I couldn't," she whispered.

"What? What the fuck do ya mean, you couldn't?"

"He would have killed us both."

"Both, what do you mean both?" Toni's voice was rising with each word.

"He told me if I ever mentioned that he was my husband to anyone, he would kill both Nicky and me."

Toni responded in amazement. "Jesus Christ!" She wanted to hit Susan Clark in the mouth.

"I couldn't let him do it. Don't you understand? He'd already wrecked Nicky's life, I couldn't let him take it away, too." Susan was sobbing now. "I only came here to ask a few more questions regarding Nicky's case."

"Listen to me, you stupid woman. Nicky may have gone through hell as a child, but the things she's done to people, and her disgusting way of life, was a conscious choice on her part. She knew right from wrong. Her real problem is, she's too much like her father, the murdering bastard!" Toni felt no pity for Nicky Clark.

"What are you saying?" Susan Clark's face had turned white, her voice trembling as she spoke.

"I'm telling you that Harvey Morris has killed five innocent women."

Susan Clark held her head in her hands as she rocked back and forth. The only sound in the room was the squeaking of the chair.

"Now get the hell outta of my sight." Toni's face was bright red, rage overwhelming her. She reached down and grabbed Susan, lifting her to her feet. She dragged her to the door, opened it, and threw her out into the hall.

The officers in the outer office were stunned. No one moved; their eyes were all on Toni. She turned and slammed the door shut behind her, then walked to the center of the office.

The blind rage and pain within her exploded. She picked up the ashtray from her desk, and threw it across the room. In a mad frenzy, grabbing everything on her desk, Toni flung the objects in every direction. The ringing of the phone startled her back to reality.

"WHAT IS IT?" she screamed into the mouthpiece.

"There's a call for you, Lieutenant," Harry said meekly. Toni pushed in the blinking button on her phone.

"Good afternoon, Toni," Captain Morris whispered.

Toni's eyes opened wide. "Where the hell are you, you sick son of a bitch," she growled into the receiver.

"Now, now, Toni, is that any way to talk to your superior?" The sound of laughter in his voice incensed her.

She took a deep breath. "Look, Harvey," she said calmly, "why don't you tell me where you are, so we can talk?"

"Do you really think I'm *that* crazy, Toni? It's not gonna be quite that easy."

"Okay, Harvey, spit it out, what do you want?" Toni knew she had to act calm now.

"Well, I've gone to a lot of trouble to arrange a quiet rendezvous for us, Toni.... I guess you could call it a deadly rendezvous." He coughed and she heard him bang down a glass or a bottle. "Besides, Sergeant Murphy wants you to come...she's here now. But she can't come to the phone." He laughed a maniacal laugh as he looked over at Sally.

"What have you done to her, you bastard?" She was screaming again. *And where is Megan*? she thought, but didn't dare ask.

"Why, nothing yet, Toni. We can't start without the guest of honor, you know." Then his voice became cold and hard. "Listen to me, you fucking dyke. This is how it's going down. When you come here, come alone. If there is any hint of anyone else around, your girlfriend is dead. So be sure you don't have any company with you."

He laughed, "And one more thing, dyke, you'd better come unarmed...and don't wear a jacket. Just bring your cuffs, understand?"

"Yeah, I understand."

"I'm at the Pussy Willow bar, I'm sure you know where that is. All you god damn queers have your own bars, right?" he snarled in Toni's ear.

"I'm on my way." She slammed down the phone.

Toni unclipped her holster and laid it on the desk. She already had a pair of handcuffs on her. She pulled up her pant leg and adjusted the velcro straps on her leg holster, then checked her small 380 pistol for ammo.

She stood up, straightened her shoulders, and strode out into the hall. Hayward was still standing there.

"Lieutenant, you look ill. Is everything all right?" He touched her arm.

Looking coldly into his eyes, Toni pulled away. "I'm just fine, Hayward. Now please, step aside, and let me pass."

"You don't look all right, Lieutenant," He persisted, a worried expression on his face.

Toni glared at him. "If you don't move now, I'm gonna..." She never finished her sentence.

Hayward blinked, and let her go. Once in the lobby of the police station, Toni walked up to Harry's desk. "Harry, I'm on my way to the Pussy Willow bar on Palm Canyon Drive. Sergeant Murphy is being held prisoner there." Toni's face was tense and drawn as she spoke. Harry sat staring at her, wide-eyed. Hayward stood by her side listening, his mouth hanging open.

"Now, I don't have time to repeat this, so listen carefully, Harry. It will take me approximately twelve minutes to get to the bar. I'm going to leave in two minutes, at one o'clock. At exactly 1:10, I want you to deploy every available unit to the Pussy Willow."

Toni straightened up. Harry was on his feet, listening intently to every word and jotting down notes.

"This is to be a silent run. My life and Sergeant Murphy's will depend on that."

"Yes, ma'am, I understand." Harry's voice was no more than a whisper.

"Park the cars far enough away so that the engines cannot be heard from inside the bar. I want all entrances covered, front and back. No noise, understand?" Toni paused to take a breath.

Hayward's eyes never left Toni's face. His hands clasped and unclasped at his sides.

"Once in position, I want the officers to move, in unison, into the building, weapons at the ready. The man we are dealing with knows all about police procedure, and he's deadly."

"Who is this man, Lieutenant?" Hayward asked quietly.

"Captain Harvey Morris, of the Riverside P.D." Toni answered flatly. Both Hayward and Harry were visibly stunned. "Do you understand everything, Harry?" Toni asked in a strong, firm voice.

"Yes, Lieutenant," he answered.

"Okay, I think you have a briefing to take care of. I'm outta here."

"Can I go with you, Lieutenant Underwood?" Hayward asked, pleadingly.

"Sorry, Hayward, not this time. You help out with the briefing. Hold a good thought, okay?" Toni turned and walked out the door.

Michael Hayward felt a great fear and depression sweep over him as he watched Toni get into her car and speed away.

Eleven minutes later, she came to a screeching halt outside the door of the Pussy Willow. Toni was out of the car almost before it stopped. Carefully, she approached the front door of the bar. Her mouth was dry, and shirt soaking wet.

Cautiously, she pushed the door open with her outstretched hand. The smell of stale beer and cigarette smoke filled her nostrils. Her muscles tightened as she quickly stepped inside and placed her back against the wall. Her mouth fell open at the sight before her.

Sally was sitting slumped in her chair, while the colored dancing lights emanating from the metallic ball swept across her limp body. Toni took a step toward her.

"Stop where you are, Toni," the deep voice barked from somewhere across the room. "Put your hands on top of your head. If you do anything other than what I tell you, I kill the pretty little Sergeant, here." The voice seemed to echo off the walls. "Now, I want you to walk very slowly to the edge of the dance floor and stop."

Squinting her eyes, she tried to get a fix on Morris' position.

"Walk up to the ceiling support pole, put your arms around it, and cuff them together." Toni hesitated. "Do it NOW!" Morris yelled. Slowly, she walked to the pole and did as she had been told.

Her mind was racing. *Can't make a move yet. Got to know exactly where he is, and make sure when I move, I have time to get a shot off before he kills Sally. Gotta hold it together.*

Surreptitiously, she had made sure the cuff on her right wrist wasn't snapped shut, but only appeared to be. She was counting on Morris not noticing, because of the poor lighting, and his distance from her. It was her only hope.

Morris walked out of the shadows, and stood next to Sally. His eyes were fixed and staring. Sweat ran down his face. "Hail, Hail, the gang's all here," he laughed. He held a knife loosely at his side.

Sally began to stir, moaning softly. She was trying to raise her head.

"Sal! Sally!" Toni yelled to her.

"Toni?" Sally sounded weak and confused.

"Christ, are you all right?" Toni shouted, her voice cracking.

"Toni, where are you?" Sally asked, as Tony's face came into view.

"I'm over here. Don't worry, everything will be all right."

"This is really touching," Morris mocked. "But we really must get a move on." His knuckles grew white as he tightened his grip on the knife.

"Look, Harvey, why don't you tell me why in the hell you've done these things? I thought we were friends." She was trying to buy time. If she kept him talking, maybe he'd let his guard down just for a minute.

"Well, why not? After all, you've worked very hard on this case, haven't you?" Morris pulled up a chair and sat down next to the half-conscious Sally.

"You know, if that fucking cunt Megan hadn't been so curious about Nicky's birth certificate, we wouldn't be here today. After I called Nicky, and she told me what happened. I knew it would be just a matter of time before one of you got your hands on it." The chair creaked as Morris shifted his weight.

"Why didn't you kill me long ago? It doesn't seem to bother you to have murdered five innocent women? What's one more?" Toni asked, still playing for time.

"That's a very stupid question, Toni." His voice changed, and grew louder. "I'm sure you've already figured out that the women I executed were all members of that highfallutin cunt organization, *Professional*...Women Against Abuse. They'd all been married and divorced, as you know. Now, they were preparing to reveal the names of their *so-called* abusers." His rage was increasing with every word.

"Men need protection from all these conniving whores! These disclosures would have ruined some well-known, highly respected men, maybe even me. I couldn't let that happen. First I thought of blackmailing them with the videos Nicky had, but there are others out there who aren't even dykes involved in this movement. So I began executing them, one...by...one. I thought maybe fear would stop the rest of the sluts. That's why I made the murders look as if some maniac was committing them. Nice touch, don't you think?" Bubbles of spit appeared at the corners of his mouth as he spoke.

"Anyway, I didn't have to kill you, you weren't important enough. I just enjoyed watching you go downhill, emotionally, over the years, with each new case I handed you. The lights continued to sweep across his cruel, distorted face.

"How did you get the victims to go with you?" Toni asked in a flat voice. Slowly she moved her feet apart and readied herself.

"Come on, Toni, you know how. I'm a cop. A police captain. Who would refuse to go with a captain of police? It was a piece of cake." Morris chuckled and shrugged his shoulders.

Then he got to his feet and began pacing as he spoke. *He's not getting far enough away from Sally,* Toni thought. Her eyes never left him for one second.

"Yeah, I used to beat Susan and Nicky regularly to keep them in their place." He paused, taking a handkerchief from his trouser pocket and wiping his forehead. "But did it teach 'em anything? NO! They still left me because I wasn't good enough. I didn't make enough money! And then Susan met some bitch dyke who was a lawyer. Then she hadda become some big shot lawyer. She knew I'd trash her and her practice with her perversion, if she said a word." He snickered and wiped his forehead again. "Always gotta find ways to keep the bitches in line...right, Toni?"

Toni said nothing. She just watched Harvey very carefully. Waiting for him to let down his guard.

"And Nicky...well you know about Nicky. At least I had my own bitches scared enough of me to keep their mouths shut. In fact, Nicky is terrified of me. She'd do anything I said." For a moment, it seemed as though he was finished with all he had to say.

Toni's heart began to race. How could she keep Harvey talking? Sally was awake now, looking at her. A trickle of dried blood showed on the side of her face. Her jaw was swollen, her eyes dazed and frightened.

He smiled at Toni, a strange twisted smile. Slowly he walked toward Sally. Then, stopping next to her, he faced Toni. "Enough of this bullshit. Let's just say killing rich, uppity women is a service to mankind. One I really enjoy. And now, you two get to join that elite club."

While he talked, Toni had slowly freed her right wrist. Time was running out. She was going to have to make her move and pray she could move faster than Morris. It was a long shot, but there was no more time; he was going to kill Sally.

He laughed loudly. "What's the matter, Toni? Not scared are you?" His laugh was that of a madman, high-pitched and hysterical. Morris raised the knife, and brought it down inches from Sally's eyes.

Then he paused, still looking at Toni. "Don't miss this, Toni, it's beautiful." He smiled a crooked, mad smile.

Toni's muscles tensed. Just as she pulled her hand free, a loud commotion came from the front of the bar, near the door. Automatically, she jerked her head around toward the noise.

At the same time, Morris' attention was temporarily drawn away from Sally.

"What the hell time does this god damn bar open?" The loud, drunken voice boomed out through the bar. "It's fucking hot outside; what's it take to get a drink around here?" The shadowy figure staggered and stumbled a few paces forward. Then the colored lights swirling through the air spotlighted the swaying figure.

Hayward! My God, it's Hayward! Toni swung her head back toward Morris. He was frozen, knife raised. The commotion had distracted him just long enough.

In one swift movement, Toni fell to one knee, grabbed the pistol from her leg holster, and fired. Morris staggered back a couple of steps, and then moved toward Sally again, still clutching the knife. Another shot rang out, and another. Blood began soaking through his shirt in a widening circle. A shocked expression flashed across his face, and then he fell face first onto the floor, still clutching the knife.

The only sound in the Pussy Willow was the soft strains of "Mona Lisa" playing in the background. It seemed like an eternity before anyone moved. The colored lights bathed Morris' body as a pool of blood began to cover the floor around him.

Then, with a loud crash, both front and back doors of the bar burst open and the place was flooded with police officers, guns drawn.

Toni jumped to her feet. "It's clear, it's clear. Everything's under control." She turned to Hayward. His gun was still in his hand, pointed at Harvey Morris. She walked up to him, slowly. "Michael, it's all right, it's over," she said quietly.

His face was ashen, his eyes unblinking as he stared at the dead body. Then, in a whisper he said, "We did it, Lieutenant, we did it." Toni took his hand and slowly pushed his weapon down.

Two officers had untied Sally, and were lowering her to the floor. Toni turned and rushed to her, kneeling down beside her injured partner.

"How ya doin', kid?" Toni asked in a soft, caring voice.

"I'm okay," Sally whispered just before she lost consciousness once more.

"Did somebody call for an ambulance?" Toni shouted.

"Yes, Lieutenant, they're on their way," an officer responded.

"Lieutenant, there's someone behind the bar, on the floor."

"Alive?" Toni yelled.

"Yes, ma'am. Looks like she'll be okay," came the answer.

Toni sat down on the floor and gently cradled Sally in her arms. Tears streamed down her face.

16

Sally's eyelids fluttered as she fought to open them. She turned her head to the side, only to have her head and jaw ache. Blinking, she attempted to clear her vision. Toni's smiling face greeted her. Toni was holding her hand tightly.

"Hi," Toni whispered. "Welcome back."

"Where am I?" Sally asked, looking around the room.

"You're in the Sunrise Hospital, in Palm Springs, but you're okay," Toni answered softly. "You got a nasty cut on the side of your head, and a very badly swollen jaw."

"How long have I been out?"

"Oh, about twenty-four hours, you lazy bum."

"What happened? Where is..."

"It's over, Sal. The serial killer is dead."

"And...Megan?"

"She's dead, Sal," Toni whispered. Tears filled her eyes. She paused for a moment to take a deep breath. "The mounted police found her car hidden behind some old desert shack near Desert Hot Springs. One shot to the head at close range." Toni lowered her head, and swallowed hard trying to control her grief. "It's okay, Sally. I'll be all right. It'll just take time."

"I want out of here," Sally said, tears streaming down her face as she tried to get up. A stabbing pain ripped through her temple as she raised up on one elbow.

"Just relax, you're going home tomorrow. I'll be here to pick you up. I brought you clean clothes, and pajamas so you can get out of that silly green hospital gown you're wearing."

"How did you get into my condo?"

"I picked the lock, of course! I *wasn't* a cop for nothin'."

"*Wasn't* a cop? What does that mean?" Sally frowned.

"I resigned, Sal. This was my last case. I just can't do it any more. I told the bastards what they could do with my badge, and quit." Toni's lower lip quivered as she spoke.

There was a long dreadful silence in the room. Sally gently took Toni's hand. "I'm sorry, Toni, I'm so sorry," she whispered, as the tears spilled from her eyes.

After a few moments, Toni cleared her throat and said, "There's an official department funeral day after tomorrow in Riverside for Megan. She had no family, except for distant relatives, so I've made all the arrangements."

"I want to be there," Sally said as she wiped her eyes.

"Are you sure you'll feel up to it, Sal?"

"I'm going to be there," was her response.

"It's at three o'clock in the afternoon. I'll pick you up at 9 a.m., and get you out of here. Then I'll have to leave for Riverside." Toni stood up and straightened her tee shirt and jeans. Smiling, she bent down and kissed Sally on the cheek. "Oh, by the way, happy Fourth of July." Toni's voice trembled, and her hands were shaking. Quickly, she turned and walked out of the room.

Sally stared at the empty doorway. "Megan's favorite holiday," she whispered.

Toni leaned against the wall outside Sally's room. She closed her eyes for a moment, attempting to gather herself together before she walked into the next room.

A nurse was standing beside T.J.'s bed. Jill Collins sat quietly in a chair next to her.

"How is she?" Toni whispered.

"She'll be okay. She has a concussion," Jill answered softly.

"When she wakes up, tell her I was here." Toni turned to leave.

"Wait," Jill said getting to her feet.

With some embarrassment, Jill looked directly at her. "I don't know how to thank you."

"Thank me for what?"

"For giving me back some of my self-respect. I didn't believe I had any left after Nicky got through with me. You helped me face myself."

"Sounds great, Jill. Stick with T.J.; she's the best."

Jill kissed her on the cheek and returned to T.J.'s side.

Toni pulled into the driveway of Bill Perry's house in Palm Springs at 2:15 p.m.. A sickening ache filled her insides. Slowly, she inserted the key into the lock and turned the doorknob. A wave of despair enveloped her as she stepped inside.

Out on the patio, Megan's bathing suit still lay over the back of a chair. The sun sparkled on the pool and the echo of Megan's laughter rang in her ears. She stood there for a moment drinking in the memory of Megan's laughing face. Then, with a deep sigh, she walked to the bedroom.

Pulling the suitcases from the closet, she quickly threw the clothes into them, all except for Megan's favorite old worn-out terry cloth tee shirt. She buried her face in it. Megan was still there; the sweet smell of Megan filled her senses. Hot tears streamed down Toni's face as she hurried from the house, still holding the terry shirt in her hand.

The day was sunny and bright. Officers from all over the state had arrived in their dress uniforms. A slight breeze touched the trees, gently caressing the leaves.

All stood at attention around the oak coffin draped with the American flag. The chaplain spoke in glowing words about Megan. Toni was pale and drawn. Her hands hung loosely at her sides. She couldn't hear a word the chaplain was saying, for Megan's sweet voice filled her mind and drowned out everything around her.

I love you Toni, and I always will. No matter what else you may know in your life, know this.

Tears streamed down Toni's face, and the ache in her chest was so intense it felt as though her heart was going to stop beating. A cold numbness held her in its grip.

The flag was carefully folded and handed to her. Rifles cracked in the background, as the mournful notes of taps rang through the air. Then all was still and quiet. Finally, everyone turned silently and walked away. All but Hayward, who slowly approached her. "I'm so sorry, Lieutenant," he whispered, his lower lip shaking.

"Thank you, Michael," she responded taking his hand. "You're gonna make it, Michael, just hang in there. You're going to be a good cop." They stood silently looking at each other for a moment, crying quietly, and then, Michael Hayward turned and walked away.

Sally waited for Toni by the car.

As Toni stood alone on the knoll, a bird fluttered into the tree above her. Slowly, she walked to Megan's coffin, and placed her hand upon it. "Sweet dreams, until we meet again," she said softly.

She stood there for a long moment, then straightened. Her shoulders were back, her head held high.Turning, she slowly walked to her car. She stopped briefly and looked into Sally's eyes.

"Keep in touch, Toni," the blonde woman murmured, gently touching Toni's wet cheek.

Without a word, Toni got in her car and drove off, alone.

The End

About The Author

Mind you, I was raised in the '40s and '50s, when lesbians were described as motorcycle-riding Amazons. And although motorcycles had always scared me, I *was* six-feet tall, and I'd loved women all my life. I just wish I'd known sooner that I didn't need to own a motorcycle to get a woman.

I was brought out in the parking lot of the Seattle Zoo, at four in the morning, but that's another story. After two years in Washington, I moved back to Southern California, where I was born.

Writing has always been my secret passion, but being a single parent, I was too busy raising my daughter and myself to do anything but work. I live alone, now—a condition I am learning to enjoy, and have lengthy conversations with my two dogs and cat, because I like the answers they give.

If You Liked This Book...

Authors seldom get to hear what readers like about their work. If you enjoyed reading this novel, why not let the author know? Simply write the author:

Diane Davidson
c/o Rising Tide Press
5 Kivy Street
Huntington Station, NY 11746

MORE EXCITING FICTION FROM
RISING TIDE PRESS

RETURN TO ISIS
Jean Stewart
The year is 2093. In this fantasy zone where sword and superstition meet sci-fi adventure, two women make a daring escape to freedom. Whit, a bold warrior from an Amazon nation, rescues Amelia from a dismal world where females are either breeders or drones. Together, they journey over grueling terrain, to the shining world of Artemis, and in their struggle to survive, find themselves unexpectedly drawn to each other. But it is in the safety of Artemis, Whit's home colony, that danger truly lurks. And it is in the ruins of Isis that the secret of how it was mysteriously destroyed waits to be uncovered. Here's adventure, mystery and romance all rolled into one.
Nominated for a 1993 Lambda Literary Award
ISBN 0-9628938-6-2; 192 Pages; $9.99

ISIS RISING
Jean Stewart
The eagerly awaited sequel to the immensely popular *Return to Isis* is here at last! In this stirring romantic fantasy, Jean Stewart continues the adventures of Whit (every woman's heart-throb), her beloved Kali, and a cast of colorful characters, as they rebuild Isis from the ashes. But all does not go smoothly in this brave new world, and Whit, with the help of her friends, must battle the forces that threaten. A rousing futuristic adventure and an endearing love story all rolled into one. Destined to capture your heart. Look for the sequel.
ISBN 0-9628938-8-9; 192 Pages; $9.95

WARRIORS OF ISIS
Jean Stewart
Fans of *Return to Isis* and *Isis Rising* will relish this third book in the series. Whit, Kali, Lilith and company return in another lusty tale of high adventure and passionate romance among the Freeland Warriors. The evil sorceress, Arinna Sojourner, has evaded capture and now threatens the very survival of the new colony of Isis. As Whit and Kali prepare to do battle with a seemingly unbeatable foe, Danu makes her own plans to avenge a beloved friend's death at Arinna's hands. Eventually, high in the Cascade Mountains, they will face Arinna's terrifying magical powers.

Once again, Stewart weaves a rich tapestry of an all-women's society in the twenty-first century, bursting with life— lovers, villains, heroines, and a peril so great it forges a bond between all the diverse women of this unforgettable place called Isis. ISBN 1-883061-03-2; 256 Pages; $10.99

FACES OF LOVE
Sharon Gilligan

A wise and sensitive novel which takes us into the lives of Maggie, Karen, Cory, and their community of friends. Maggie Halloran, a prominent women's rights advocate, and Karen Weston, a brilliant attorney, have been together for 10 years in a relationship which is full of love, but is also often stormy. When Maggie's heart is captured by the young and beautiful Cory, she must take stock of her life and make some decisions.

Set against the backdrop of Madison, Wisconsin, and its dynamic women's community, the characters in this engaging novel are bright, involved, '90s women dealing with universal issues of love, commitment and friendship. A wonderful read! ISBN 0-9628938-4-6; 192 Pages; $8.95

LOVE SPELL
Karen Williams

A deliciously erotic and humorous love story with a magical twist. When Kate Gallagher, a reluctantly single veterinarian, meets the mysterious and alluring Allegra one enchanted evening, it is instant fireworks. But as Kate gradually discovers, they live in two very different worlds, and Allegra's life is shrouded in mystery which Kate longs to penetrate. A masterful blend of fantasy and reality, this whimsical story will delight your imagination and warm your heart. Here is a writer of style as well as substance.

ISBN 0-9628938-2-X; 192 Pages; $9.95

ROMANCING THE DREAM
Heidi Johanna

This imaginative tale begins when Jacqui St. John leaves northern California looking for a new home, and cruises into the seemingly ordinary town of Kulshan, on the Oregon coast. Seeing the lilac bushes in bloom along the roadside, she suddenly remembers the recurring dream that has been tantalizing her for months—a dream of a house full of women, radiating warmth and welcome, and of one special woman, dressed in silk and leather....

But why has Jacqui, like so many other women, been drawn to this place? The answer is simple but wonderful—the women plan to take over the town and make a lesbian haven. A captivating and erotic love story with an unusual plot. A novel that will charm you with its gentle humor and fine writing.
ISBN 0-9628938-0-3;176 Pages; $8.95

YOU LIGHT THE FIRE
Kristen Garrett

Here's a grown-up *Rubyfruit Jungle*—sexy, spicy, and sidesplittingly funny. Garrett, a fresh new voice in lesbian fiction, has created two memorable characters in Mindy Brinson and Cheerio Monroe. Can a gorgeous, sexy, high school math teacher and a raunchy, commitment-shy ex-singer, make it last in mainstream USA? With a little help from their friends, they can. This humorous, erotic and unpredictable love story will keep you laughing, and marveling at the variety of lesbian love.

ISBN 0-9628938-5-4; 176 Pages; $9.95

DANGER IN HIGH PLACES
An Alix Nicholson Mystery
Sharon Gilligan

Free-lance photographer Alix Nicholson was expecting some great photos of the AIDS Quilt—what she got was a corpse with a story to tell! Set against the backdrop of Washington, DC, the bestselling author of *Faces of Love* delivers a riveting mystery. When Alix accidentally stumbles on a deadly scheme surrounding AIDS funding, she is catapulted into the seamy underbelly of Washington politics. With the help of Mac, lesbian congressional aide, Alix gradually untangles the plot, has a romantic interlude, and learns of the dangers in high places.

ISBN 0-9628938-7-0;   176 Pages; $9.95

WE HAVE TO TALK: A Guide To Bouncing Back From a Breakup
Jacki Moss

Being left by your lover is devastating. Suddenly, your world has been turned into something almost unrecognizable and barely manageable. That's the bad news. The good news is that you are not the first person to be dumped, and most of those who unexpectedly find themselves in the same predicament live to love and be loved again. It's not easy. And it's not fun. But this upbeat guide with a sense of humor shows you how to survive, and eventually, even thrive.

WE HAVE TO TALK is the first interactive guide designed specifically for lesbians, to help you rebuild your life. You will recognize many of your own thoughts, feelings and fears, and find new ways of dealing with the small things in a breakup, that left unchecked, develop into big things. You will even find reasons to laugh again.

ISBN 1-883061-04-0;   160 pages; $9.99

CORNERS OF THE HEART
Leslie Grey

This captivating novel of love and suspense introduces two unforgettable characters whose diverse paths have finally led them to each other. It is Spring, season of promise, when beautiful, French-born Chris Benet wanders into Katya Michaels' life. But their budding love is shadowed by a baffling mystery which they must solve. You will read with bated breath as they work together to outwit the menace that threatens Deer Falls; your heart will pound as the story races to its heart-stopping climax. Vivid, sensitive writing and an intriguing plot are the hallmarks of this exciting new writer.

ISBN 0-9628938-3-8; 224 pages; $9.95

SHADOWS AFTER DARK
Ouida Crozier

Wings of death are spreading over the world of Kornagy and Kyril's mission on Earth is to find the cause. Here, she meets the beautiful but lonely Kathryn, who has been yearning for a deep and enduring love with just such a woman as Kyril. But to her horror, Kathryn learns that her darkly exotic new lover has been sent to Earth with a purpose—to save her own dying vampire world. A tender and richly poetic novel.

ISBN 1-883061-50-4; 224 Pages; $9.95

DANGER! CROSS CURRENTS
Sharon Gilligan

In this exciting sequel to *Danger in High Places*, freelance photographer Alix Nicholson is looking forward to teaching photography at Pacific Arts, a college idyllically located on California's North Coast. But as she quickly discovers, there are ugly goings-on beneath the surface beauty of her surroundings.

When her landlady, a real estate developer, turns up dead, and the police arrest Leah Claire, the woman's much younger lover, Alix is rapidly drawn into a complex web of intrigue and murder.

As she frantically searches for a way to free Leah, Alix unexpectedly finds herself at the dawn of a new romance ... and on the brink of her own destruction. A satisfying, well-crafted mystery.

ISBN 1-883061-01-6; 192 pages; $9.99

HEARTSTONE AND SABER
Jacqui Singleton

You can almost hear the sabers clash in this rousing tale of good and evil and passionate love, of warrior queens, white witches and sorcerers.

After the devastating raid on her peaceful little village, Elayna and her brother are captured and nearly sold into slavery. Saved from this terrible fate by the imperious warrior queen, Cydell Ra Sadiin, Elayna is brought to the palace to serve her. The two are immediate foes.

But these two powerful women are destined to join forces. And so, when rumblings of war reach the palace, Cydell, ruler of Mauldar, and Elayna, the Fair Witch of Avoreed, journey to Windsom Keep to combat the dark menace which threatens Cydell's empire and Elayna's very life. But along the way they must first conquer the wild magik of their passionate dreams, learn the secrets of the heartstone, and accept the deep and rapturous love that will transcend the powers of evil.

ISBN 1-883061-00-8; 224 Pages; $10.99

EDGE OF PASSION
Shelley Smith

The author of *Horizon of the Heart* presents another absorbing and sexy novel! From the moment Angela saw Micki sitting at the end of the smoky bar, she was consumed with desire for this cool and sophisticated woman, and determined to have her...at any cost. Set against the backdrop of colorful Provincetown and Boston, this sizzling novel will draw you into the all-consuming love affair between an older and a younger woman. A gripping love story, which is both fierce and tender. It will keep you breathless until the last page.
ISBN 0-9628938-1-1; 192 Pages; $8.95

How To Order:

Rising Tide Press books are available from you local women's bookstore or directly from Rising Tide Press. Send check, money order, or Visa/MC account number, with expiration date and signature to: Rising Tide Press, 5 Kivy St., Huntington Sta., New York 11746. Credit card orders must be over $25. Remember to include shipping and handling charges: $4.95 for the first book plus $1.00 for each additional book. Credit Card Orders Call our Toll Free # 1-800-648-5333. For UPS delivery, provide street address.

Our Publishing Philosophy

Rising Tide Press is a lesbian-owned and operated publishing company committed to publishing books by, for, and about lesbians and their lives. We are not only committed to readers, but also to lesbian writers who need nurturing and support, whether or not their manuscripts are accepted for publication. Through quality writing, the press aims to entertain, educate, and empower readers, whether they are women-loving-women or heterosexual. It is our intention to promote lesbian culture, community, and civil rights, nationwide, through the printed word.

In addition, RTP will seek to provide readers with images of lesbians aspiring to be more than their prescribed roles dictate. The novels selected for publication will aim to portray women from all walks of life, (regardless of class, ethnicity, religion or race), women who are strong, not just victims, women who can and do aspire to be more, and not just settle, women who will fight injustice with courage. Hopefully, our novels will provide new ideas for creating change in a heterosexist and homophobic society. Finally, we hope our books will encourage lesbians to respect and love themselves more, and at the same time, convey this love and respect of self to the society at large. It is our belief that this philosophy can best be actualized through fine writing that entertains, as well as educates the reader. Books can be fun, as well as liberating.

Writers Wanted!

Rising Tide Press, Publisher of Lesbian Novels, is Soliciting Quality Fiction Manuscripts

Rising Tide Press is interested in publishing quality Lesbian fiction: romance, mystery, and science-fiction/fantasy. Non-fiction is also welcome, but please, no poetry or short stories.

Please send us the following:
- One page synopsis of plot
- The manuscript
- A brief autobiographical sketch
- Large manila envelope with sufficient return postage

RISING TIDE PRESS

5 KIVY ST • HUNTINGTON STA NY • 11746
(516) 427-1289